The
Mermaids
Singing

Lisa Carey

VIKING

VIKING

Published by the Penguin Group
Penguin Books Ltd, 27 Wrights Lane, London W8 5TZ, England
Penguin Putnam Inc., 375 Hudson Street, New York, New York 10014, USA
Penguin Books Australia Ltd, Ringwood, Victoria, Australia
Penguin Books Canada Ltd, 10 Alcorn Avenue, Toronto, Ontario, Canada M4V 3B2
Penguin Books (NZ) Ltd, 182–190 Wairau Road, Auckland 10, New Zealand

Penguin Books Ltd, Registered Offices: Harmondsworth, Middlesex, England

First published in the USA by Avon Books 1998
First published in Great Britain by Viking 1998
1 3 5 7 9 10 8 6 4 2

For my Nana
Helena Margaret Carey (née Cullen)
1909–1993

Acknowledgments

First, I thank my parents, Thomas and Ann Carey, for their generosity, patience, and humor, as well as the literal and figurative support they have given me during the writing of this novel. And my brother, Tommy, for being another artist, thus deflecting their frustrations.

I am grateful to the following for tea, shelter, palm readings, constructive criticism, personal loans, faith, and, in one fashion or another, for giving me the island I fell in love with:

Bernard and Mary Loughlin of the Tyrone Guthrie Centre at Annaghmakerrig, Ireland; The Hawthornden Castle International Retreat for Writers; the staff and faculty of Vermont College; the Islanders; Dana Brigham and Gang at Brookline Booksmith; Alan Paciorek, Sandra Miller, Gary Miller, Matt Swig, Justin Barkley, Noreen Ryan, Terry Byrne, Bridgid Walsh; Sara O'Keefe and her family; The Drisko Girls and Jim; Dr. Judith Robinson; Donald and Norah Alper; my agent, Elizabeth Ziemska; my editor, Jennifer Hershey; and my mentor, Douglas Glover.

Last, because it's our favorite spot, my Best Friend, Sascha.

When you are old and grey and full of sleep,
And nodding by the fire, take down this book,
And slowly read, and dream of the soft look
Your eyes had once, and of their shadows deep;

How many loved your moments of glad grace,
And loved your beauty with love false or true,
But one man loved the pilgrim soul on you,
And loved the sorrows of your changing face;

And bending down beside the glowing bars,
Murmur, a little sadly, how Love fled
And paced upon the mountains overhead
And hid his face amid a crowd of stars.

— WILLIAM BUTLER YEATS

CHAPTER 1

Grace

It is only at night now that she has the strength to wander. Rising quietly, so as not to disturb her lover, Grace pulls a sweater over her pajamas, slips her feet into running sneakers. Stephen had bought her the sneakers to wear in the hospital after she refused to put on the regulation blue foam slippers. She is not a runner but she likes the height of them, the curve of the soles which roll her forward like a boat lifted by waves. She wraps a scarf around her gruesome bald head.

She passes through the cottage quickly, without looking at the tacky furniture—leftovers from someone else's life. Stephen had rented this place so Grace could be near the sea. Sometimes she calls it "the hospice," in an attempt to be the blunt, witty sort of dying person she would like to be.

She goes first to the water, down the damp sand and over to the barnacle rocks, which she climbs gingerly, still surprised by the weakness of her limbs. She wants to stand on the rocks, dive into the cold water and swim the pain away, but she can only sit, watching the moonshine catch the waves, feeling the salty damp seep into her clothing and skin, breathing it; it is thick and familiar in her damaged lungs.

The sea does not speak to her in the daytime. When Stephen manages to coerce her into a walk, the sunlight, harsh on her yellowed skin, distracts her. The beach feels dangerous with Stephen, because of the way he clings to her elbow, guiding her over shells and rocks, assuring that the foamy tide does not wash against her fragile ankles. On these walks she feels like a captive, like a creature held just out of reach of her watery home. She wants to shake him off, as passionately as she used to want to creep into his body because his hands on her skin were not enough. She hides the impulse to push him away, tells herself it is the cancer that makes her feel this repulsion. Though it is not the first time she has felt like a prisoner.

On the nights she escapes, the sea becomes hers again; the rhythm of the waves aligns itself with the thrust and ebb of her heart. She looks over the silver water and imagines another beach across the Atlantic, an Irish shore, the landscape a mirror reflection of this one. There, the wind in the coves was a chorus of the island mermaids, who moaned with the hopes of capturing a sympathetic man. She used to swim there, that moan in her blood, longing to leave. Now, though she has been gone from Ireland for twelve years, it is appearing to her, dropping in heavy folds, swallowing her present life. She thinks how odd it is, that the strongest convictions, like possessions, can lose all meaning when you are dying. Everything that she thought she was about has slipped from her, and the things she never wanted are clinging to her memory like the seaweed in the crevices at her feet.

Her mind is a collage of faces. She sees her mother, whose early wrinkles looked like crevices in rock, whose mouth was constantly clamped in a stern line, who always fought to keep her face expressionless. Grace hated that blank face, she raged to get it to register something—even anger—anything. Now she misses her mother, longs for her like a lonely child. But she escaped from that face and it's too late now, she believes, to ask for it back.

Another face her husband's, an Irish man. Though she has spent several years trying to erase him from her memory, his features come back to her in perfect detail; he glows like a stubborn ghost when she closes her eyes. She wonders why she ever left, why she can't remember what went wrong between them. He was kind, she knows. Had that not been enough? It means more to her now, kindness.

When she feels her body crawling toward sleep, far too soon, she goes back to the cottage, slips into its silence. She opens a bedroom door, checks on her daughter—a teenager who sleeps like a child, her limbs sprawled, mouth gaping, the sheets twisted like vines around her ankles. The glinting black curls on the pillow are her father's. At one time, Grace might have righted the bedding, smoothed the masses of hair away from her daughter's face. But tonight she only stands there, afraid of waking her. They avoid each other now, these two, as intensely as they once clung together.

She closes the door, walks across the dark living room. At a table in the corner she sits, switching on a miniature desk lamp. There is an old typewriter here, a stack of crisp white paper beside it. She winds a sheet through, and types out a note, flinching at the sound of keys, like gunshots in the night.

Gráinne, she types.

> *Please pick up cereal and matches if you pass by the G.S. today. If you have any clothes that need washing—and you must by now, kiddo, unless you plan to keep wearing those stinking jeans—give them to Stephen, he's going to the laundromat.*
>
> *—Love, Mom*

She props the note on the refrigerator with a lobster-shaped magnet. She doesn't know why she continues to compose these strange communications, why she cannot say anything she really feels. She wants to ask her daughter if she's all right, wants to know what she does all day and half the night when she's away from the cottage. But Grace has lost the ability to ask anything. Once, she had prided herself on speaking bluntly, honestly to her daughter. Only recently has she admitted that she's been lying all along. She lied by never telling Gráinne about the people she had left behind them: Gráinne's grandmother, her father, her family. Grace used to think that she was all that Gráinne needed. Now she feels guilty, inadequate, resentful. She is dying, her daughter is living on, and they hate each other for it. They cannot figure out what to say. So they leave notes—hanging them on the refrigerator like sheets of hieroglyphics that neither one of them knows how to translate.

With barely any energy left, her body disintegrating into exhaustion, she sets a place at the dining table. Plate, salad plate, napkin, two forks, two knives, a spoon at the top. A water glass glinting in the moonlight from the window. She has made too much noise, because Stephen opens the bedroom door and calls to her. He thinks that she lays this place for him or for Gráinne, for breakfast, but it's for neither. It is the extra place she always set as a child, a tradition she copied from a book about an old Irish castle, a book she found in her mother's drawer. At the castle, an extra table setting was always laid for the Gaelic queen Granuaile, even if she wasn't expected. A pirate and a warrior, Granuaile was known to appear without warning at the gates with her crew of hungry sailors, assuming she'd be welcomed. Long after Granuaile had died, the castle staff continued to leave a place for her, not wanting to offend the spirit of such a woman.

Grace hasn't thought to set Granuaile's place in years. Once, she did so with a childish hope that she would be able to sail off with the queen after dinner. Then she grew up, and grew to believe that only she could save herself. She performs the ritual again now—the instinct, long dormant, has risen with an ease that frightens her. She no longer believes in pirate queens, in safety. But she can think of nothing else, save those useless little notes, to leave behind her in the night.

She follows the sound of Stephen's voice, returns to the warmth of the bed, the resented comfort of sleep. As she drifts off, Stephen's solid body pressed against her bony back, she listens to the waves, eternally crashing on the beach, hushing, calling, their currents drawing her body away and pulling her mind backward.

CHAPTER 2

Clíona

On the Aer Lingus ticket, someone has spelled my name *Clíodhna*. At the departures desk in Shannon, I consider correcting it with the available pen, but I don't, for fear it will get me in some fix with the authorities. What their rules are, I am not certain—it's been so long since I've even left Ireland—and I don't want to cause myself any more trouble. It is to my daughter Grace's funeral I am going on this airplane. Nothing like my last trip to America, by ship passage, when I was young and had life rather than death waiting on the shore for me.

Clíona is my name. I was baptized Clíodhna but I dropped the silent consonants when I entered primary school. (My mother accused me of breaking the Fourth Commandment—*Honor thy father and thy mother*—heightening my fear of hellfire, but this could not compare to my dread of ridicule.) You can find both spellings in those wee dictionaries of Irish names; they're the rage in all the shops now on account of the fashion of naming children in Gaelic rather than English. In my day, on the island where I grew up, my name was right strange. All of my friends were called Mary, Margaret, or Joyce. When I had my daughter in America, I baptized her Grace, with the hope that a normal name would help her fit in. Of course, she grew up despising me for it, for giving her such a diminished, compromising name, as she called it. I suppose it wasn't the name that bothered her so much as my intentions, you know the sort of way. She called her own daughter Gráinne, after the pirate queen of Connaught. I often wonder if the girl hates her for it, if the cycle has come round again, as it tends to do in families.

You can read in these name books the story of Clíodhna, who eloped against her parents' will and sailed off in a curragh with her lover. He left her alone in the boat while he went hunting, and a great wave came roaring in and drowned the poor woman. From then on she was said to be the fairy of the sea. A guardian, of sorts, who existed to save others from similar tragedy. When Grace was a teenager, and at her most vocal in her hatred of me, she used to say that the name Clíodhna suited me perfectly. She believed my life was defined by a pitiful and unimaginative subjection to others. She never understood me. But I am as much to blame as anyone for that.

I can remember her as a child, eating her supper at the polished wooden table in the Willoughbys' kitchen in Boston, where I was employed. She always refused to eat unless I sat at the table with her. She laid an extra place setting beside hers, even though I never had time for my tea until later on.

"Don't stand above me, Mom," she'd say, "I hate that. I hate it!" Sure, I was too busy to sit idle, but I humored her; I'd always humored her, that ridiculous little temper. She was a scowling, moody child, but gorgeous, with her thick ginger hair and sea-green eyes. She would grow to be so much more stunning than I ever was.

In one particular memory, Mrs. Willoughby comes into the kitchen. I stand and ask her if everything is all right and she waves her graceful fingers.

"Sit, please, Clíona." (*Cleeoona*, she calls me, and I've never bothered to correct her.) "Don't let me disturb you."

I sit back down across from Grace, who'd automatically stopped eating while I was standing, but resumes again when my bottom touches the chair.

"Just when you get a chance, Clíona, could you fetch us a hot plate? It seems there is one missing from the dining room table." She swings back out the door.

My daughter freezes as I rise to take a trivet from the cupboard and bring it to their table. Mrs. Willoughby takes the gravy pitcher off its saucer and places it on the trivet. I have learned not to question her American sense of table manners. When I rejoin my daughter in the kitchen, she does not resume eating.

"Work away, now," I say, but she stares at her plate, at the potato jackets and meat buried in gravy, her brow crouching like an animal over her eyes.

"Why do you let her talk to you like that?" she says to me.

"Like what?" I say. Sure, even at eight years of age, her voice carries so much more weight than mine.

"Like that, like that!" She waves her fork in the direction of the swinging door. "Like she does all the time. Like you're not good as her or something."

"Hesh up, now, and finish your supper," I say. "Selfish child. You'll learn to show some respect before I'm through with you." She looks at me as if she loathes me.

I hadn't meant to sound so cruel. But it was my daughter who was acting high and mighty, who thought she was better than those around her. The Willoughbys weren't perfect, sure, but they'd given me a job and my daughter a home, and I was grateful for that much. I didn't expect to be coddled. But Grace, well, there was rarely a human being, myself included, who could meet her standards.

My daughter is dead now. It was a man named Stephen who rang me to say so. Her lover, I suppose, but I do not judge.

"Was there an accident?" I said to him, hearing the echo of my voice in the bad overseas connection. "Sudden, was it?"

The man paused. "No," he said. "She'd been sick for a while."

"I see," I said. That was how it would be, so. My daughter denying me her death as she'd denied me her life. I was not surprised.

Sure, with all that's passed, I did not have to board this plane to Boston. I could have thanked your man for giving me the news, and gone back to the life I've had without Grace for years now. But there was the child to consider. Gráinne. And her only fifteen. Though this Stephen assured me that there were many friends of Grace's who would be glad to take her in, I knew that was not a proper solution. No grandchild of mine will be farmed out to some American family. And of course there was that image that flashed across my mind of a dark-haired girl who curled in my lap and slept there, trusting that I would not move away. My little Gráinne, still tugging at my heart after all these years.

I decided so. I boarded Eamon's ferry, which I take every week to the mainland grocer. I watched my island grow smaller and saw how a foreigner might think it ugly on first sight—the rusted quay, the treeless, rocky landscape that from a distance appears diminished under heavy power lines. From this angle, a foreigner would not see the spectacular black-and-green cliffs on the west end, or the white expanse of Mermaid Beach where seals bask at dawn. A new visitor might find the smell of Inis Murúch—a blend of netted fish and turf fire which hangs thickly in the damp air—hard to stomach. Or the complex accent of the islanders frustrating. My daughter had found Murúch so. This had been a mystery to me, after all my years in America, where I had longed for the scent and music of my home.

I bought this ticket to Boston. It's a ticket I've thought about purchasing for years, hoping to find my daughter again. I tell myself, as the plane flies over the Atlantic, that though it is too late to change some things, there is always the chance of beginning others. I am all Gráinne has left in the world. And, as far as any connection with my daughter, Gráinne is all I have left as well.

CHAPTER 3

Gráinne

At the wake—in a room where my mother's body was displayed in a coffin, her hands contorted in mock prayer, a string of beads tied like a shoelace through her fingers, and a thick red wig lying like a pelt between her head and the silvery pillow—a woman I had thought was dead came to fetch me.

I was sitting alone in the front row watching Stephen, my mother's boyfriend. He was kneeling by the side of the casket, reaching over to finger the sleeve of her dress, and then, with a gentle stroke that made me nauseous when I imagined the feel of it, he touched her earlobe. Behind her head was the wreath of white and yellow roses, draped with a satin ribbon inscribed *Mother* in purple cursive. Stephen had ordered it, as well as a heart-shaped arrangement of pink carnations, that resembled an oversized box of Valentine candy, with a ribbon that read *Beloved*. I'd had this strange feeling all morning that the ribbons were like flash cards, meant to remind me in all the mugginess of funeral arrangements who I was and why I was there. This is your mother. You are her daughter. Your mother is dead.

The old woman came in by the doorway to the right of the wreaths. She was not exactly fat, but solid-looking, with thick, bleached hair tied in a loose bun. Her face was intricately lined, the deepest wrinkles leading from the edges of her mouth to her chin— an outline like the wooden mouthpiece of a puppet. She was one of those old people that you can tell were once beautiful. She looked briefly at the casket and then at me, and for a moment she looked confused, and I thought she must have come into the wrong viewing room. But instead of turning back, she walked over to me, her puppet mouth hanging open in preparation to speak.

"Is that Gráinne?" she said, and I was surprised, not only that she knew my name, but that she pronounced it correctly. It's the name of a sixteenth-century Gaelic queen, pronounced *Graw-nya*, with a roll over the *r*, but no one ever knows this unless I tell them, and then they rarely remember anyway.

I was too freaked to answer the woman, but she read my silence as a hello and sat down.

"Clíona O'Halloran is my name," she said. She pronounced it oddly, with a clicking sound at the beginning. Her voice skittered over the syllables so quickly that I couldn't get a picture in my mind of how it would be spelled. "I'm a relation of yours from Ireland," she said.

There was something very familiar about her voice. It was like the difference between my mother saying my name and a teacher or new friend. In my mother's voice my name sounded musical, like poetry; there was a rhythm that no one else ever seemed to reproduce. All of this woman's words sounded like my mother saying *Gráinne*.

"You're who?" I said. I had no relatives—none in America, let

11

alone Ireland. It was always just me and my mother. My mother said she came from nowhere and I came from her.

"I'm your grandmother," the woman said, and she looked over at the casket, where she must have seen my mother's wigged head—and Stephen, crouching beside it. "Your Mum is . . . ," she said, then stopped and looked down, looping the thin black strap of her purse over her fingers. "Grace was my daughter." Her hands were brown and old, the delicate bones starkly visible beneath the loose skin. Her fingers, though callused, were long and graceful, bare except for a polished gold band. I thought of my mother's long fingers, holding a cigarette like it was a part of her, hovering delicately from her mouth and away from her face and back again. And my mother's waxy fingers now, tied together by the white beads and silver links of what Stephen said was called a rosary, which I'd never seen before.

The woman sighed. "Have you no words?" she said. What did she expect? "Grandmother," "relation," these were words that had never had anything to do with me. I hated this woman suddenly, for coming in and changing the silence of this room in which it seemed I had sat for ages.

"I suppose Grace told you nothing," she said, and I felt a tight sob advancing in my throat. My forehead ached as I tried to stop it, and I saw my mother's and Stephen's faces blur and waver as if under water.

"My mother tells me everything," I said, my voice breaking. Then Stephen seemed to wake up from his trance, turning around and looking at me with so much pity that I stood up, ready to fight him off. "My mother tells me everything," I said again, to Stephen this time, and he nodded. I'd said this to him before, I'd said it to him only last month, last month when my mother was still alive. Then too I had known it wasn't true.

I started to back away, moving toward the doorway behind the rows of chairs. The woman stood up and they both stepped forward, as if they were stalking me.

"Gráinne," the woman said in her musical voice.

"Gráinne," Stephen echoed, flatly, though he'd always put more effort into saying it correctly than any of my mother's previous boy-friends. "Why don't we go back to the apartment and discuss this over lunch," he said. "You should eat something," he added, when he saw I was glaring at him, "before we come back for the evening service."

I shrugged and let him take hold of my arm. He'd been trying so hard, for so long, to coordinate the little things, as if by doing so he could make me believe everything was normal. He guided me outside, the tips of his fingers a gentle pressure against the small of my back. I imagined the old woman was watching Stephen's hand, as acutely aware of its position as I was.

When we reached the car, Stephen put her suitcase in the trunk and went around to the passenger side, to hold the door open for her. I got in the rear seat by myself. When he climbed in and started the coughing motor I watched the backs of their heads, thinking about how many times I'd viewed Stephen and my mother from this angle. Before, when her hair was a mass of silky, rust-color curls, and later, when the knotted end of a scarf covered the base of her bald skull. I stared angrily at this woman's cheaply dyed blond bun and thought: *I* should be sitting in the front now.

The woman shifted around and caught me watching her. She smiled queerly and made a gesture with her fingers to her hair. I realized she was referring to mine and I reached for my neck, pluck-ing at the meager strands.

"Gráinne Mhaol," she said, "was the pirate queen's nickname. It is told that as a young child she begged to be taken along with her father's ship sailing to Spain. When her mother told her that ships were not the place for young ladies, Gráinne cut her hair like a boy's. They called her Gráinne Mhaol, bald Gráinne, after that."

I ran a hand through what was left of my hair. At the last minute that morning, Stephen had trimmed it, trying to even out the mess I'd made when I'd cut it all off, myself. In the end there was not much he could do to fix it, so I had slapped some of his gel on my

head, and combed it down. I knew I looked ridiculous and I certainly
didn't need to be reminded.

"What's your point?" I snapped, and Stephen jerked his eyes up
to the rearview mirror.

"Gráinne!" he said, and the woman turned back around, putting
her hand in the air to quiet him, as if I were some poor little orphan
who needed to be humored. I crossed my arms and slumped back
in the seat, watching the featureless highway whiz by. I wondered
if this woman thought she was moving in with us, if she had come
to replace my mother out of some guilty obligation. If she thinks
I'm going to make it easy for her, I said to myself, she knows nothing
about my mother, and even less about me.

"Please eat something, Gráinne," Stephen said. "You've got to
be hungry by now." He had stopped by Legal Sea Foods on the
drive home and picked up clam chowder, salad, and warm rolls. He
must have remembered that, last year, this had been my favorite
meal. But in my bowl the thick soup looked like curdled milk,
littered with chunks of potatoes and clams. Orange grease amoebas
floated on the surface.

"I'm not hungry," I said, but he kept watching me, so I selected
a relatively clean piece of lettuce from the mound of overdressed
salad and forced it into my mouth, letting my saliva well up so that
when I chewed, the taste wouldn't be too strong.

Mrs. O'Halloran, who had insisted on setting the kitchen table
and doling out the food, was now eating with such graceful and
spare movements that I waited eagerly for her to slip up and dribble
chowder onto her suit. Stephen was hunkered over his bowl, his
eyes darting guiltily back and forth between the two of us.

When they had finished eating, and my soup had cooled to a
custard, Mrs. O'Halloran cleared the dishes and made us tea. She
had to search through the cupboards to find my mother's old ceramic
teapot, which she rinsed with boiling water from the kettle before
dropping in the Salada bags. She brought cups and saucers and tea-

spoons to the table, as well as the milk carton and a cereal bowl she'd filled with sugar. Stephen and I watched her in silence. She seemed to be performing some sort of religious ritual, like the priest I'd once seen on Sunday cable, with white crackers, water, and wine, all laid out in preparation. My mother, when she drank tea, poured water— before it boiled—into her "#1 MOM" mug, plopped in a tea bag, and, without waiting for it to steep, added skim milk. She sipped it still standing at the refrigerator, a cigarette in her other hand, the Salada octagon hanging out of the mug like a price tag.

Mrs. O'Halloran sat down to pour the tea, and we passed around the sugar and milk in silence, Stephen and I swirling our teaspoons carefully, as if they were dangerous weapons. The gentle clinking was like some foreign music around the table. The tea spread with an unbearable heat through my throat and stomach, while Stephen asked Mrs. O'Halloran a few stupid questions about her flight—how long was it and did she spend much time at Logan, blah, blah, blah. It was becoming more obvious to me that Stephen had something to do with this—that he'd known this Irish woman was coming for me. He asked her if she was tired and told her she'd be staying in my Mom's room.

I hadn't spoken yet, but when the woman stood up, ready to go settle herself into the room like she belonged there, I couldn't stand it anymore.

"Are you leaving tomorrow?" I said. The funeral was tomorrow; maybe she was just here to say good-bye. She looked at Stephen before answering me.

"Not tomorrow, no," she said. "I'm staying on awhile, to sort out your mother's affairs and . . ." She stopped, began clearing the cups and saucers.

"And what?" I said. I was really getting fed up with this take-charge crap. Who the hell did she think she was?

"Sure, we'll talk this through later on," she said. "It's rest you should be getting now."

"No," I said, ignoring Stephen's don't-be-rude look. "What else do you think you need to sort out?" The woman sighed, putting the cups back on the table.

"I'm sorry, Gráinne," she said. It was the beginning of the same speech I'd been hearing the last two days: I'm sorry, Gráinne, that your mother died. . . . "It's obvious that Grace did not tell you much about where she came from. But the only family you have now is in Ireland. I think arrangements should be made for you to come back with me. When you're ready."

"My mother didn't have any family," I said. "Just me."

"It's your grandmother I am, I tell you."

"My grandmother died when I was three years old." As I said it, she looked pained, and I was glad, in a vicious sort of way, that I'd hurt her.

"That's what your mother thought, yes," she said. She sounded exhausted.

"So, what, you've been pretending to be dead for twelve years? And you're just showing up now?" Mrs O'Halloran looked at Stephen again. I was getting tired of this conspiracy shit, I really was.

"No, Gráinne," she said. "I haven't been pretending, your mother has. She wanted me dead, so." She said it like it was nothing. As if she hadn't just told me my mother had been lying to me for most of my life. I looked at Stephen. He was sitting down again, holding his forehead with one thin hand.

"How long have you known about this?" I said. He dropped his hand and looked up at me. He looked exhausted, too. It seemed everyone was exhausted but me—exhausted *with* me, maybe.

"Not long," he said.

Well, fuck you both, I thought, but I couldn't say it. I just left the two of them in the kitchen, went to my room, and slammed the door. I could hear my mother's response in my head. *Why don't you slam it a little harder*, she always used to sing after me. *Maybe you'll convince me your anger is justified.*

★   ★   ★

16

That night, after we had returned from the evening "viewing," and Mrs. O'Halloran had gone to bed, I opened my door wearing only my nightshirt and walked across the dark living room. Stephen was lying on the couch, with a blanket covering his body and his feet sticking out at the end over the arm cushion. He'd let his long brown hair out of the ponytail and taken his shirt off. He had one arm flung across his eyes but I could tell he was awake by the careful way he was breathing. When I stepped up next to him, he peeked out from beneath his wrist, then sat up, swinging his feet down to the floor to make room for me on the couch. He was wearing his New England Conservatory sweat shorts, the ones my Mom always teased him about. ("What do a bunch of wimpy musicians need with gym suits?") I sat down on the warm cushions and he sighed, attempted a sad smile. He smelled like he'd been drinking, and I saw on the table the bottle of whiskey my mother opened only when she had a cold. I could barely see his features, but I could fill them in from memory, I'd been looking at him for so long.

"Can't sleep," he said, a statement for both of us rather than a question. He combed a hand through his hair. At the evening service, while we stood in the receiving line, I had focused on that hand, watching him clasp the palms of my mother's friends and the long procession of her former boyfriends. I had felt that the motion of his fingers squeezing and releasing, was what sustained me, that it was his hand that was powering mine to do the same. I had never been to a wake before, never suspected that my mother would have wanted rosaries and little prayer cards. But she had decided on the arrangements; Stephen had told me so. Maybe she had even imagined me standing in that line, had predicted that when I shook hands with the priest I would have to listen to Stephen to know to call him "Father."

Mrs. O'Halloran had not stood with us, but sat in a chair by the coffin, staring at my mother's body. Probably, I figured, she didn't want to keep explaining herself to people.

"I want to talk," I said to Stephen. I knew if I sat there in the dark with him much longer, the quiet would become too thick and I would have to leave without saying a thing.

"Yep," Stephen blurted out. "Okay."

"Why didn't you tell me?" I whispered, conscious of Mrs. O'Halloran in the next room. "Why didn't Mom tell me?"

"I don't know, Gráinne," he said.

"I don't like her," I said.

"Give it some time."

"I don't want to give it any time. I don't want to give her anything. If she really is my grandmother she must be a horrible person because Mom obviously couldn't stand her. She wanted her dead." I stopped at that word, *dead*. It was coming up so often now, a small, flat, unanswerable word.

"That doesn't mean she's a horrible person, Gráinne. She was a mother, Grace was a daughter. Shit happens. Competition, resentment, personality clashes. You can't understand because your Mom's always been your best friend." Stephen blushed.

Until she started dying, we were both thinking.

"She can't make me go," I said. "She can't just take me to another country. It's probably not even legal."

"You don't have to go right away. Take some time to talk to her before you act like you're being kidnapped." I didn't answer that, just sat seething and hating him for a moment. But when I glanced over he looked so tired and miserable that I felt an odd stirring that swished away my hatred. I plucked at the seam of the couch cushion.

"Can't I just stay with you?" I whispered. I'd been thinking that sentence, and dreading it, for months.

"Oh, Gráinne," he said, like he was about to cry, and he turned and put his arm on the back of the couch behind me. "I'm not your father, Gráinne. I couldn't be your father. I'm a twenty-eight-year-old musician. I don't know what your mother saw in me, but it certainly wasn't a substitute dad for you." When he'd shifted, the blanket had fallen, exposing the outline of his long leg in the darkness. I was watching it and, without thinking, moved my own smooth thigh so it brushed against the hair on his.

"But I thought—" I started. He put his hand on my shoulder and pushed me very slightly away.

"Don't, Gráinne," he said. I had heard that before, my name like a scold coming out of the darkness. "I was your mother's boyfriend. Your mother's boyfriend. Nothing more."

I felt like my insides, which had been numb for days, were splintering apart with his voice, slicing their way to the surface. I stood up, my legs hot and weak, and walked with effort over to my bedroom door. Won't you miss me at all? I thought. Won't it hurt you when I go, too? But the room was silent. "Nothing more," he had said.

In my room, lying curled up like a cat on my bed, I listened for hours to the faint sniffling and shuddering of breath that was Stephen, crying about something, with his face in the sofa.

CHAPTER 4

Grace

"I think Gráinne wants something from me," Stephen says. He's rubbing Grace's back, running his palms up and out, like waves over her skin. He has to rub gently now, because if he presses too hard she feels as though her organs are being bruised. She can hear the tide coming in on the beach, and she wonders if Gráinne is swimming in it.

"Grace, are you listening?" Stephen says.

"Gráinne's fine," Grace says. Stephen's rubbing loses its rhythm; he has never been able to talk and move his hands at the same time. As if all his coordination goes into playing the piano, and he doesn't have the concentration for the tasks which are left over.

"She's angry all the time now," Stephen says. "I think she's afraid of being alone."

"She won't be alone," Grace says, rolling away from him.

"I thought maybe she was looking for a father," Stephen says, barely petting her back.

"She's done fine without a father for twelve years," Grace says. "She likes you, Stephen, but I think you're underestimating her."

"Maybe," Stephen says. What he means, she can tell by his tone, is: Maybe *you* are.

When she closes her eyes, Grace can see her daughter clearly: three years old, sitting at the scarred wooden table in their first apartment in Brighton. She threw tea parties with the set Grace had bought for her at Woolworth's. Plastic plates, saucers, cups, and a teapot with a rose pattern, which had begun to flake off from too much use. Gráinne prepared the pretend tea the way her grandmother did—scalding the pot, shaking in some oregano that represented the loose tea they'd drunk in Ireland. During tea parties, their kitchen would smell like a pizza parlor. Gráinne set places for her dolls, one for her kitten (who stayed because of the milk in her tiny saucer), and gave the least battered pieces to her mother. She always laid one extra place, reverently, opposite Grace, and left the chair empty.

"Who's that for, sweetie?" Grace asked once. "Is it for the pirate queen?"

"Nope," Gráinne said, pouring the flecked green water into the tiny cups. "Dada."

The smell of oregano and warm milk turned Grace's stomach.

"You still think Dada's coming?" Grace whispered. Gráinne gave the empty seat a sugar cookie.

"First he's gotta escape from the mermaid pirates," Gráinne said. "Will you take sugar?" she added, in her grandmother's accent, holding a spoon out to her mother's cup.

Grace said nothing else the whole year during which Gráinne performed this ritual. Sometimes, watching the determination in the girl's face as she laid the table for tea, Grace would shiver, and look toward the doorway, half-expecting their absent guest to appear. Gráinne never mentioned her father except at these tea parties, and

21

Grace debated with herself about the best way to handle the subject. How do you explain something you don't understand yourself to a three-year-old? A year later, when Gráinne lost interest in her tea parties—and, it seemed, her missing father—Grace was relieved.

I should have talked to her then, Grace thinks now. Stephen has stopped rubbing her back, but he's still here, waiting for something. She should have explained to Gráinne, or tried to, about why she left Ireland, about how one could feel trapped, captured, even where there were no pirates or mermaids. But she'd waited. And Gráinne had forgotten, never asked about her father except for an occasional, almost journalistic inquiry when she reached puberty—what color was his hair, that sort of thing. No more "Dada"—just a man about whom she was mildly curious.

Now Grace's pain is beginning again. Actually, it is always there—at different levels, from bearable to almost surreal—and at the moment it is escalating to a degree that will require the pills which keep her from thinking clearly. Soon, she knows, the doctor will give her a supply of morphine shots, which Stephen will have to administer. The pills no longer work the way they used to.

Stephen knows from the sweat on her forehead, and from the way she begins to thrash against the sheets like a fish, that it is time to hand her the tablets. Time to help her sip the water which he leaves at room temperature, because cold liquids make her feel like her teeth are cracking.

When the edges of the pain begin to smooth, she tries to think of Gráinne as a little girl again, to think of a time when she knew what she was doing as a mother, when she believed in the logic behind her lies. But it is herself as a girl she remembers instead, not as a whole being, but as a reflection in the scraps of what surrounded her. Herself next to a boy named Michael, whom for years she thought of as her brother, though she knew they weren't related in any traditional sense. Michael had his own mother and father, but Grace's mother was also his mother, in a way that no one had bothered to explain, other than to say she was his "nanny." Which hadn't made any sense to the young Grace.

Grace's own father was dead and had been dead, as her mother put it, for longer than Grace had been alive. Grace liked to imagine that they had spent time together in heaven, when she was just the soul of a baby waiting to be born. When she thought of her father, she pictured an angel. A winged man who looked like Jesus without the exposed, thorny heart. At least, that was how she imagined him before she found out her mother had been lying to her.

It was Michael who told her. Every night, he snuck into her bed and they pulled the sheets over themselves like a tent, lighting the inside with a flashlight they stole from the kitchen. If it was late and the grownups were in bed, Grace and Michael would take their pajamas off and trace their fingers over their identical upper bodies, giggling at the way their nipples puckered and shrunk like dried fruit. One night, when Michael had taken off his underwear too, and Grace saw the extra globes of flesh, she laughed so hard that Michael got mad at her.

"Your father's not in Heaven," he had said. "He's in Hell because he never married your mother." When Grace stopped laughing and just looked at him, her pupils throbbing, he tried to take it back. But she punched him in the mouth anyway. There was a little blood, and he cried, which brought Grace's mother, who smacked Grace for having no pajamas on as well as for being a bully.

After that, Grace's father was gone. She never pictured the angel again. And her mother, who had always been a stern but slightly unfocused presence in Grace's life, became the expressionless face that Grace learned to mistrust, and, later, to hate.

Grace loses the memory as Stephen pulls the sheets up over her back, smoothing the wrinkles she made in her pain. She wants him to pull them up farther, so she can make a tent, but she is too tired to explain why. Stephen requires more explanation from her than any other man she has ever loved.

"Do you understand what I wrote down about the arrangements?" Grace says to him. She is afraid he hasn't read her notes. He does not like to discuss the details of her dying.

"I was Catholic once, too," he says. "I know the routine. I just don't understand why you want it."

"It's not for me," Grace says. Stephen closes his eyes, as he does a lot lately when she says something that seems to sting.

"It's not too late to talk to her," he says. At first she thinks he means her mother, but then realizes he's talking about Gráinne.

"No," Grace says, "it's too early."

"What does that mean?" Stephen says, but she closes her eyes. He doesn't understand. He was somebody's child, but he has no children. He doesn't know that things you swear you will never do become the things you *must* do, for reasons you never counted on. He doesn't know that if she tells Gráinne the truth now, she will die in her daughter before she even dies in herself.

CHAPTER 5

Gráinne

Stephen had lived with us for the longest of any of my mother's boyfriends. He wasn't the first of them that I'd had a crush on, but he was the first crush I'd dreamed about. Sexy dreams that left me blushing and frightened in the morning. Like once, I dreamt that he took off my shirt and lifted me up onto his piano, stood between my legs and kissed me wetly down my breasts and stomach and back up to my neck. I couldn't look at him for days after that one.

I hid my feelings well, I know, because my mother didn't tease me. In the past she'd had fun with me when I started watching and thinking about her boyfriends. Never in front of them, so it was pretty harmless. She didn't try to embarrass me, but instead acted like her lover was some boy at school and we were two girls talking about how cute he was. That's the way my mother was with me—a best friend, a conspirator.

"We're both boy-crazy," she'd say. She said I'd inherited her sex appeal, but I knew I could only wish to be as sexy as she was. She'd always had a man or two in love with her. I could remember most of her boyfriends, and we used to have arguments about our memories—she hated to admit that she had forgotten a man. I'd learned long ago not to ask her about my father, simply because he seemed so unimportant. It was as though he had never really existed for her: our life was the two of us in the center and men on the outside. Men she was never secretive or embarrassed about.

Like one night when I was eight, I woke up to what sounded like a man being strangled—grunting, breathless noises coming from my mother's bedroom. I got out of bed, went to her door, and knocked, calling for her. She came out, tying her robe, and took me back to my room. She told me she'd been having sex with Bob, the guy who had come for dinner. I already knew about sex. I wanted to know about the noises.

"Bob was having an orgasm," she said. Her voice was slightly musical, with that ever present hint of laughter underneath: it was the voice that told me everything. "He was pretty funny, wasn't he?" Bob had been listening from the hallway, and when he heard her say that, he got really mad and yelled something about my mother being a sicko, then left our apartment, slamming the door.

"I'd like to know what he would have told you," she said, snuggling under my covers. I can remember the tingly warmth of her hand on my arm, and the smell of her cigarettes and the sage oil she wore as perfume. There was another scent clinging to her, a strange combination of her sweat and a mustiness I thought must be left over from Bob, which I knew would be gone by morning.

Stephen, from the beginning, was different than the others. He was the first man who ever belonged to us. The other few that had moved in, they were all right, but they came and they went and we never missed them much. My mother usually managed to stay friends with her men, so occasionally I'd see the nicest ones coming back for dinner or at one of her matchmaking parties. She liked to pass them off to her single girlfriends. I'd never worried about my mother losing some man, until Stephen came. And technically, I guess, she never did lose him.

When my mother first found out she had breast cancer, she told Stephen to move out. She packed his duffel bag and called the piano movers and locked him out of our apartment. He sat on the stairs out front for hours, sent the truck away when they came for the piano. My mother had me checking out the window every hour to see if he had gone yet. By the time she let him back in it was late at night and Stephen was so cold his face had purple spots. She wrapped him in a blanket and laughed.

"Are you trying to impress me?" she said.

"I'm the stable, trustworthy type," he said through chattering teeth.

He was with her when she had her first, small operation and a session of chemo, and after that she got better. It was months before the next lump. When it came she said to him: "You can leave any-time."

She finished dying in a cottage on Singing Beach that Stephen had rented for the three of us. It was a long summer. At the very end she'd checked into the local hospital, and it was Stephen, not me, who went with her.

That first morning after we moved to Singing Beach, I woke up and lay frightened for a minute until I recognized the little bedroom I was in. The walls were papered in a faded yellow rosebud print. The bed frame and the bureau were lime-green and lumpy, painted over many times. Nothing in the room was mine except my clothes, which were already in the closet. At home I had photographs clipped from magazines and my favorite poems written in blue marker on the wall next to my bed. I hadn't wanted this place to be anything like home. That morning I wished I had brought something, any-thing, to anchor me.

I looked for the bathroom—which I had forgotten was on the

other side of the single-floor cottage, off the kitchen—then pushed open the gray-paneled door without knocking. My mother stood in front of the sink, her nightgown dropped to her waist, the gauze bandages on her chest pulled away from a deformed sunken welt of puckered skin and stitches. I hadn't seen my mother naked since the operation, so I just stood there, shocked. She lowered her head and covered the screaming ugly spot with her upper arm.

"Gráinne," she scolded, and when I didn't move she pushed the door closed with her foot, forcing me back into the kitchen. "I'll be out in a minute, honey." I didn't wait but hurried back to my room.

There was a wicker-framed mirror above my bureau, painted the same lumpy green as the furniture. I stood in front of it and unbuttoned my nightgown, dropping it down to my hips. I ran my palms across my breasts and watched my nipples pucker up, red and hard and deformed. I remembered the first time I had noticed them doing this, when I was eleven, how I had run crying to my mother. I had thought there was something wrong with my new, growing breasts, that I had cancer. She'd laughed and explained how it works—that my nipples would always respond to cold and to excitement. Later, if it happened when I was with a boy, I would concentrate, trying to figure out which I was—excited or cold.

My mother no longer had a nipple.

I covered my chest and stared hard at my image in the mirror. "My name is Gráinne," I whispered, and repeated it over and over— a trick I'd learned when I was six. If I said it enough the sounds became meaningless and my face evil and unfamiliar, like some naked witch in a stranger's mirror.

When I woke again later, Stephen was practicing, and the thundering of his piano rattled the gray floorboards in my room. I put on a T-shirt and cutoffs before opening my door. The house was elevated above the high-tide mark on pillars, and one wall was glass doors that looked out onto the beach. From where I stood it looked like the waves were crashing right behind Stephen's head.

"Good morning, good morning!" he sang out when he saw me, playing a silly tune with single keys. The piano looked monstrous and out-of-place in the tiny room, luxurious mahogany next to a couch with a fisherman's navigation map embroidered in blue on the fabric. The piano was the only thing in the cottage that reminded me of home.

"Should we have a lesson this morning?" he asked.

"I don't think so," I said. He shrugged and went back to playing. I grabbed a nectarine and went out on the beach.

Stephen had been teaching me piano on and off since he'd moved in with us. I used to love our lessons, mostly because I got to sit so close to him on that smooth bench, and because he touched me a lot, showing me how to move my fingers and wrists. He slid the tip of each of my fingers gently along the ivory keys before pressing down. I had imagined kissing him and thought that his mouth would feel like those keys, cool, soft, and tense, hovering just above something powerful. I'd stopped the lessons awhile back, to prepare myself for when he decided to leave us. My mother had given him permission, what she called her "get-out-of-jail-free card"; he didn't even need an explanation to take off. Each day I half expected him to be gone before breakfast, leaving my mother bleary-eyed but affectionate; she'd say things like "It's so nice to have my freedom" and "There are plenty more where he came from" while pouring my cereal. It had also occurred to me that if Stephen left, my mother might *not* say the usual things, might not start dating someone else right away, or not get out of bed to pour my cereal at all. Either way I didn't want to torture myself with any more sensuous piano lessons. I didn't want to have more to miss when he was gone.

When I'd finished the nectarine and buried the pit in the hole I'd been digging in the sand with my toes, I went back up the porch steps. I stopped and peered in the sliding door. Stephen wasn't at the piano, he was helping my mother sit down in a chair by the dining table. She was wearing her purple scarf, and some red bangs, fluffed up to look thicker, poked out over her forehead. She turned her face up to Stephen and smiled weakly. He touched her, his fingers resting on the side of her neck, his thumb grazing her earlobe. I decided not to go in and went back down to the beach. I walked along the edge of the waves—not looking ahead where I was going, but down at the seaweed, shells, and foaming water at my feet, thinking eventually they'd lead me somewhere.

I sat on the cement wall that lined the public beach strip, watching the swarms of tired, sweaty families carrying coolers and umbrellas and L.L. Bean canvas bags. I kept an eye out for the teenagers, strutting in tight groups back and forth from the general store, some of the boys playing volleyball with a fierce energy. I saw one boy, tall and spare, with tan shoulders, and hair in a thick ponytail like Stephen's. He played volleyball well but nonchalantly; he had a cigarette propped in the sand by his feet and in between serves he picked it out and dragged on it. He looked older than me, maybe seventeen, and confident—the type that would look straight into your eyes for a while before he kissed you. I lit a cigarette and watched him play.

"Man-hunting," my mother would have called this if she'd been there. Flirting was something she liked and knew she was good at. But this thing I'd been doing since my body had gone berserk with strange longing felt like something else entirely.

It had started with dreams. Not dreams about being with boys or anything specifically sexy; those dreams didn't come until Stephen moved in. In these earlier dreams I'd be alone, usually sitting on a park bench, and between my thighs this bubble would begin to grow, a swollen, living thing that was frightening even though it felt so good, because I was not sure if the bubble was a part of me growing outward or something dangerous trying to get in. Eventually, even the fear didn't matter and I would press my thighs together, trying to keep the bubble from escaping, willing it to move harder against me. I'd always be struggling to keep a straight face because people would be walking by with their dogs. Occasionally, some man or boy would sit down and try to talk to me and I would close my eyes and wish him away so that I could finish alone. Often I would wake with echoes in my stomach and thighs, my underwear slippery.

I knew what it was. I'd read *Our Bodies, Ourselves*; I'd had many explicit conversations with my blunt mother. I wanted to find that feeling when I was awake. I tried touching myself, late at night with my covers pulled up over my head like a tent, my underwear down at my ankles, wetting my fingers in my mouth and probing around. And sometimes I'd manage a minor explosion, a muscle spasm, that was so unlike what I'd dreamt that I'd end up crying, feeling stupid and disgusting. I'd fall asleep smelling myself on my fingers.

Then, last year, after Stephen moved in and I started having dreams about him, I fooled around with a few boys. But the only time I felt anything was before they touched me, when I was anticipating their touch, imagining it. Passion, I decided, wasn't this gropey sex stuff, it had nothing to do with a tongue in my mouth or fingers plunging around in my pants. Ecstasy, or the closest thing I could get to it, came right before a kiss, in the swollen bubble of space between lips that crackled and pulled, when I could still imagine the feel of a boy's mouth, before it actually clamped down, real and slimy, sucking on my teeth in a fearful hurry. I was experimenting more than my mother even knew, looking for the perfect kiss, and I had it so clearly orchestrated in my mind that I knew I would not fail to recognize it when it came.

The volleyball boy was looking at me, although at first it was with only sidelong glances, and I had to torture myself trying to figure out if he was going to look again. I arranged my legs out along the wall so their length would be noticeable. I don't think of myself as pretty, but my mother always taught me to emphasize my best features—and I've been told that I have her long legs and her breasts, that my dark, curly hair is exotic. I've realized that these are things that boys like, though occasionally, when someone is first looking at me like the boy on the beach was, I feel deformed, and I imagine

31

my legs are spindly, my chest a lump of fat, my hair frizzed out like the Bride of Frankenstein's.

He was definitely looking. Lingering now, obvious; he wanted me to notice. The ball came toward him and he botched the shot, distracted. I laughed and he grinned at me. I was already plotting the rest of the summer. We would walk by the waves at dusk, our elbows purposefully brushing, the last of the sunlight outlining our skin in orange. He would stop, turn, move closer, gaze into my eyes. He would kiss me, perfectly, and my summer, the rest of my life, would fall in the shadow of that kiss, a warm powerful pressure that would sustain me.

"I'm Mark," the boy said. He was standing in front of the wall, twirling the volleyball in one hand. It sounded like *Mac* the way he said it, with a heavy Boston accent. Not the best name. Not necessarily the name of someone who'd change your life, but I forgave him for it. You never knew.

"I'm Grace," I said, giving him my mother's name. I didn't know why, exactly, maybe I didn't want to have to say "Gráinne" five times over, or maybe I dreaded the mess his accent would make of my Gaelic name.

"You're too pretty to be sitting all alone, Grace," he said, and he smiled at me. It was that easy.

I spent the rest of the day with him, sparkling with anticipation. I really barely heard anything he said, I was so caught up in trying to figure out when he would kiss me. I was constantly wetting my lips, checking my breath, sucking in my stomach in case he suddenly put his hands around my waist. It was exhausting, this waiting, and I had moments of doubt, where I would suddenly feel I had been mooning over someone who had no interest in me. Then I would be mean to him, I'd be tough and unreachable, and he would try even harder.

After sunset, we walked to a bonfire, which was on a secluded stretch of beach, beneath high stone cliffs. About twenty kids were there, with radios and blankets, and they all seemed to know each other. There were a few girls my age who looked disappointed or vicious when they saw Mark's arm around my shoulders, and I imagined they'd come out that night with satin bras on under their flannel shirts, hoping maybe he would notice them.

We sat cross-legged on a rough blanket, drinking Budweisers and lining up the empty cans so they sparkled in the firelight. The beer was bitter in the back of my throat. Mark was getting bolder; he'd given me his jean jacket to wear—it was slimy from too much sea air—and he was leaning into me, speaking with his mouth right up against my ear. The flames of the bonfire shot up toward the night, making a slapping noise like laundry in rough wind. The waves crashed, invisible behind us, and when it was quiet I could hear the foam sizzle down the sand like embers.

When we were drunk we wandered up to the cliffs, out of the light of the fire. It was cold there and I tried not to shiver when Mark passed me the beer can. We sat without saying anything for a while and I felt myself moving beyond impatience—I was desperate. I wanted to shake him and cry out, "Are you going to kiss me or what?" In the moonlight I could see that he no longer looked sexy or confident. He looked cold and his forehead was strained in concentration. I looked away as he slugged the last of the beer, thinking that in a second I'd get up and walk back to the fire. I looked back and he lunged at me. Our lips met, though his didn't feel like lips so much as two fat slugs pressed together. He tried turning his head back and forth, and I did it too, but we were going in totally different directions. I tried to think back to what I'd imagined all day, but eventually it was just me with my shirt shoved up to my neck, my back sticking to the cold sand, my cheeks and chin covered in slobber, and Mark on top of me, clamped around my leg, rubbing up and down so fast I could hear a whizzing noise from the zipper of his jeans.

"Oh," he moaned into my cheek, "unhh." The cute boy had transformed into a strange ugly thing that was smothering me. I thrust against him, trying to get him off, but he only moaned louder.

He seemed to like it, so I did it some more, trying to quicken things so it would be over.

"Grace," he whispered, and for an instant I was alone in my bedroom listening to the sounds of Stephen making love to my mother.

"Ah! Ah!" Mark blurted out then, squeezing his eyes shut, a look of painful disappointment contorting his face. I'd learned, from being with other boys, that this expression was actually ecstasy.

"Shhh!" I hissed, suddenly mortified that we could be heard at the bonfire. He stopped moving, paralyzed on top of me. I heard a giggle in the distance. I pushed at Mark's shoulder and he rolled away.

"Sorry," he muttered when his breathing was normal.

I wouldn't let him walk me home. I ran most of the way, disgusted and terrified, the sand squealing and singing beneath my rubber soles. When I got to the cottage, a faint blue light was coming up over the water. No one was waiting up for me. I entered the house silently, went into my green-and-yellow room, and peeled off smoky clothes that dropped to the floor with a whish of trapped sand and pebbles. I crawled under the nubby blankets that smelled like mothballs, and the sun rose higher and glowed orange like fire through the white curtain. No one knocked on my door or crawled into bed with me to nap for the rest of the morning.

CHAPTER 6

Gráinne

By July, I hardly saw my mother anymore, though her hair was in the bathroom wastebasket in clumps, like rusty birds' nests. Sometimes I snuck toward her closed bedroom door and listened for coughing or movement. Once, Stephen caught me and said, "You can go in, she's awake." But I backed off. I wasn't going to catch her off guard, without the straw hat that she wore when Stephen walked her down to the water. I imagined the bald spots on her head were infected, puckered like her missing breast.

"If she wanted me in there, she'd have left the door open," I said. Which was stupid, because Stephen told her. After that the door was always ajar and I had to tiptoe by to keep it from swinging open.

She wandered the cottage at night. I could hear her pacing, and sometimes she stomped, rattled things, which is what she used to do when she was mad and wanted me to come out of my room and face something I'd done—like being a wiseass or not loading the dishwasher. That pissy act hadn't worked on me since I was ten. It always worked on her boyfriends, though, and at the cottage, Stephen would eventually come out and whisper, "What's the matter, babe?" and she would follow him back to bed.

Once a week, Stephen drove her into town for chemotherapy. He tried to give me updates: how much she'd thrown up afterwards, that the doctors were debating more surgery.

"Don't you want to know how your mother is doing?" he asked me when I showed no reaction.

"My mother tells me everything I need to know," I said, although this was no longer true.

"What are you waiting for?" he said. I thought it was a funny thing to say. I wasn't waiting for anything.

To make him feel better I let him give me piano lessons again in the mornings. We sat with our hips and elbows brushing together. After practices, we went swimming, and I let him lift me above the incoming waves and drop me down, his hands under my arms and almost around my breasts. I imagined that he was trying to seduce me. I pictured him showing me things like he showed me piano. *Like this, Gráinne*, he would say, and his lips would be perfect on mine.

I didn't go back to the bonfires. I was afraid someone would remember me. I spent my nights at a little diner downtown where mostly old people hung out. I chain-smoked and drank coffee until my hands shook, copying down poems in my notebook. I hadn't brought any books with me, so I tried to remember the poems on my wall at home.

My mother started leaving me notes on the refrigerator; I would find them early in the morning before I went out on the beach.

Gráinne,

Please buy eggs and Pepto-Bismol at the G.S. (Remember

George, who always had a capful with his omelets?) Stephen will
give you money.

—Mom

Gráinne,
   Do your busy Mom a favor and sweep up the line of sand that
leads from the front doorway to your room. Just because you were
named after a queen, doesn't mean I'm going to treat you like one.
Your feet are beginning to look like your father's—his little toes did
that too, curled long and thin past his big one. It's a sign of intel-
ligence.

—Mom

   P.S. I have seen my Country Road nail polish on your toenails.
Return it immediately you little thief!

She typed these notes on the old Corona that sat on a desk in
the corner of the living room. They were creepy, those tiny letters
on a large white page, like an anonymous threatening note. She had
never mentioned my father so casually, and without bitterness. It
frightened me, though I wasn't sure why. I imagined her stealing
out of bed in the night, peering at my toes and composing notes
while I slept.

   One morning I turned the paper over and scribbled a line from
Anne Sexton:

So it has come to this—
insomnia at 3:15 A.M.

My mother's next note was longer, chatty, like a postcard about
her trip to the beach. I began to leave her quotes every morning,
typing them up on fresh white paper that she left for me.

I shall wear white flannel trousers, and walk upon the beach.
I have heard the mermaids singing, each to each.

I imagined that my mother was taping these pages neatly on the wallpaper next to her bed. If she knew the poem, she left me an answer: *I do not think that they will sing to me.*

At night we glided by one another like blind ghosts on our ways to and from the bathroom. In the white porcelain sink, I occasionally found blood clots clinging on the edge of the drain, like miniature marooned jellyfish. I ran the water until they lost their grip and swished away.

Halfway through the summer, the doctors stopped my mother's chemotherapy—and I couldn't eat anymore. Stephen was cooking like some mad gourmet, meals which he and I sat down to alone because my mother slept through them. Everything he put in front of me looked rotten, curdled, or regurgitated. I started seeing microscopic insects shifting all over my vegetables, maggots eating their way through my steak. The bites I managed to take refused to go down, I was always gagging. Stephen would jump up and run behind my chair like he was going to perform the Heimlich maneuver. I had to spit into my napkin when he wasn't looking, finishing the meal with a handful of crud seeping through the paper. Eventually, I stopped showing up for dinner. He didn't ask why, just left me a plate of food, sectioned perfectly into food groups, a film of plastic wrap smeared across the top. When I came in I would scrape the contents into the garbage can outside, covering the evidence with crumpled-up paper towels.

I began shrinking. My breasts were lost in my C-cup bra, my stomach became concave. I looked at myself naked in the mirror every morning and it looked good, my fleshlessness, my ribs strong and sharply pressed against my skin. The yawning emptiness in my middle warmed me, energized me, made me want to swim, which

I did, for hours, in the waters below the sandbar. I was growing smaller and smaller, disappearing. Stephen noticed me less, stopped leaving me plates of food, forgot to say good morning when I passed by him as he practiced at the piano. I was invisible.

One morning I walked out the sliding door and almost tripped over Stephen, who was sitting hunched up on the steps. He was rocking himself, his arms wrapped around his knees, and he didn't move when I let the screen door slam behind me. I walked halfway down the steps. He was crying, or close to it; his face was screwed-up and twitchy, though there were no tears. I tried to walk past him but he stopped me, slapping his hand down on my sandal.

"I don't want to talk about anything," I said, "but I'll sit here with you if you want." Stephen nodded and half smiled up at me, and I sat down and scooted over so our shoulders almost touched. He didn't say anything at all for so long, I wished I hadn't asked for quiet. I cleared my throat and leaned sideways, peeling the leg of my cutoffs from the back of my thigh. This made him look over at me, at my legs, and he moved his hand and played on my kneecap with his fingers like I was a piano. It made me glad I had shaved my legs earlier. The old longing returned, instantly.

"Thanks for sticking around," I said after a minute. Stephen snorted and pulled his hand away. He looked out at the shoreline; the waves were huge that morning, loud and crashing, each one trying to be bigger than the last.

"How could I go?" he said, threading his hair back behind his ears.

"You could go," I said. "I mean, you could be in lots of places right now." I wanted to tell him about the list I'd once made in my notebook: options of who I would live with if my mother didn't get better. There was my mother's friend Lucy, who lived in California; she had no kids and had always been jealous that my mother had me. I could track down my father with a private detective. My first choice was to stay with Stephen. I thought that when I was eighteen he might want to marry me, but I wasn't going to tell him that part.

He turned to look at me and when he did the sun caught the auburn strands in his hair. I was thinking how much more beautiful he was than any boy I'd ever kissed.

"I liked it better when we weren't saying anything," he said, and he reached up and touched me lightly, with his index finger, right below my eye. "Look how pretty you are," he whispered. "Just like—" Then he stopped and frowned. "Just right." His face was so close and he was looking at my mouth, then my eyes, then my mouth again, and I thought he wanted to kiss me, was probably just a second from kissing me, and I felt like crying just at the closeness of his face.

Then the screen door squeaked. We turned and my mother was there, in her purple kimono and that floppy straw hat. Stephen stood up and brushed off his butt.

"Hey, babe," he said. "Want to walk down?" She wouldn't look at him. She was looking at me. If I could have, I'd have bolted right down to the water and into it.

"Hey, kiddo," she said in this phlegmy voice, and then she coughed. Her face was yellow and bruised under the eyes, her forehead went up way too high before it hit the hat, and I could tell she was now completely bald. Her collarbone, like mine, was deeply outlined, though hers looked like there wasn't much keeping it from popping out and falling down the front of her robe. The wind blew up from the water and the purple fabric lifted briefly above her ankles. I saw a half inch of black stubble on her legs. I thought of how we used to shave our legs together, sitting on the edge of the tub with our toes on the wall grip, writing our names in the creamy soap on our calves.

I stood up and bounded down the stairs. "I have to go to the G.S.," I said.

"Gráinne," my mother said weakly, "wait."

"We're out of milk," I said, backing away. I never should have sat down.

"Maybe tonight we can all have dinner together," she said. The sun glared off the skeletal lines of her face.

"I have a date," I said. I don't think I'd ever said that to her, not in all the time she'd been saying it to me. I hurried off down the beach. I could have sworn that I heard my mother's musical laughter behind me, though it might have been the wind and the sea.

One night in August it was unusually cold, like autumn was beginning early. When I came home my mother and Stephen weren't there. The car was gone, the house was silent, the porch lights had been left on for me. I took my time getting into the kitchen to check for a note. The black rotary phone by the piano rang like a fire alarm throughout the cottage. I had never heard it ring before and decided to ignore it. I sat on the navigation couch, took my sandals off and cleaned the sand from between my toes, letting it fall into the seams of the round braided rug. The phone kept ringing, so I got up and went into the dark kitchen, opened the fridge, and took out the lemonade. I was so thirsty I couldn't stand waiting for a glass, so I guzzled from the pitcher, and the sticky liquid spilled out over my jaw and into the neckline of my shirt. It made me sick and dizzy, the foreign thickness coating my empty stomach.

I closed the refrigerator door and pulled the ceiling light string. Tacked to the usual spot on the freezer was an ordinary piece of lined notepaper, with the logo of the local Mariners newspaper, a dolphin, printed in blue across the top. The handwriting was miniature and messy—it was not my mother's.

Went to the hospital. Call there immediately.

—Stephen

There was a phone number. I took the note off and turned it over. That was all.

The phone rang again, or maybe it had never stopped, and I went into my bedroom and closed the door. I would read some poetry from my notebooks and wait. The phone rang sixteen, twenty-two times. It rattled so loud in its stand that I could hear a faint vibrating hum from the piano. I lay down on my bed and felt paper crinkling beneath me. I turned on the light and pulled the page out from under my butt. It was clean white typing paper, four lines in faded ink down the middle.

> Go and leave me if you wish to,
> Never let me cross your mind.
> And if you think that I've proved unworthy,
> Go and leave me, I don't mind.

For a second I thought it had to be some sort of joke. It wasn't a poem but a silly little song she used to sing whenever she'd broken up with a boyfriend. She'd always sing it loudly, gesticulating, trying to make me laugh. It usually worked. I had no idea why she'd left it for me now. Did she think this was funny? Was she pissed at me? I wasn't the one going anywhere, for Christ's sake. I squeezed and twisted the paper until no words were showing and dropped it on my bed. I left my room and walked toward the bathroom, past the phone that was still ringing—but softer, like it was losing its voice.

In the bathroom, I opened the medicine cabinet and took out my mother's bandage scissors. I used them to cut my hair, as close to my head as I could get it. Masses of it, like little black animals, skittered over the countertop. In some places, I ended up with uneven tufts, like the brittle hair that used to poke from my mother's hat. When I was finished I washed my face, and then wrapped my shrunken chest in some gauze which I found under the sink.

I went into my mother's room and looked at myself in her full-length mirror. I put my face right up to the glass. "Gráinne," I said, and I repeated it over and over until I did not know that voice, until even the eyes were unrecognizable. I went over to the closet and took out Stephen's flannel shirt, my mother's jeans, and her running sneakers, the soles of which were caked with sand. When Stephen had first moved in, I'd seen my mother sipping tea early in the morning, pulling the collar of his shirt over her nose and inhaling deeply. I did that now. It smelled of sea air, smoke, and sage. It smelled like my mother.

I went out to the living room and sat down at the typewriter. I took a fresh sheet of paper that had been left there for me and wound it in the machine. I typed out a few lines and looked at them. I'd made some mistakes, so I typed them out again. Satisfied, I yanked the paper out and folded it, and put it in the shirt pocket.

The phone started that ringing again. I went over to it, lifted it from its base, and set it on the floor. I took the little wooden stand it had been on and one of the dining chairs and hefted them behind the piano. I opened the sliding glass door and carried them outside, down the beach, stopping at a safe distance from the water. I dropped the furniture and stomped on it. The wood was old and the seams unstable, so it wasn't hard for me to smash the table and chair into appropriate-sized pieces. I filled a trash bag with some firewood and kindling that was under the porch, took my notebooks from my bedroom and the folder of typed pages I'd collected from the refrigerator door all summer. I built the fire like a Lincoln Logs cabin, and when it was roaring, started to drop in pages, watching them liven then crinkle.

There was a sound behind the fire, coming up to me in a rhythm like waves; a sound that went high and then low, like lonely laughter. I remembered another time I had heard it, on the beach with my mother when I was a little girl.

Mermaids, my mother had said. I must have been very young, because in the memory I try to repeat her, but the word does not come out right.

By the time Stephen came home, I'd burned all the chairs, a wicker basket, the laundry drying rack, and a pile of wooden utensils from the kitchen. The fire was still going strong, licking at the dark air, its base a squealing lake of embers. Stephen came out the sliding door and walked down the steps slowly. I took the paper out of my pocket and read what I'd typed.

Time held me green and dying
Though I sang in my chains like the sea.

I imagined this was the note my mother had left. That the hand holding the fluttering paper was my mother's graceful one. That I was the one who was dying. I dropped the paper in the flames.

"Gráinne?" Stephen said, his voice thick like he'd been crying. I watched the orange snapping, the sparks like fireworks disappearing in midair. Stephen moved closer, looking at my head in the firelight.

"God, Gráinne, what did you do to yourself?" he whispered.

"Shhh," I said, listening to the fire. It groaned and whimpered like a wounded animal. He looked at it briefly, maybe hoping he'd see something more.

"I tried to call you," he said, and his voice broke.

I turned to him and put my hands around the back of his neck, pulling his head toward me. He grabbed me fiercely by the waist and cried into my naked neck, kneading and clasping my back through the flannel shirt. I started to kiss him. On his earlobe, his cheek, his soaking eyelashes. He stopped breathing. I could feel heat glowing from his mouth, and when I pressed my lips against it, he was shaking.

It only lasted an instant, there was the faintest promising pressure as he moved in toward me, and then it was gone, his hands were on my shoulders, holding me away.

"Don't, Gráinne," he said. "God." And his face changed, as though it had just occurred to him that what we'd done was disgusting.

So I stood there, suspended in the air around the fire, feeling

nothing but his cold palms against the bones of my shoulders, wanting to run but not able to back away, listening to the sounds from
the sea which rolled and crashed and built up like a familiar anticipation in my throat.

CHAPTER 7

Clíona

A strange session, my daughter's funeral is. Men everywhere. All former boyfriends, from what I can gather. It is clear that Grace's popularity with the lads never waned.

It's a Catholic ceremony, at least. I'm relieved that Grace has kept up some connection with the Church. Though it puzzles me, for religion was one of the things she always rebelled against.

At the grave's edge, I dedicate my rosary to the Sorrowful Mysteries and begin the prayers. Between each decade I recite the Fatima Ejaculation: "O, Jesus, forgive us our sins, save us from the fires of Hell, and lead all souls to Heaven, especially those who are most in need of your mercy." I recite the prayers mechanically, my fingers moving over the beads like those of a blind woman reading braille. It's a long time since I've felt anything when I pray.

Gráinne is glaring at me. She has the same vicious look her

mother had. And God only knows what she has done to her hair—chicken-scratch, what's left of it, though you can still see that it's violet-black the way mine once was. She's so thin she looks like a picture of a famine victim or one of those diseased girls there is talk of nowadays: anorexics. I long to feed her potatoes, rashers, butter, cream.

She certainly has not received me with any affection. She seems suspicious of me, like I'm an impostor, but I suppose it's only natural since Grace kept me from her, in memory as well as presence. It's quite obvious from the way she spoke to me yesterday that Gráinne does not remember anything about her first three years, which she spent in Ireland with me. Sure, everything will come out in its own time.

Hard to understand, this granddaughter of mine. Not as brash as her mother, a little frightened really, but there is some toughness, a resilience underneath. It's there in the way she says her name, when shaking the hands of the mourners she's never met before, *Grawnya*. Perfect Irish pronunciation. She says it boldly, with a certain pride, rather than flattening it or making it sound American, as I did with my name when I first moved to Boston.

I try nodding at her, but she shifts her eyes and seems to focus within, as if she is refusing to see what is before her. This girl wears an armor which won't be easily breached. Her mother had that absent look once—it came from keeping to herself too much. Stephen tells me Gráinne and Grace were the best of friends, but this girl looks as though she hasn't had a friend for some time.

The service has ended. We walk back toward the cars, my heels plunging into the soil, making my progress precarious. Gráinne and Stephen walk just ahead of me; he is holding her by the arm, though she seems perfectly composed and able to walk on her own. There is something inappropriate between these two. Nothing scandalous, maybe, but Gráinne definitely has an infatuation with him. Grace felt similarly about a man that I was once involved with, not Marcus of course, but before him, an American man.

What worries me is not the girl's infatuation so much as that your man does not appear completely immune to it. He is younger than Grace by a few years; perhaps he has not gotten that boy-wildness out of his system. And again, there is the grief, and grief can do strange things to a man, just as drink can, and I've seen Stephen take a bit of that since I've been here as well. All things, I think these two would be better off with an ocean between them.

Stephen, who is not lacking proper manners, opens the car door for me. We drive off and I do not look back at the graveyard, but at the road ahead of me that leads out of it. Gráinne, I notice, does the same. Later, when I am alone in my daughter's bedroom, or even when I get home to Ireland, I will let myself cry for Grace, I will release this grief which I fear is so much stronger than the grief I have felt for her all her life. But not now. Now I have other things to occupy me.

This is how I win Gráinne over initially: with snaps. I have brought three albums with me. The first is full of old family pictures, the second of snaps from our home in America, the last from back in Ireland: Gráinne as a baby. I lay them out on my daughter's sitting room table and leaf through them one at a time, while Gráinne storms the flat in her stocking feet. She is intrigued, I can tell, because she's watching me; occasionally she walks behind the sofa to sneak a look over my shoulder.

"Will you look on?" I say during her third lap around the room. She glances around the room and shrugs. Stephen has gone to the university, so there is no one to witness if she weakens. She sits at the far end of the couch and I move down, handing her first the album with the snaps of Grace as a child. "This is your mother," I say, pointing to a thin, scowling Grace at eight years old, "when we lived here in Boston." Gráinne looks at it skeptically.

"Why is she wearing a wedding dress?" she says.

"It was the day of her First Communion," I say. "Did you not have one yourself?"

"No," Gráinne snorts. It's as I feared: Grace has not raised her a Catholic. It was thanks to myself that Gráinne was even baptized.

"Who are the other kids?" she says. Three blond children, a boy Grace's age and twin baby girls in their pram, are beside her.

"Those are the Willoughby children," I say. "I was employed by the family and we boarded in the house until your mother was the age you are now."

"Like a servant," Gráinne says. It's cheeky she's getting again, but I let it go, I don't want to scare her off.

"Ah, not a servant. I raised those children. We were a part of the family, your mother and I." Still, she seems doubtful—her mother's ideas of my position coming through, I see.

"Where did you go after that?" she asks. "Did you get your own house?"

"When Grace was fifteen years of age, we went home to Ireland. To Inis Murúch, the Island of the Mermaids, off the West, where I was born. It was then I married my husband, Marcus."

"What about my mother's father?" Gráinne accuses. "Where was he?"

"I was widowed when your mother was very young." Gráinne folds her arms and shoots me an evil look from under a brow that frighteningly resembles her mother's.

"My Mom said you never married her father, that she was just some accident that happened when a man passed you in the night," she said. This was becoming difficult, trying to bond with a child whom I just wanted to slap.

"Think what you like. Your mother had a habit of reinventing the past to suit herself." That shuts her up. She flips through the rest of the album, quickly, searching for something. I hand her another one. On the opening leaf: myself, Grace, and baby Gráinne. She squints at it.

"That's me?" she says, and I nod. "Where is this? Did we visit you in Ireland?"

"You were born in Ireland, Gráinne. You lived there until you were three years of age." Perhaps I should have put it more gently. She drops the album, stands up and backs away from me.

"I don't remember," she says. She is frightened; I am sorry for her.

"I know, it's all right, child."

She walks quickly to her room, and I think she is going to lock herself in there again. But she returns with a framed snap in her hand. She gives it to me, but does not sit down.

It is a close-up of her face, a toddler's rounded face, violet-black ringlets hanging about her ears. She is laughing—pure delighted laughter—her eyes squeezed shut from the effort.

"I remember this one, sure," I say. "From my own camera, it is. Taken in my garden, just a few weeks before you left." Gráinne shifts her weight from one foot to the other. She pulls at her short hair, brings her fingers around to gnaw at her nails. Her face is a battleground of expressions—she cannot decide between confusion, sorrow, and self-righteous anger.

"Who is my father?" she says, quietly. "You know him?"

"I do. I know your father well."

"Is he in Ireland?"

"He is."

"Near you?"

"On Inis Murúch, yes."

"How come he didn't marry my Mom?" she says. The anger is starting to win in her features.

"He did, Gráinne. They were married before you were born."

"Why didn't my Mom tell me any of this?"

"Perhaps she wanted to forget it. She left Ireland; she did not look back."

"Why? Is it a horrible place or something?"

"No, Gráinne, it's a lovely place."

"Then why?"

"I don't know." I look away from her. Not everything at once, God help me. I can't go through all of it in an instant. We're quiet for a moment, there is only our harried breathing, as if we've both been exercising. Gráinne takes her picture back from me.

"I'm going to my room now," she says, and it is just that little bit, that attempt on her part at manners, that lets me know I've gotten somewhere at last.

CHAPTER 8

Gráinne

"I have a father," I said to the thin reflection of my face in the mirror. I'd been in the bathroom for an hour, avoiding Mrs. O'Halloran and Stephen.

I had an Irish father, grandmother, maybe even cousins. I hadn't even known that my mother was Irish. My Gaelic name was from a book she'd liked. She had never told me where we came from, just that we would always be together.

I remembered that when I was in the second grade, I was supposed to draw my family tree and trace my ethnic heritage.

"What are we?" I had asked my mother. "Are we Jewish?" All my friends were Jewish and their families came from places like Russia, Poland, and Lithuania.

"You're whatever you want to be," my mother had said. "It's not important where you come from, Gráinne. What matters is where you take yourself." She'd gotten the teacher to excuse me from the assignment. While the other students had stood in front of the class and explained the intricate trees they'd traced to manila paper, I had drawn a picture of two thin tree trunks entwined together, and told myself that no one else had a mother like mine. She was beautiful, she laughed all the time, she never nagged me, she asked my opinion on everything, and took it seriously, too. She was my best friend.

She had lied to me. There were other people, besides us, people I had known until I was three. I had assumed that my father was a random boyfriend who'd left my mother when she got pregnant. I had never known that she'd married him. She had always told me that she was not the marrying type.

From my hideout in the bathroom, I could hear Stephen and my grandmother conferring. They've already decided what to do with me, I thought. There are strangers in another country who want to be my family, and Stephen seems to have forgotten that he ever wanted me in the first place.

"Why did you lie to me?" I said to the mirror. But there was no answer from my mother, only this new, mean face of mine, staring at me as if she didn't know me at all.

"I'm going," I said to Stephen, at the end of that first week after my mother's funeral. "I'm going back with my grandmother."

"Great!" he said quickly, then calmed down, like he was ashamed of his enthusiasm. "I'm glad for you, if that's what you want to do." We were sitting on the couch again in the dark living room. This was the only way I could talk to him now—in darkness.

"Like I had much choice," I said.

"Oh, no, Gráinne. If you were set against going, I'd help you figure something out, you know I would."

"Yeah, all right," I said. I wanted so much to believe him.

"You feel better about her now—your grandmother, I mean?" I shrugged.

"She's not why I'm going. My father's there."

"Your father? Oh."

"I guess you already knew that," I said, as Stephen rubbed his eyelids roughly with his thumbs.

"No." He sighed. "No, I know nothing about your father."

"But you knew about her," I said, gesturing toward the room where my grandmother was sleeping.

"Your mother gave me a name and a phone number. She didn't tell me anything, just to call when . . . well."

"When she was dead," I said.

Stephen ignored that. "Anyway, I knew nothing really, nothing," he mumbled.

I was remembering when he'd first moved in, how he'd gone out of his way to talk to me, to hurry up in the bathroom, to include me when he and my mother went out on the weekends. He was worried, I'd been able to tell, that I'd resent him. My mother and I had laughed about it. About how little he knew about us.

"Mrs. O'Halloran says there's a high school on the island. It would be good for you, I think, to meet some people your own age."

"I'm not going for the social life," I said. "I want to find out why my mother lied to me." He nodded, opened his mouth to say something, stopped. He thought for a while.

"You might never find out," he said. "What people lie about, well, sometimes it only makes sense in their own minds."

"I bet my father knows," I said. Stephen nodded, but I could tell he was holding back. Jealousy, I thought. He doesn't want to think of any man knowing more about my mother than he does.

I should get up and go to bed, I thought, because there's nothing left to say. But I lingered. I had to give him an extra moment just in case the impossible was only a little late in coming. I wanted to touch him, to hold his hand, which was lying lost and useless in his lap. But I knew better. My body, which had once seemed to have so much effect on him, now meant nothing.

I got up, walked the length of the living room and turned back to say good night. For a second, with his face looking after me, expectant and inquisitive, he resembled the boys I had known, who didn't understand why I no longer liked them—as if he was wondering what he'd done wrong.

"We should write," Stephen said. "Will we write?"

I opened my bedroom door and, with my hand on the molding, looking back, I whispered: "You have no idea how much you're going to miss me." It was the kind of thing my mother would have said, had said in the past, boldly, loudly, with laughter in her eyes. I said it, but my hand was shaking when I closed the door. I moved my mouth, silently muttering: *I can't believe I said that, why did I say that?* I felt my cheeks and ears go up in flames.

CHAPTER 9

Gráinne

My father wasn't at the airport when we arrived in Ireland. I had a moment of panic—maybe he was dead, too, maybe he'd never existed and was just this woman's ploy to get me across the ocean. As though she knew I was panicking, Clíona spoke up and eased my fears.

"They'll be meeting us in Galway," she said. "We'll take the bus there."

I readjusted my fantasy. I would not meet my father in an airport (though Shannon airport was smaller and less dramatic than I'd imagined), we would be reunited in a bus station. Not as romantic, but romance was becoming less important. What I wanted. . . . What was it I wanted? First to see his features, I suppose, to see if I was in them. Then, answers.

At the bus station in Galway, my grandmother left me alone and went searching for her husband, who was somewhere in this maze of luggage and plastic-framed schedules with my father. I stood by the newsagent, looking at a postcard rack. The cards showed first names and their meanings, with Celtic designs around the border. When I was in the fourth grade, all my friends had things with their names on them: pencils, mugs, key chains, and stationery. Names were fashionable accessories. Of course, nothing ever had my name on it, but I'd got into the habit of looking. Here, for the first time, I found my name on a rack with the rest of them.

"Gráinne"
The most popular interpretation of this name is: "She who inspires terror." The best known owner of the name is the pirate sea queen, Gráinne Ní Mhaille.
Gráinne Ní Mhaille, also called Granuaile or Grace O'Malley, was the daughter and wife of two legendary Connaught chieftains of the O'Malley and O'Flaherty clans. Gráinne, after the death of both men, took on their responsibilities, ruling the sea and the land with infamous courage. She commanded a respect and fear that no other woman in her time in Ireland had.

Reading that card made me uneasy. I knew my mother picked my name to instill me with courage and independence, but my whole life I've sort of gotten it backwards and thought that the terror I inspired was in myself.

Would my father, who had probably helped my mother name me, expect me to be so fearless?

"I see Marcus," my grandmother said, coming up behind me. I reached up to smooth my hair, forgetting I had almost no hair left to smooth.

"Grab your gear now," she said. I had only a large blue suitcase and my backpack, and most of the space in the suitcase was taken up by my poetry books. In my backpack, with my notebooks, Walkman, and tapes, I'd stashed the little box with my mother's ring, a heart-shaped ruby surrounded by gold hands and a crown. She'd kept it in a drawer for as long as I could remember. My grandmother, when she saw it in Boston, told me it was my mother's engagement ring from my father, Seamus O'Flaherty.

Marcus, my grandmother's husband, patted her arm awkwardly, as though he was too embarrassed to hug or kiss her in front of me. He was a gigantic man, tall and thick, with red hair and a redder beard, and a smile that pushed his cheek up past the lower lids of his inky-blue eyes. He was alone.

"Howaya, Gráinne?" he said, then followed the greeting with something I couldn't decipher. His voice was deep and rhythmic; his words ran together into one long sound, and his lips barely formed them. I nodded, pretending I'd understood him.

"You're welcome," he added, though I couldn't remember saying thank you. Did he expect me to be a meek and thankful orphan? I wanted to smack the sympathy from their faces. Marcus tried to take my suitcase, but I backed away.

"Where's my father?" I said. Marcus looked at Clíona, who grabbed my suitcase impatiently, hefting it with a thud into the trunk.

"It seems Seamus had to work," she said. "You'll see him at home." Marcus nodded as if he thought she'd given a good answer. They got in the car and I hesitated before following them. They were conferring in the front seat. Listening to them murmuring to one another (Marcus, like my grandmother, spoke sentences as if he were singing them), I began to worry that I spoke too loud, that my voice sounded ugly as a fart in a quiet room.

We drove for two hours down a road so bumpy I had to stick my hand out the window, the way my mother had taught me, to stop from feeling carsick. When we started, the land was acres of green fields divided by brush walls. I saw sheep, cows, a few white, bare-backed horses. After about an hour on the road the scenery changed drastically. Craggy mountains rose above valleys, the fields were scabbed with gray rock that seemed to grow right up out of the grass, low stone walls ran like veins impossibly high up the mountains. Piles of what looked like stacked rectangular manure stood tied together at the sides of muddy pits. I smelled a sweet, dense burning, like a fireplace but not wood, something unfamiliar and moist.

"We're in Connemara now, girl," my grandmother said. There were no free-growing trees, just occasional squared-off groups of pine that looked purposeful, like Christmas tree farms. The sun broke through in patches high on the mountains, illuminating purple grass. Some clouds were so low they were oozing over the mountaintops. We began a descent into a vast valley, and between the two mountains ahead there was a thick, bright rainbow. I'd never seen a whole one, only pieces blocked by buildings or trees. Something about the gray stone pushing up like pimples from the soil, and the sight of sheep standing at suicidal angles on the slopes, and those ridiculous but painstakingly constructed walls, made me feel like sobbing. It's not that it was ugly, it wasn't. It just made me feel lost. My mother had left this, and would never be back. I shouldn't be here, I thought. I don't belong.

I closed my eyes and tried to picture my father. In the photos Clíona had shown me, he was always slightly out of focus: his hair was long, dark ringlets like mine before I cut it, but his face was a bright white empty space except for the dark contrast of his eyes. I wondered what he would do when he saw me, what expression would be on those features that were missing in the photos. Would he cry and try not to, like Stephen? When he opened his mouth and said my name, would I remember him instantly?

"We're almost there," Clíona said, and I opened my eyes. A sign pointed our way: INIS MURÚCH FERRY. The name was spelled differently from how it sounded. Irish words seemed to have more letters than they actually used.

Marcus parked the car in a lot beside the dock. He brought our bags over to the moss-smothered stairway at the water's edge.

"We've been waiting on you, Marcus," a man on the boat called.

He then said something which I didn't understand, but which made the other men on the boat and Marcus laugh loudly. None of them looked like he might be my father, though they smiled and nodded at me.

The boat was very small, the open deck piled with crates of milk and juice cartons. I walked carefully down the slimy steps and climbed over a rope into the boat. The man who'd spoken to Marcus took my hand to keep me balanced; the skin of his palm was thick and rubbery.

"This can't be the little girl I know," the man said, grinning at me.

"Ah, that's her, all right, Eamon," Marcus said, looking proud, as though I were a puppy he was showing off.

"Aren't you just the image of Seamus when he was the wee lad," Eamon said. He winked at me and turned to untie the boat before I could respond. He had hair on his cheekbones, and I could see where he'd shaved just beneath it, leaving patches of fur under the hollows of his eyes.

Clíona and I sat inside on cracked plastic seats. The air was thick with the smell of gasoline. Someone started the engine, and the boat groaned forward, rising up with the waves.

"How's your stomach?" Clíona yelled to me after a few minutes. "Your mother was a brilliant swimmer, but she got fierce seasick on this boat." I didn't like her knowing things about my mother.

"My Mom doesn't get seasick and neither do I," I said, though the smell of the gas was giving me a headache. I climbed out on deck, avoiding the cluster of laughing men at the back.

Clíona was right about one thing; my mother was like a fish when she entered the water. It had always disappointed her that, even though I could swim from the time I was four, the sea still terrified me. "Stop grabbing me," she'd say whenever we took a ferry in Boston. "You're not going to fall in." I'd never explained to her that my fear was not of falling. Instead I was afraid of pitching myself in, afraid that my body might hurl itself directly into what scared me the most.

The dock faded into miniature, and as I watched the silver water and gripped the cold, rusty handrail, I imagined my mother lifting her delighted face to the sea air.

The boat passed the high cliffs behind the island and turned in to a thumb-shaped harbor, where the water was clear and calm. At the point where we turned in, there was a half-ruined castle, the same gray as the stones jutting up from the land. At its base, a sheet of rock angled steeply into the ocean. The walls looked like they were about to slide into the ocean any minute.

"Granuaile's castle," my grandmother said. She'd come to join me on the deck.

I didn't say anything, but she smiled when she saw me looking.

"Your woman had castles all over Connaught and the islands. They say Gráinne and her crew hid in this one, rowing out in curraghs to capture Spanish ships on their way to Galway. Gráinne would climb aboard and demand a passing fee. If the captain refused, she'd steal all their gear."

The tumbledown structure didn't look like a queen's house. A new picture of Granuaile was forming in my mind: a rough-looking woman with no hair, a bloody sword at her side. Maybe chewing tobacco and spitting like a man.

"There's our hotel," Clíona said, pointing to a long yellow building with red trim, just up the road from the dock. Next to it was a brown cabin with O'HALLORAN'S PUB painted in white across the roof. The island, like the mainland, had no trees, just bushes and rock and varying shades of green and purple climbing toward the sea on the other side. The houses were single-stories, paint chipping off cement, lined along a road that twisted out of sight. Power cables hung like an ugly web over the populated tip of the island.

"Is that it?" I said, thinking the place looked depressing, but Clíona nodded proudly.

When the boat docked, Marcus drove us up the graveled road in a pickup truck. At the back of the hotel was a red-and-gray stone extension, smoke puffing out of its piped chimney.

"Home," Clíona said, looking excited. She opened the door to a swarm of people, most of whom jumped up to kiss me and introduce themselves. I couldn't keep them straight. All the woman said they were my "anties." They kept saying, "You're welcome, Gráinne," which I figured out was a greeting rather than an answer to "thank you." Most of the middle-aged men and women were Marcus's children and their spouses. They had Marcus's blue eyes, and two names apiece: Mary Louise, John Patrick, Anna Mariah. I started to get that dizzy, detached feeling I'd had at my mother's funeral. I had the instinct to reach for Stephen.

"Which one is my father?" I asked Clíona when she took my jacket.

"He's not arrived yet," she said, slipping away from me.

Someone gave me tea, which I drank. It was sweet and milky and something to concentrate on. The Anties left me alone finally and went to laughing among themselves. They spoke like Marcus, rhythmic voices out of mouths that barely moved. Even my grandmother sounded as though she'd switched languages now that we were here. I sat on the stone shelf in front of the fireplace and waited.

A boy came slamming in the back doorway to my right. He had a long, fluid-looking body, shining black hair, and a pale face with those inky-blue eyes, which he fixed on me, blinding me to the rest of his features.

"Howaya?" he said, smiling. I nodded and looked back at the fire. I knew he was still watching me.

"Liam!" Clíona yelled from across the room. "Don't you take another step in this house with those Wellies." He was wearing long rubber boots that were discolored with mud on the toes.

"Is that Gráinne?" he asked her, gesturing at me.

" 'Tis, sure. The girl's home now."

"Jesus, Nana," Liam said, looking at me again. "What did you do to her? She looks knackered." I sat up straighter, glaring at him. He wasn't bothered, he just grinned and winked at me.

"God help you, girl," Clíona said, walking over to me. "You must be dying to get to bed. Are you tired?"

"I'll wait until my father comes," I said. Liam looked at the ceiling and whistled. Clíona seemed embarrassed.

"Your father won't be back until late," she said. "You'll see him soon enough." She looked away when I glared at her.

"He's not out on the trawler, is he?" Liam said. "If he's fishing with my father could be ages before they get back."

I looked at Clíona. "He's only joking, he is," she said. "Don't be teasing the girl, Liam."

"I'll wait, then," I said, my voice sounding distant, like an echo in my ears. "I'm not tired. I'll wait."

"You'll want to see your room, sure?" Clíona said.

My room? I didn't have a room here. Didn't this woman get it? I didn't want her house or her family or any of it. I wanted to meet my father, find out the truth, and go home to Stephen.

I turned my back on her and headed for the door. The family was quiet now, watching me.

"Are you going for a walk?" Clíona said in a falsely cheerful voice. "Be certain you return before dark, child, for you don't know the island—"

I slammed the door, shutting her up.

I ran toward water. There were a few men at the harbor shore, tying up black rowboats, who looked at me and smiled. I slowed down and veered away from them. I slogged through the deep sand, along a beach that looked out toward the mainland. The wind was so strong that it pounded my temples and screamed in my ears. I thought of building a fire but realized I had no matches.

I must have walked halfway around the island before I noticed it was dark. My fingers were stiff and my cheeks felt thick from the cold. Though I had not touched the water, my clothes were damp, and when I licked my lips I tasted sea tears.

Up ahead, outlined by the moonlight, I saw cliffs of rock growing out of the water. The screaming wind changed its pitch and from the rock's crevices I could hear a rhythmic moaning.

For an instant I thought it was my mother. I ran to the cliffs, but as I reached them the sound moved behind me.

Stupid, I thought, and I started crying. I sat down in a tiny cave and tucked my legs into my chest. They were too thin to shield me.

I fell asleep wedged within the cliff and woke when Marcus and Clíona found me. Their mouths were moving, but I could not hear them because my ears were ringing with the echoes of moaning wind and sea. Clíona covered me with a waxy coat and Marcus lifted me. They carried me back toward the truck, their voices blending with the music that still sloshed in my head.

CHAPTER 10

Clíona

She's going to be a handful, this granddaughter of mine. Hardly here a day and she's after running off by herself—straight to the sea, just as Grace used to do. Ever since that plane touched down, Gráinne has had the look of an immigrant child, lost and longing for home. I want to take her in my arms, though I can see she wouldn't allow this. It is only because she's exhausted that she lets Marcus carry her back to the truck, and wrapped in his coat she looks no bigger than ten years of age.

I was not much older than you, I want to tell Gráinne, when I traveled on that ship to America. Eighteen. I certainly felt young when I arrived, though at home I'd been an adult for ages.

My childhood is a common enough story in Ireland. I am not of the generation that blames present hardships on things gone past. God does not give you more suffering than you can handle. I said that to Grace once and her smart response was: "No, but your family does."

My father was a fisherman like all the island men. My mother was with child almost constantly from the time she was sixteen until she was thirty. She bore nine children, with a miscarriage between each two. We were neither a large family for our island, nor a small one.

When I was thirteen years my mother got the cancer. It killed her quickly. (It was probably the same cancer, once removed, that killed my daughter. I myself have always been healthy.) I did not mourn my mother deeply. I'd loved her, be sure, but she was a harsh woman, an unreachable woman, and I did not know her well. She was born in the North and met my father on a holiday in Galway. She was an outsider on our island and she had a habit of treating her children with the same suspicion the locals had for her. My brothers, sisters, and I obeyed our mother but adored our father.

Da was the only one who seemed to suffer by her passing, and after that I always believed that he missed a younger version of my mother, that perhaps she'd once been lighthearted and lovable. He was a great man, my father, a funny, passionate man who always seemed mismatched with my mother's sternness. He never remarried.

After her death, the wee ones were farmed out to aunts on the mainland. My sister, Maeve, took over the care of my brother Colm and our father. It was lucky I was to be old enough to stay on the island and help Maeve. It was difficult for the wee ones who grew up like charity children in someone else's family, though it was common enough at the time.

When Maeve left for Boston two years later, I took over the keeping of the house. I remained until my sister, Róisín, was old enough to move back to the island. I was the thrilled one, following after Maeve on a boat to London then Boston. It was not difficult for Maeve to set me up with a job—caring for the Willoughbys' first baby boy—and I did not suffer as an immigrant in America. The country was always good to me. I stepped off the boat and the next morning I had a job, a home, a future.

My plan was to work for a while, saving money, then apply to St. Elizabeth's to study nursing. I'd long dreamed of becoming a nurse. (I may appear at times cold and undemonstrative in my affections, but I have a brilliant bedside manner. Marriage proposals I've had, helping the island men to health.) I hoped someday to return to my island and take over the position of the existing nurse, Mariah O'Malley, a cousin of mine. She was getting on in years and was eager to defer to me. You see, I never planned to stay so long in Boston, I never thought to live there permanently. It was an opportunity for employment and schooling, nothing more. I did not run back to Ireland with my tail between my legs as Grace once suggested. I'd wanted to go back all along; it was my decision.

Mr. Willoughby was from London originally; he'd come to America for his schooling in law, and worked in a real estate firm in Boston. Mrs. Willoughby was an American. She worked as well, as a clothing designer, and she looked her job, sure. So fashionably dressed I was in dread of spilling something on her whenever I served them their dinner. They lived on Beacon Hill, in a flat that was as large as a mansion. They gave me a cozy little room in the attic, with my own toilet. Sound enough people, they were. Just not much time for their baby boy, so I was happy to help in that area. They were Protestants, but this was America, not Ireland, and they did not mind my being a Catholic, and I treated their religious persuasion with the same respect. On Sundays, they took little Michael to services and I went to Mass at St. Joseph's alone. When I wrote to my father, I let him assume they were Catholic, because he was not as open-minded as I.

I spoiled little Michael, and he adored me. It was easy enough to give him attention, there being just himself. At home, before my mother died, I'd been swamped with children and it was enough to get them bathed, dressed, fed, undressed, and bathed again, that I didn't have the time or even the desire to have a favorite. But Michael and I had each other to ourselves. I sang to him, told him fairy stories when he was ready for bed; even on my day off I'd buy him sweets at the shop. By the end of my first year with them, when Michael was learning to speak, he sometimes called me Mama by accident. Mrs. Willoughby, you can imagine, was not thrilled. She spent a few moments before dinner every night, correcting him.

"I'm Mama," she'd say, pointing to her jeweled and powdered neck. "That's Cleeoona," she'd emphasize, pointing to me at the stove.

"Mama!" Michael would call, reaching in my direction.

"No, no," she'd say, annoyed. "Ma-ma, Ma-ma," stabbing her chest with his pudgy little hand. To my relief, Michael eventually relented, calling his mother by her proper title. But he wound up calling me "Ooma," which was close enough to "Mama" to annoy your woman. Eventually, though, she forgot about it, and sometimes slipped up, calling me Ooma herself.

They paid me well, and I scrimped, so after eighteen months I had enough money saved to put me through my first semester at the nursing college. When I told the Willoughbys that I would be leaving in the fall, they were desperate.

"You can't leave us, Cleeoona," Mrs. Willoughby said. "How would we get along without you?"

It's a bit shocked, I was. I had told them my plans when I'd taken the employment, but somewhere along the way they had forgotten—they'd gotten used to me being there, I suppose.

"What about Michael?" Mrs. Willoughby said. "Children his age are very impressionable. You can't just up and rip yourself away from him, can you?"

I reminded her that the child would still have his parents. "I want to be a nurse," I said.

"A nurse!" Mr. Willoughby bellowed. "What the devil for? So you can earn an unfair wage and be treated with disrespect by the entire medical community? Nonsense, Clíona, you're much more appreciated here. We need you. I'll double your wages. You can have half Wednesday off as well."

In the end I agreed to stay on another year. With the extra wages I'd be able to save enough for the entire nursing course, plus living expenses. Then I'd be fit to get through school without having to take a job that would interfere with my studies. It wasn't that hard a decision. I liked my job, and I would have missed that boy dreadfully. It didn't occur to me, until after I was trapped, that the Willoughbys were never concerned with what was best for me. That was their way, sure, and I lived with it.

I still wonder, at times, what my life would be like now if I had made it to the nursing college. I would have returned to the island just the same, but I believe other things would be different. It's not Marcus I'd have married, though as good a husband you cannot find on God's green earth. I might have had a more romantic, younger marriage, a house full of my own children, a career that kept my mind busy as well as my body. I am not the one to mourn over lost opportunity—your life is what you make of it, with God's grace, the good and the bad. But still, I sometimes indulge myself and think, What if? What if I had never met that Patrick Concannon, had not gone dancing on that particular Saturday with Maeve and the girls, had not let myself feel what I felt or do what I did. What sort of woman would I be now?

He was a gorgeous fellow. Dark brown hair with shimmers of copper, forest-green eyes, tall, so tall I could rest my head below his neck. He was Irish, as well, which was an attraction for me. I liked my job, but I'll not fail to admit that I was a bit lonely. Maeve was newly married and hadn't much time for me—only occasionally it was that I had a night out like the one where I met Patrick. He was from Connemara, like us, except from the mainland; he was studying medicine at MIT. His accent was cultured, but still familiar to me. Especially when he slipped into the expressions of our county.

"Let's get pissed," he whispered to me that first night at the disco. "Show these Americans what proper drenkin is." And he won me, so easily it's a wonder I wasn't ashamed of it sooner.

He called for me every Saturday for two months. We had picnics on Boston Common, carriage rides around the city. He took me to concerts at Symphony Hall, to dinner in expensive Italian restaurants. He seemed to have loads of money for a boy from Connemara. When I protested at his extravagance, he told me he had a rich American uncle. I let him spoil me, let him hold my hand in the carriage, kiss me with his hips crushed into my stomach when he dropped me at my door. No boy had ever paid such attention to me. It made me feel beautiful, womanly, dangerous. I loved every minute of it.

I was so taken that once, in the middle of a roasting August afternoon, I agreed to follow him to his dorm room in Cambridge. On a narrow bed covered with dirty linens, I let him lie on top of me, kiss my breasts, which he let loose from my blouse and bra. I still remember the look of my own breasts, large, white, and foreign, without feeling, like something he had borrowed from me, removed from my body for his amusement. Like the carved mermaids I'd seen as a child, their stone bosoms exposed and deformed looking. I let him keep going, thinking all along that he would stop, knowing in my mind that I was sinning but feeling as though it were happening to someone else. Like what I saw was being described to me in gossip of some loose girl on the island, and I was saying: She did what? You're only joking!

I was so convinced of my detachment that I was terrified when I realized we were both completely naked. Even when he entered me, and the pain seared through that inner flesh where I had never before felt anything—which I had hardly known was there—even then I thought: This can't be happening. He was in and out of me, as though he was plagued with indecision; he was huge, he was hurting me, frightening me. At one point, near the end, he looked as if he might be having a stroke: his face welled up red and purple, his eyes bulged, he moaned as if in pain, as if something within me was ripping him apart as well. Then he collapsed on me. I lay there, trying to grasp the shards of my soul which had been thrown off from me, soiled now I knew, during the splaying and thrashing of limbs.

Patrick rolled off me and I gasped for air. He smiled, nuzzled my neck, kissed me with an exaggerated smack.

" 'Twill get better," he said. "A lady's first time is always the worst." I tried to pull a sticky sheet up to cover my breasts.

"If you think I'm going to do *that* again with you, Patrick Concannon—" I started, but he burst out laughing. Apparently he thought that I was only slagging him.

I have told my family, just as I told Gráinne, that I was a young widow. Only Maeve and the Willoughbys knew the truth, and Grace, who figured it out eventually. I was never married to Patrick Concannon, but he did die. A stupid, clumsy death. He toppled off the roof of his dorm while drunk, crashed through the top of a passing taxicab. When Maeve rang to tell me the news, I had already been vomiting for three mornings. I like to believe that he would have married me, if only out of a sense of obligation. So I don't feel like I'm lying when I say I've been widowed, not much so.

Mr. and Mrs. Willoughby were not as appalled as I feared they would be. Shocked, yes, surprised a bit, but after all, this was 1961 in America and I was not the first girl to get herself in such a fix. Sure, on the island I would have caused the scandal. When I told them, they calmly excused me, discussed it between themselves, then called me back into the room.

They would help me, they said. I would stay with them for as long as I needed to. I would continue to work for them, I would raise my child in their house, we would tell all visitors that I was a widow. I was family now, they said. Of course, my wages would go down a bit to compensate for the cost of my child's board and lodging. But I had their support. My child would grow up with Michael and whatever siblings of his happened to come along.

I could only nod and cry, trying to breathe over the fear that had shrunken my insides. Why was I not relieved, I wondered, or even grateful?

Mr. Willoughby handed me his handkerchief. Mrs. Willoughby patted my hand.

"We're delighted you'll be staying on with us," she said.

When Grace was born, she nearly tore me in half. I was in labor for thirty-four hours at the Lying-in Hospital for Women. There were some complications, some hemorrhaging, I was told, and in the end they had to remove my womb. Coming from a family of nine, I found it inconceivable that I would have no more children. No legitimate children. When they brought the baby to me for the first time, I looked at her red, flattened face and thought: This is all. This is all I will ever have.

Until I got back on my feet, the Willoughbys hired a housekeeper to look after them and Michael. For most of that time I was alone in my attic room with Grace. A dreadful few weeks it was, a prison from which I thought I'd never escape.

I was bottle-feeding because, at that time, the breast was not fashionable. Grace was a terrible eater. She couldn't seem to get the rhythm of the business down, always pulling away from the bottle, spitting up, not burping, then screaming for days on end with colic. I'd never had such difficulty with a baby. They say when it's your own you love them no matter what, but this was not the case. I despised my child in the beginning, with an intensity that horrified me. Every time I looked at her there was something wrong, she was wailing or rashy, even when she slept she had this permanent scowl contorting her tiny features. I looked at her and I thought of everything she'd taken away from me: a nursing career, other children, marriage—for in truth, who would marry me now? All given up for this unattractive, contrary child. I longed to get back to work, to Michael who smiled at me and brought me drawings while I was cooped up in the attic. Sure, I thought at times, he was more my child than Grace was.

Of course, nowadays they would say this was postpartum depression. It ended when I woke up one morning and Grace, for the first time, was sleeping peacefully in her crib. I suppose I just stopped feeling sorry for myself; I ceased to blame my daughter and began to love her. She grew to be a fierce, dramatic child whom I couldn't help but admire. A fighter, she was. You were the lucky one if you had Grace on your side.

I worried, when she got older and began to hate me, that maybe I had damaged her somehow during those first few months of her life. That she had known, even when it was over, that her mother had resented her, and she was getting me back for it.

She was ashamed of my job, looked at my position in the household as that of a slave. It drove her mad that we ate in the kitchen while the Willoughbys ate in the dining room. That was my doing, though she never believed it. I had told the Willoughbys early on that I would prefer to eat separately. They invited me to join them all the time, in the beginning. I never did it, and not because I "knew my place" or anything degrading, but because it was a job after all, we weren't family, and later because I didn't want Grace to grow up confusing herself as the Willoughbys' child. It would have been more difficult to leave; I still believe that.

Grace tolerated Mr. Willoughby, and Michael was like a brother to her, but Mrs. Willoughby—well, let's say I had a time keeping her from torturing the woman. I myself had always taken to Mrs. Willoughby—not with any great affection, mind you, but she was kind to me in the beginning, and I felt sorry for her, sure. She'd married above herself in Mr. Willoughby, and I believe she was always trying to hide this fact. She never had her own mother over the house, but visited her in Dorchester once a month with Michael. Even with all her nitpicking, I know she appreciated me. But by the time Grace was seven years old, Mrs. Willoughby was already growing ill, and she had changed drastically. Grace could never understand that your woman was sick—she thought Mrs. Willoughby's episodes were part of her personality—but I knew better and didn't take them to heart.

When Michael was nine and Grace seven, Mrs. Willoughby gave birth to twin girls, Sarah and Lindsey. It was a difficult pregnancy for her; she was confined to bed for the last three months of it, and it was this time that gave Grace her bad impressions. The woman was uncomfortable, and bored—she had never been the one for just lying around. She was very demanding of me, nothing I did seemed good enough—the food was inedible, my cleaning sloppy, I did not come quickly enough when she rang the bell at her bedside. Michael avoided her during this time, and she began to resent me for the time I spent with him. She was going a little off her head already, I believe. Once, when I was sweeping her bedroom carpet, and Grace was in there with me, holding the dustpan, Mrs. Willoughby started glaring at me murderously. Not a word, mind you, but she didn't take her eyes off me. It made me uncomfortable and I tried to sweep up quickly. When I heard the front door slam, I told Grace to see if it was Michael.

"He'll be wanting his lunch. Tell him I'll be down in a minute so." Before Grace could move, Mrs. Willoughby let out this noise, a growl from what it sounded like.

"He's my son," she spat. She looked possessed, her eyes red, hair on end.

"Pardon?" I said.

"If you try and take him from me I'll rip your ugly Irish head off," she yelled. I ushered Grace out of the room, but we could hear her still screaming, all the way down the hall. "You hear me? I'll rip your ugly Irish head off and feed it to the dog!" She'd no dog. I couldn't imagine what had gotten into her.

Grace became hysterical. She was crying, smearing snot all over her cheek with the back of her hand.

"Hesh," I said, stopping at the bottom of the stairs. "No tears now, it's only joking, she was."

"Was not," Grace said. She was angry now, red-faced, on the

verge of one of her tempers. "She tries and I'll rip her head off first," she sneered.

"God help us," I said. "Don't be ridiculous." I went into the kitchen to Michael. He was looking at me like he'd heard it all and was terrified, but I pretended nothing had happened. What stayed with me all that day was an image of this crazed woman and my mean little girl, ripping at each other like lions. I could see it, sure as it was happening before my eyes.

When the twins were born, Mrs. Willoughby almost died. When she'd recovered, the smaller girl, Lindsey, was not expected to live long. She had to stay in the hospital for months. Mrs. Willoughby was never the same again, even after Lindsey came home, frail but healthy. Something had loosed in the woman's mind, probably when she was still pregnant. She was not as easy to live with after that. She no longer worked, but shuffled around the house in a robe like a zombie. I was the one looked after the twins, hoping that she would snap out of her mood, but it went on for years. When the twins were eight, Mr. Willoughby had a promotion that made him richer than I think he'd ever dreamed, and he moved us all to a seaside house in Scituate, where they had a private beach, a tog room with a fireplace for changing out of swimming gear, and acres of green lawn and gardens.

It didn't seem to make any difference to his wife. She had strange outbursts—there were a few episodes where she was almost dangerous, but it was not so bad as Grace would have people believe. She exaggerated, because she needed reasons to keep hating the woman. Her first memory of Mrs. Willoughby would always be that uncomfortable scene in the bedroom, and Grace couldn't forgive her that. We had our differences, but the truth is that my daughter grew up fiercely protective of me. She'd never admit it, but she was always my little warrior, a step in front of me with a sword, ready to rip the head off of anyone who stood in my way.

Despite this, or maybe because of it, Grace prided herself on being my exact opposite, in personality and in action. The worst insult you could bestow on her was to point out some similarity between us. "I'm *nothing* like her," she'd say. She looked more like her father, with the same green eyes, and the rich red hair that must have come from his copper strands. She certainly was too brash and fearless to resemble my composed demeanor. When I moved her to Ireland, after Mrs. Willoughby's accident, she hated everything about the place. She would have left as soon as she turned eighteen, but by then she was pregnant with Gráinne, and it turned out that as far as our mistakes went, we weren't so different after all.

This is what I want to tell Gráinne, without exposing the whole sordid story: Mistakes were made. Compromises followed. My daughter, as it was, resented me for them. Sure, she made her own mistakes as well. There is nothing that says that Gráinne needs to suffer, no reason that she must hate me as her mother did. We can begin again, this girl and myself; I can give her Ireland the way I tried to do with Grace, who would take nothing from me. Gráinne has the suspicious look of someone who has been lied to altogether, but if I'm careful with what I tell her, this can change.

As I drive back to the hotel on Murúch's only road, Gráinne is shivering from the damp; she's too thin to stand this island weather. She glares at me from beneath the jacket draped over her head; she has struggled free from Marcus's arms and is sitting alone by the passenger window.

"We're almost home," I say, and I turn my head back to the dark road, giving her privacy, as she presses her forehead to the glass, trying not to cry.

CHAPTER 11

Grace

When she sleeps, she moves. She swims in quiet coves, or in the undertow of the open water, the pain in her limbs a welcome pain, her arms and her heart hammering the same rhythm in her hot ears. She makes love in her dreams to countless, faceless men. She knows them only by the way they touch her, the way they enter her, gentle, teasing, or with desperate urgency. It is Stephen who runs his fingertips and tongue over her body as if she were an instrument, her husband who holds her hips and legs above the sand and pulls her toward him again and again until they are both moaning louder than the sea behind them. Often it is Michael, her first lover, his hands shaking, so cautious, so sweet and terrified.

She knows she is awake before she opens her eyes because the pain is back. She thinks it is the pain that translates to the sensation of movement while she is sleeping. She hates to sleep, fights it because it means she has to wake up and continue dying. It eats at her, this pain, like something ripping at her muscles and organs with sharp relentless teeth. On her worst days, everything is an effort, and she tries not to breathe, not to think, because breathing and thinking fuel the pain. Stephen is a hazy figure to her then, a voice that she resents because she cannot relax enough to listen to it, a touch that sparks like a burn on her arm or her neck. She doesn't take the injections as often as she is allowed because they frighten her, lower her defenses. She emerges from them not knowing how to handle the pain.

When she does allow Stephen to give her the shot, she is able to speak to him for a few minutes. She rambles, trying to fit everything in. It confuses him and this angers her, that he cannot decipher what she knows she means.

"Has my mother come?" she says, and Stephen looks frightened.

"You told me not to call her until. . . . Do you want me to call her now?"

"No, you're right. I keep thinking I'm dead and you're here telling me how it's going."

"Grace," he says, but she has no time to listen.

"Where's Gráinne? Why doesn't she come in?"

"She's out again. She's scared, I think. It would help if you asked her to come."

"Nope, I'm scareder. That's not a word. I can't help her today. Maybe tomorrow."

"Listen, Grace, this thing about calling your mother. I'd feel better if you told Gráinne first. I'm in a weird position here."

"You want my position? You die; I'll tell Gráinne all the dirty family secrets."

"Grace, don't, please." She's gotten so mean. She knows this, and it makes her even more mean, the knowledge of it.

"My mother is not a nice woman. I don't want you to call her. But she loves Gráinne; I know she'll take her in. I want you to keep in touch with Gráinne, write to her. She'll need some . . . affection."

"Of course I will."

"She'll be a queen, my little girl. They'll give her a boat, she'll rule the sea. She'll steal anything she ever needs."

"Grace, try and get some sleep."

"You don't know what I'm talking about. You don't believe she can do it. You know nothing of these women, what they are capable of."

"What women?"

"Island women. Oh, they are hard. Even my mother—and I thought she was the weak one. Now I know she was hard. Gráinne is one. I should tell her. Remind me to tell her when I wake up, okay?"

"Okay, sweetie, go to sleep now."

"She tried to kill me, you know."

"Not your mother?"

"No, Mrs. Willoughby. She tried to kill me because I was fucking her son."

"Who is Mrs. Willoughby, babe?"

"Didn't you meet her? I'd take you by there, by the old house. Except she's dead so there wouldn't be much point in you meeting her now. You can say that about me someday."

"Shhh," Stephen says, stroking her head. "Please be quiet, please go to sleep." She wonders why he wants her to be quiet. She could tell him so much, now that these memories have come back to her. She wants to tell it all, but she cannot remember the order of things, what the beginning is, where to reveal the details that become pertinent later on. The logistics of telling a story have slipped from her, she can only remember images, and whenever she tries to share them, he tells her to go to sleep.

"Stephen?" she whispers.

"Here."

"Is it me that's dying or is it Gráinne?" He doesn't answer. She opens her eyes but closes them fast because she is having hallucinations. Michael Willoughby is at her side, looking older than she remembers him. His cheeks are wet, like he's just been swimming, or crying, and has forgotten to wipe his face.

CHAPTER 12

Grace

When Grace was fifteen years old, she began to swim. She had learned years before at the YMCA pool, but she didn't love it, not until she found the ocean. The Willoughbys' mansion was right on the beach in Scituate; Grace left her clothes in the swimmers' cabin by the shore and dove naked into the cold waves. She could go for hours, swallowing up the miles of beach with her stroke. She took pride in being stronger than the water, in beating it down with the curve of her arm. She imagined her arms were the oars of a boat, sweeping the pirate queen Granuaile along the water. (Though she rejected most things Irish, Grace had always liked the Irish sea queen. Granuaile was a woman completely opposite from anything Clíona stood for.) Grace stayed in the sea way past the point when she thought she might collapse. Under the water, her mother's criticism could not reach her; with the waves sloshing over her back, she was not the servant's illegitimate girl. She was a sea creature.

When she wasn't in the water, her legs ached from the restraint, she could not stand still, had to flex her ankles and bend her knees or her muscles would quiver. "Stop that fidgeting!" her mother would snap. "Sure, you can sit like a lady with some effort?"

On the weekends, Grace spent the morning helping her mother with the housework, cooking breakfast and lunch for the twins, Michael, and their mother. The twins were seven and they rarely spoke to anyone but each other and Clíona. Lindsey was a smaller, paler version of Sarah, and they still dressed alike. At the table they looked like two dolls, next-to-motionless and made-up. They were equally afraid of their mother.

For as long as the twins had been alive, everyone had feared Mrs. Willoughby. Everyone pretended to be concerned over her, but only because it contained her outbursts. Grace hated her, and she was sure Michael hated her, too, but he was afraid to show it.

Lunchtime was torture for Michael without his father there. When Grace was in the house she had a habit of fussing over the table, interrupting the meal and giving Michael a secret wink so he wouldn't feel alone. Michael had always been her friend, though Mrs. Willoughby didn't like it.

"Michael," she said one day, "is it absolutely necessary that that girl come in here every two minutes while we're eating?" Mrs. Willoughby rarely spoke to Grace directly, they'd had too many clashes over the years. Michael tried not to smile.

"I don't know, Mom," he said. "Grace, could you get me the mustard?" Grace smiled and went through the swinging door to the kitchen, leaving it open so she could still hear them.

"You're very cruel to me, Michael," Mrs. Willoughby said.

"Mom, it's only mustard."

"You don't have to pretend. I know how much you hate me." She spat the words out, her face growing red and dangerous.

"Mom, I don't—"

"I know I've been a horrible mother, I know it well enough."
She began to sob, in that instant, hysterical way that terrified everyone. It paralyzed them when she was like this, when her face played
like a film of emotions, changing from threatening to helpless and
back again. When Grace came in with the mustard, the tears stopped.
Mrs. Willoughby looked at no one, but poured herself more tea.
The wet drops that still slid down her cheeks looked out-of-place,
like someone had splashed water on her. Grace rolled her eyes at
Michael and went back into the kitchen. The twins did not look up
from their sandwiches.

"Michael," Mrs. Willoughby said loudly, startling the girls,
"where is your father?"

"Uh, work, maybe?" Michael said, sarcasm slipping into his
voice.

"Don't be fresh with me. He's not at work. Your father's the
laziest man alive."

"What's he got an office for then?"

"Deception." She banged her teacup in its saucer.

"Mom, cut it out."

"You think that man sits at a desk all day? He's dropping his
pants all over the city."

"What's wrong with his pants?" one of the twins asked. Michael
only stared at his mother.

"Just as I thought," his mother said. "No sympathy from you.
You're just a man, after all. Like father, like son. Depraved."

Grace, who'd been lingering behind the door, walked in and
swiped the mustard bottle from the table. Mrs. Willoughby looked
at her viciously, intending to scold, but Grace looked back just as
fiercely. The woman turned instead to her son.

"You won't need an office, though, will you dear?"

Michael came down to the beach at dusk while Grace was swimming. He skipped stones in front of her path until she stopped the
crawl stroke to tread water above the sandbar. He walked out on

the dock where she'd left her clothes and towel and climbed into the tied-up motorboat.

"Are you coming in?" Grace said, arching her neck backward so the waves smoothed the hair off her forehead.

"My mother's fucked," Michael said.

"No kidding." Grace laughed.

"I'm serious. She's a nutcase. I can't stand it anymore. I keep thinking it's a whole year before I can get away from her."

"Don't take yourself so seriously. Everyone thinks their own mother is crazy."

"Your Mom's nice."

"Yeah, to you maybe." Michael could do no wrong as far as Clíona was concerned. Grace, on the other hand, was a constant disappointment. She always needed correcting—her clothes, her posture, her tone of voice or vocabulary. She'd been smacked, by hand or wooden spoon, almost every day until she was thirteen. Clíona sometimes looked at her like she was some evil alien child that had swallowed up the fantasy daughter she would have preferred.

"Grace?" Michael said, "Do you think she's right? Do you think my father has affairs?"

"Would you blame him?" Grace said, but she felt bad as soon as she saw his face. It hadn't occurred to her that this would bother him so much. She stopped treading and dropped her feet to the sand. "I doubt it though," she said. "Your Mom's totally paranoid." She started wading up toward shore, wringing her hair out behind her, and she felt Michael's stare before she saw it.

"When did you get those?" Michael said, smiling at first but then blushing and turning away. Grace looked down at her naked breasts, nipples puckered from the cold, the water beading where she'd slathered herself with oil for speed. Until that moment her breasts, which had grown quickly over the last year, had been an annoyance. Some days she had to swim in a bathing suit or else her whole chest ached afterwards. The boys at school looked at her breasts as if they wanted to remove them, take them away for some perverted experiment. With Michael's blush, she knew suddenly that they were an attractive part of her. She was not embarrassed but delighted. She took pleasure in her body, in her flexibility, the definition of her muscles, the smell of her salty skin after swimming, or the new odor, born with her breasts, that left its evidence on her underwear. She hadn't thought how it would feel to have someone share in the admiration.

"Do you like them?" she asked, to get him to look back at her. She was making him nervous, which excited her even more.

"You look like a mermaid," he said, and she laughed when he threw her the towel.

Grace managed to avoid her mother on most days but Sundays. Clíona, whom Grace thought of as fanatically holy, never missed Mass. Grace considered herself lucky because they were too poor for her to attend the local Catholic school. Still, every Sunday since she was four, she'd had to endure Mass and Catechism school through her First Communion, and then her Confirmation at thirteen. After that she was supposed to have earned the right to be responsible for her own religious actions, but Clíona kept dragging her to Mass anyway.

Grace would have liked the church had there been no people or priests in it. The ceiling was a mural of plump, mischievous-looking angels. She liked the smell of candle wax, the stained glass light that colored her hands, the tinkle of the gold bell at the offering. She imagined, though she knew Clíona would think her blasphemous, that the church would be a good place for kissing. While the priest droned out the sermon, Grace had fantasies of boys mouthing her backward onto the smooth wooden pews.

But she despised the girls she'd gone to Catechism with, who'd been rough and catty, made up like little saints in their Sunday best. And the boys—who had tried to push her hand down their pants, their tongues wagging at her in a gruesome attempt at sensuality—

those boys closed their eyes in profound holiness as the priest placed the Body of Christ on those same tongues. Even the priests seemed to be part of the act. They smiled and patted Grace's head on the church steps, after terrorizing her in Confession with judgmental grunts and guilt-inspiring silences. One had gone so far as to call her a "little tramp" before dispensing penance and shutting the screen.

Grace was always trying to get out of the Sunday ritual. She tried disappearing on Sunday mornings, but came back in the afternoon to her furious mother, who would only force her to go to Confession, and to morning Mass the next day.

"The Church is your guardian for when your morals as a young lady are tested," Clíona said when Grace tried to tell her she was too old for Mass. "Sure, it's time we spoke of the birds and the bees."

"Oh, please," Grace moaned. "Mom, don't. I know how it works."

"Sure, they told you the facts in that school of yours. Did they tell you that relations before marriage is a mortal sin?"

"Give me a break," Grace said.

"A girl can get herself in trouble on earth, as well."

"You should know," Grace muttered.

"I'll have none of your cheek, miss. You'd be well off to learn from my mistakes rather than casting stones. It's hard-pressed you'd be to find a man to marry you when you end up in my position."

"Michael will marry me," Grace said.

"It's fooling yourself you are if you think that boy would look at you. He's too rich for your blood. And I don't think his folks would take to his marrying a Catholic."

"He doesn't care what they think," Grace said. Her eyes were a wild green anger.

"Even if he fancies you, doesn't mean he'll do right by you."

"You don't know anything about it," Grace said.

Every Sunday started with a similar argument. Grace was infuriated by her mother. To her, Clíona was a dinosaur, despite the fact that she was younger than most of her classmates' parents. Grace promised herself that she would never end up like Clíona, an ignorant slave in someone else's country.

Michael began to come swimming with Grace. He would walk down at twilight, strip quickly to his shorts, and wade out to meet her. At first he could only manage a clumsy dog paddle; thrashing at the water, he fought it like he was afraid it was trying to swallow him. He arched his chin with a panicked expression that made Grace laugh.

She had him float on his back and made him believe her open palms were holding him up. She taught him how to give himself to the rhythm of the water, to immerse his ears so he could hear what she heard: the sea speaking over the beat of her heart. She showed him how to curve his arms with a strength that propelled him through waves. Before long, he was letting the swells wash over his face and swimming with a confident, though messy, crawl stroke.

Every day they swam miles along the beach, and Michael could not conceal his pride at his growing shoulder and arm muscles. At the end of the swim they would rest in a cove that was hidden from the view of the house. The water there was warm and still, the bottom covered with fine sand and soft seaweed.

One night at sunset, they knelt in the cove so the warm water came up to their necks. Amber rays illuminated their bodies beneath the surface. They had been talking, but as they floated closer they fell silent, watching each other. The beaded water on Michael's face was glinting in patterns like some sort of coded message. He looked down from Grace's eyes to her breasts, which were magnified by the water's surface.

"Can I . . ." he whispered, moving one hand slightly forward.

"Can you what?" she asked, teasing. Michael blushed.

"You know," he said, but she only smiled again. She wanted him to say it. "Touch," he said, his mouth barely forming the word. She floated closer and took his wrist, gliding his weightless arm upward. His palm cupped the outside curve of her breast and he squeezed slightly and moved a thumb across her nipple. Grace swallowed a noise. It was as if his touch was in two places at once, grazing her breast and pressing between her legs. Michael brought his other arm up, closing his eyes and moving his face to her cheek so she couldn't look at him. Grace put her hands just below his armpits, pulling him closer. For a few moments they held each other like this, Grace's body careening with sensations in all the places he wasn't touching. Michael twitched suddenly, letting go of her breasts, and pulled her to him like he was trying to stop her from falling away.

"Are you okay?" she whispered, and he nodded into her neck. When he leaned back he was blushing, his eyelids heavy, his expression clear evidence to her that something was permanently changed. Michael was in love with her.

She kissed him. His mouth tasted of salt combined with the flavor she recognized as the smell of him, an odor that was as familiar to her as the scent of her own body.

That summer, Grace and Michael stayed in the water every day until their lips were lined in blue and their fingers mushy as old fruit. They would swim a mile in case anyone was watching, then hurry off to the cove. At night, they walked around the house blushing and avoiding each other. Mr. Willoughby looked at them oddly, but only Clíona went so far as to comment.

"Sure, you young ones will find no good soaking in that sea all day," she said. "When was the last time either of you read a book?" So Michael went to the library and checked out a stack of novels. From then on, he would leave the house with a hardback clenched to his chest. "I'm going to the beach to read, Ooma," he'd call, and she would cluck praisefully after him. He would abandon the book at the swimmers' cabin.

Grace and Michael had barely enough self-control to keep from mauling each other. They held back only because it felt better to go slowly. For the first week they knelt facing each other in the cove, an imaginary line at their waists which they wouldn't go below. One day Grace couldn't stand it anymore, the pull to lie down next to him—or even better, beneath him—was too strong. She took his hand and floated toward the shore. They lay sideways in the shallow water, their heads cushioned on a nest of bubbled seaweed. Michael kissed her and whimpered occasionally. She thought it hurt him as much as it did her, not being able to get close enough. So she pulled off his bathing suit. She had to extend the elastic and maneuver it over his penis, which was pushed at a hard angle toward her.

"Grace?" Michael whispered, looking terrified.

"Shhh," she said, moving up to kiss him. She kissed his neck and down his chest until he let his head fall back on the seaweed, looking to the sky in panic like he expected a guillotine. The hair below his penis was softly moving like the locks of a mermaid. Grace put her hand there and his penis jerked like it was startled. She stroked and pulled the way a boy in Catechism had taught her. She had whacked that boy off a few times, never looking at his penis, considering the action repulsive practice for the real thing. Michael was moving his hips now, in a graceful flow that reminded her of a swimming dolphin. It wasn't long before she felt the snaky throb of a vein at the base of his penis, and she watched as a milky eruption blurred the seawater. She'd never seen this part, and hadn't imagined semen would look so tasty. She kept her hand on the shrinking penis and moved up to lie next to him. He kissed her, sighing, his embarrassment gone. After a few minutes he rolled her over and, with his leg separating her thighs, stroked until she swelled beneath his fingers, finally settling on a spot which he touched long after she could not lie still beneath him.

The summer passed quickly and Grace began to dread the beginning of school. She would be starting her sophomore year at Scituate High School and Michael would be a senior two towns away at the boys' academy. What would happen during those hours they were apart? Grace took comfort in the knowledge that he would rarely meet other girls, but she also knew he was obsessive about his studies and often stayed at the school library until dark. Soon it would be too cold for them to swim, and meeting in the house was too risky. Grace didn't mention her worries to Michael, mostly because she was afraid he wasn't worried himself.

The weekend before school started was Labor Day, and the Willoughbys had their annual party. Since Mrs. Willoughby's illness, they had entertained less frequently, but the Labor Day weekend was a tradition they held on to. Mrs. Willoughby was a strange caricature of her former self at these parties: she dressed extravagantly but something was always wrong. Her lipstick would be a shockingly ugly color, her hair unwashed, or she would mismatch her once fashionable accessories. The guests were condescending and spoke loudly to her as though she were deaf. She spent most of the party bothering Clíona about imaginary details. Grace almost felt sorry for her, the way the guests reduced her. She hated Mrs. Willoughby, but, after all, it was her party, and they treated her like a retarded dog.

When they were children, Grace and Michael would sit on the landing in their pajamas during these parties, listening to the clinking, hooting, and gruff laughter below. This year, Michael was forced to dress in a suit and be introduced to the guests. After helping Clíona and the caterers with the food preparation, Grace didn't have the heart to sit and listen with the twins, so she stayed in her attic bedroom, pretending to read one of Michael's library books.

Three hours into the party, Michael came upstairs and knocked on her door. He paced her little room, his hair grazing the rafters.

"Did you meet any nice young ladies?" Grace said. His eyebrows answered that he appreciated the joke, but he was too distracted to smile.

"Mom's in rare form tonight," he said. "She keeps dragging me into the kitchen to ask me who Dad's talking to. Then he goes to walk someone to their car or something and she freaks out. She wants me to go find him. Fuck if I'm going to follow him around all night."

"She just needs the scheming to keep her busy," Grace said. "No one else even talks to her."

"Well, I'm not gonna help her anyway," Michael said. "Fuck this. I've got her in one ear and some old fart telling me Harvard stories in the other. Then I get introduced to this pig they call a girl, who they want me to show the *garden* to."

"You have better things to do?" Grace asked. It gave her a little thrill when he called that girl a pig.

"Yeah." He grinned. "Let's go swimming."

They snuck down the back stairs and took the path behind the swimmers' cabin in case guests were down at the dock, which was where they usually dove in. Approaching the cabin, Grace noticed that its lights were on.

"The party's moved to the tog room," Grace said. The term was her mother's, and it always made Michael laugh.

"What would people go in there for?" he whispered.

"What do you think?" Grace nudged him. Michael dropped his mouth, exaggerating shock. "Let's look," she said, and pulled him toward the window before he could answer.

Through the small pane they had a perfect view of the couple on the daybed. They were naked, their skin jaundiced in the lamplight. The woman was on top of the man, moving up and down, her torso and loose hair moving in circles, like a dancer's. Grace was fascinated. She watched closely, clutching at details and memorizing them—the way the woman's hands kneaded the man's shoulders, the circular thrust of her hips.

"Oh, God," Michael moaned at her ear, and for a moment she thought he was as aroused as she was. Then she looked at the man under the woman. It was Mr. Willoughby. His glasses were gone and his naked chest revealed that he was smaller and hairier than he seemed when dressed, but it was definitely him. He craned his neck toward the woman's hand and sucked her middle finger into his mouth, rolling it over and under his tongue.

Michael turned from the window and retched into a mound of beach grass.

"Hey," Grace said, putting her hand on his shoulder. "Relax." But he pushed her away, disgusted.

"I have to get out of here," he said, and he ran off, down the path that led to the main road. Grace could have caught up with him easily, but his push had startled and momentarily paralyzed her, so she just watched him vanish in the shadow of trees.

Michael didn't come home until four that morning. Grace had helped her mother clean up, and after all in the house had gone to bed, she stayed in the dark kitchen thinking about Michael. She was trying to understand why he'd been so upset. She enjoyed finding out that Mr. Willoughby, who'd always seemed so proper and boring, had a sexy side. She didn't have a father, so she couldn't imagine what it would be like to catch her father cheating on her Mom. Maybe Michael felt he should be loyal to his mother, even though he despised her. Really, she thought, Mr. Willoughby should have been inside being nice to his wife, when no one else was willing to do it. Or maybe seeing his father having sex just disgusted him. If Clíona ever had sex, Grace certainly wouldn't want to witness it.

But he'd acted like he was mad at Grace, and that wasn't fair. Even as a little boy, Michael had been like this—easygoing to the point where you thought you couldn't affect him, and then, without warning, violently against you.

She decided she wouldn't get mad about how he'd shrugged her off. She needed to stay on his easygoing side. Michael's parents would never consent to their relationship; they thought she was beneath him. If Michael really cared what his parents thought he'd have to dump Grace eventually and marry someone like the pig at the party. But if he hated them—and it seemed he was beginning to hate his father as much as he despised his mother—then he would think of Grace as his family, and he could take her away. Grace was desperate to leave that house and Clíona's suffocating judgments. She figured her only chance with Michael was if his parents kept fucking things up. If he wanted to believe his father was a bastard for sleeping around, then it was to her benefit to encourage him. She didn't think of it as manipulative, just as the best way to get what she wanted.

When Michael slipped in the pantry door, she stood up and kissed him before he could speak. She moved her tongue deeply in his mouth, pressed her crotch against his in the way that always hypnotized him. She'd never kissed him in the house before, and she briefly entertained the fantasy of throwing him on the kitchen table and straddling him. Michael pulled away and put his mouth beneath her ear.

"I'm sorry about before," he whispered, and she nodded. "Is everyone asleep?" he asked, and she smiled and kissed him again, backing him toward the door. "Where're we going?" he said, but she signaled for him to be quiet.

She pulled him outside. "It's a surprise," she said.

She brought him to the swimmers' cabin. He hesitated at the door but she managed to coax him in. The room was blue with moonlight, the daybed and pillows now carefully fluffed to look innocent. Grace tried to kiss him.

"This is the last place I want to be," Michael said, sounding angry. Grace pulled off her T-shirt and stepped away from him. The blue light from the window curved over her breasts. Michael, distracted, leaned forward and ran his lips briefly over her nipple. Grace twined her arms around his neck. When he lifted his face, he looked like he was trying not to cry.

"Your father would hate it," she whispered, "if he knew you were here with me."

There was a pause in which Michael shut his eyes tightly and a tear dropped off his cheekbone. Then he was kissing her. They didn't bother to go slowly. They stripped off their clothes so fast their sneakers got tangled in the ankles of their jeans and they had to fall on the daybed to kick off the rest. Grace raised her knees and he was right there, pausing just long enough to ask: "Is it safe?" She nodded, thinking he meant would anyone catch them. It didn't hurt the way she'd been told it would. There was a brief hot sting and then she was filled with him. Even when it was over, after Michael had mashed his face in the pillow to keep from screaming, she touched and kissed him relentlessly until he was ready to do it again. She rolled on top this time, enveloping him. It came as no surprise to her that, at her orgasm, her insides squeezed and clung. As she watched Michael's face below her warp with love and misery, she clamped on with every part of her body, with all the strength and determination she'd been saving up.

CHAPTER 13

Gráinne

In the morning, still half-blind from sleep, I thought I was in the cottage again. I could smell the sea, and Stephen cooking breakfast. I'd get up and check for a note from my Mom, then leave before Stephen saw me.

My eyes focused on an unfamiliar room, my blue suitcase looking like washed-up debris from another life. I was sweating from the heavy comforter and the aftermath of bad dreams. I'd dreamed there was a phone screaming under dark water and I couldn't find it to answer.

I got up. Outside of the bed, the air was freezing. I pulled on a sweater and jeans and looked around the room. Twin beds with colorful wool blankets and comforters, an antique-looking wood dresser and desk. Above the desk, hung by a piece of fishing wire, a carved black piece of wood. I looked closer.

The ridges formed a woman in the bow of a boat, a cloak covering her head, one arm raised and pointing a finger forward. I took the block off the wall. The natural hues of the wood were in just the right spaces to create shadowing in the picture. Scratched into the back was the name *Granuaile*, and under that, *Grace and Seamus O'Flaherty*. I wondered if my father had made the carving or just given it to my mother. It was the first object I'd ever seen, besides the engagement ring, that connected me to my father. Proof that he existed.

I opened the door slowly, afraid of who I might see, or not see, on the other side. I found the bathroom, which was damp-smelling, and wiped away some fog to look at myself in the mirror. I was still shocked whenever I looked at my bristly head. I found some hair spray and plastered down the hairs that stuck out on one side. I wished I could stay in that bathroom, lock myself in until someone came to take me home.

When I'd dragged myself downstairs, Clíona was baking bread. She took a huge round loaf from the oven and left it to cool on the breadboard. She started, putting a floury hand to her chest, when she saw me in the doorway.

"You walk as quiet as a ghost, girl," she said. "Good morning to you." She motioned for me to sit at the table, which was laid out with plates for breakfast. "You're an early riser, like your mother and myself."

I felt lost and stupid in that kitchen, with no notes to tell me what to do. I sat down; at least it was warm in here. Clíona filled a large metal teapot with loose leaves and water from an electric kettle.

"I'm making breakfast for himself," she said. "Will you have one?"

"I'm not hungry," I said. Clíona wiped her hands briskly on a towel and turned to glare at me.

"See here, now. I don't know what you're after doing to yourself. Starvation, from the looks of it. But you won't be wasting away while you're in this house. Three meals a day and tea in the afternoons. Sure now, if the Irish breakfast's too rich for you, you can have brown-bread and fruit. I'll put something in that stomach of yours before you leave this table, God as my witness, I will."

She seemed mad about the food, but didn't mention my taking off the night before. It would be like my Mom and Stephen, then. She'd leave me alone.

"I'll have some bread," I said. She slathered some grainy bread with too much butter and set it down in front of me.

I'd sort of assumed I'd want to eat again once my mother had died. But since her funeral it had remained something to focus on: not eating. Like I was accomplishing something by leaving my stomach empty. I broke the bread into sticky pieces and moved it around my plate.

"That's a start, now," Clíona said, looking suspicious. She started frying up slices of fatty pink meat and a chain of linked sausages. I hid some of the bread in my napkin.

"You told me my father would be here," I said. Clíona looked embarrassed.

"He will," she said. "He'll be at Mass."

"What's that," I said, covering my grumbling stomach with my hands, "church?"

Clíona nodded. "You'll be joining us, will you not?" she said, avoiding my eyes.

"What's my father like?" I said. What I really wanted to know was what was wrong with him. Why my mother spent all that time acting like she'd forgotten him.

"Oh, he's a grand fellow altogether," Clíona said. She was stirring the bacon and sausages furiously. "Quite handsome. Dark, like yourself. His father was a fisherman from the island, and his mother from the North, God rest them. Poor woman. Died while having him, she did, and him her first child. Seamus was a lovely little boy, though. I'd mind him on the odd weekend. His father did a fine job, being on his own as he was. Seamus went to university in Dublin—the smartest one around, that lad."

97

"I thought he was a fisherman," I said. I didn't think of fishermen as the kind of people who went to college.

"Sure, it takes more than an education to pull the love of the sea from a man. Writing's how he spends most of his time, though. Articles for newspapers in Dublin and such. A bit of the poet, himself. He travels quite a lot, as well. But Seamus is an O'Flaherty, sure enough. You'll never see him long from the water."

He didn't sound so bad. I thought there must be something she wasn't telling me, but I didn't say so. Marcus came into the kitchen.

"Howaya, Gráinne? Sleep well?"

I nodded. I vaguely remembered his thick arms sheltering me from the wind. He was wearing a brown wool suit, and his neck looked pinched in his white collar and print tie. Clíona put a plate piled with fried proteins in front of him, poured him a cup of tea.

"Ah, you're a lovely woman yourself, Clee," he said, squeezing her middle with one arm. She batted him away, smiling, and returned to the stove. Marcus winked at me. I wondered whether they still had sex.

"You're lucky I've time to make you breakfast at all, with the state that hotel's in," she said. "I'd a guest looking after toilet roll this morning."

"It all falls apart without you," Marcus said, his mouth full of sausage. I thought they might start arguing, but Clíona was hiding a smile.

"Liam may call in later," Clíona said to me. "He's happy to see you back."

"Who is he anyway," I said, "your son?"

Clíona laughed. "God, no. Your Mum was my only child, though I raised most of Marcus's pack, as well. The twins and Tommy are living in England, and you met Stephanie and Mary Louise last night. They work at the hotel as well. Liam is Mary Louise's boy. You're the same age; Liam was born just two months before you. He was your best playmate when you were just a wee girl."

God, I hated the way she said that. Like she knew so much about me.

Marcus clinked his silverware on his empty plate, sat back in his chair, and burped loudly.

"Mind your manners," Clíona said, rising and clearing his plate. "Or, sure, your granddaughter will think she's living with a pig."

I'm not living here, I wanted to say. Only visiting.

At ten o'clock, we went to Mass, walking up the graveled road toward the steeple. People were swarming at the door, greeting one another. I was introduced and fawned over by women in shapeless dresses. I heard them murmuring about me as I passed through; saying I looked like my father. I saw Liam standing with a pack of teenage boys. They all wore baggy jeans like the boys at my school— jeans that hung so low, the bottoms of the back pockets lined up with their knees. Liam's mother, Mary Louise, kissed me and said I looked "fresh and well."

I hadn't really looked at her the day before. She didn't look much like Marcus; she had his gold-red hair, but her face was thin, with a delicate nose. She looked me right in the eyes, which made her seem more trustworthy than the rest of them.

"Have you seen my father?" I said to her, and she frowned.

"I haven't," she said. "And I'm none too happy about it."

I didn't get a chance to answer because Clíona hushed me as we entered the church.

Inside, the one large, high-ceilinged room was dimly lit by stained glass windows with images of religious people; blue and red light puddled on the smooth brown pews. Up front, where a robed priest waited silently, there was what looked like a miniature and ancient city, white carved steeples and windows lined in gold. In the center was an ornate golden door, like a little recessed treasure chest. The scent of wax and burning wicks passed through me.

Other than my mother's funeral, I'd never been to church in my life. I had to watch Clíona so I'd know when to stand and kneel and bow my head. The crowd chanted out foreign music around me.

> Ár nAthair atá i Neamh, go naofar d-ainm,
> Go dtágtar do ríocht,
> Go nDeantar do thol,
> Ar an talaimh mar a nDeantar i Neamh.

" 'Tis the Our Father in Irish," Clíona whispered, afterwards. "You'll learn it soon enough."

"What's the Our Father?" I whispered, and she looked angry.

"A prayer, girl."

I wondered if it was a prayer for fathers; if my father would have taught it to me had I ever known him. I looked back toward the doorway every few minutes to see if he was there.

At one point the priest asked the audience to "think of Gráinne O'Flaherty, who has returned home to us all." It took Liam and the others nodding at me to realize that it was me he was talking about. At first I was only shocked: I didn't think anyone was singled out in church. Then I got mad. My name wasn't O'Flaherty. My mother and I had the last name Malley, without the O. Who did these people think I was, some kidnapped waif returned to civilization? I slumped in my seat, tried to glare at Clíona, but she wasn't paying attention to me.

When the priest began the water-and-wine ritual, everyone around me seemed to plunge into serious thought. They knelt on the cushioned knee platforms, stopped fidgeting, hung their heads between clasped palms. My grandmother's mouth moved almost imperceptibly along with the priest's.

He was telling the story of the Last Supper, mechanically, as if he'd memorized it. I had seen paintings of the Last Supper in the Museum of Fine Arts in Boston. They had been my mother's favorites; she used to look enviously at the group of men gathered at the table. She said she had a soft spot for table settings—which was why she had so many dinner parties, and had developed the bad habit of dropping small fortunes at Crate & Barrel.

The priest poured red wine and water from crystal pitchers into a gold goblet which he held high in front of him.

"Jesus took the wine and offered it to them, giving thanks and praise. He gave it to his disciples and said: 'Take this, all of you, and drink from it. This is the cup of my blood. The blood of the new and everlasting covenant. It will be shed for you and for all, so that sins may be forgiven. Do this in memory of me.' "

The priest raised the goblet over his head and a ringing echoed throughout the church. When it was quiet, I noticed one of the robed boys at the altar trying to set down a little bell without jingling it further. The priest took a sip of the wine and then wiped the goblet rim with a cloth napkin. He held up a white wafer the size of his palm.

"Jesus broke the bread. Again he gave thanks and praise. He gave it to his disciples and said: 'Take this, all of you, and eat it. This is my body. It will be given up for you.' "

The boy rang the bell again. The priest broke the wafer in half, sweeping the crumbs into the wine goblet, and crammed one large piece into his mouth. He lowered his head and chewed with difficulty, his eyes closed, his palms clasped in front of him.

I thought it was all very odd, and I was embarrassed because I didn't know what it meant. I looked at the monstrous cross hanging above the priest, Jesus' bruised and bony body, blood running down his palms and feet. He looked starved, like he'd been ill for a long time. Not like those paintings of the Last Supper, where he glowed at the head of a table full of food.

After it was over (everyone but me got to go up front and get a sip of wine and a small wafer), I was introduced to the priest, "Father Paddy." Away from the stage he was a plump, bald man with a nice smile. I was suspicious of him, though, after how he'd announced me.

"I'm sorry for your loss, child," he said quietly, shaking my hand.

He turned to someone else before he could see that I was almost crying. I swallowed it, breathing deep.

In the corner, to the left of the stage, was a line of candles on a brass shelf. Behind them stood a statue of a woman, with dark circles under her eyes and an appealing look. I walked over to it. There were fresh bouquets of flowers surrounding her. SAINT BRIGID, the plaque said. She looked hungry, too.

"Do you want to make an offering?" Clíona said, coming up behind me. I turned around.

"My name is not O'Flaherty," I whispered meanly. "It's Malley. And I'm not the returned property of this place." Clíona looked hurt, but I didn't care. She deserved it.

"He was just trying to make you feel welcome, he was. You go by any name you like." She gave me a twenty-pence coin, and showed me the slot in the middle of the candles.

"Make an offering," she said. "Your man Stephen says you're fond of the poetry. Brigid is the patron saint of poets," she added, leaving me there.

I stood seething for a moment, then put the money in the slot, conscious of the loud clank. There were wooden matches and fresh candles in a little drawer beneath the brass holder. I put my candle in the center, struck the match and set it to the wick. I wasn't sure what I was supposed to offer, other than the coin. Maybe I should have said a prayer, but I didn't know any. Where's my father? I asked the saint instead. The candle flame flickered. I wondered if my mother had ever prayed here, and who it had been for. I stood there until the wax began to gather in a puddle and drip down the candle's sides.

When I got outside, I saw Clíona and Marcus across the lot; they were speaking in a close, secretive posture to the priest, who looked silly standing on the gravel in his robes. The priest handed Clíona an envelope; she opened it and read the paper inside. Marcus was shaking his head. I went up to them.

"Look," I said, startling them, "do I have a father here or not?"

Clíona sighed. "It seems your father's been delayed in Dublin," she said. The priest and Marcus were avoiding my eyes. I snatched the note away from her and, before I could open it, I saw the priest looking at me strangely, as if he couldn't decide whether to scold me or laugh.

> *Dear Clíona,*
>
> *I've gone away to Dublin to do some work for the paper. I'm not ready to face Gráinne yet. All these years of imagining it, I never once thought Grace wouldn't be there to reacquaint us. Please explain to her.*
>
> *—Seamus*

My father's handwriting. His letters were carefully formed; he followed those old rules of penmanship my mother used to use. I stared at those lines for a long time. Not ready to face me. As though I were a chore. An interruption in his otherwise contented life.

"He doesn't want to see me?" I said. No one answered.

I put the note back in its envelope and thrust it at Clíona. I started walking away without them, in the opposite direction from the hotel.

"Gráinne?" Clíona called out, but I didn't look.

"Let her alone," I heard Marcus say. "She won't go far."

Fuck you, I thought. I can leave anytime I want to.

I walked on the road past the cliffs I'd found the night before and came to a strip of ocean that reminded me of Singing Beach. There was the same squealing sand, the seaweed in bubbled piles on the barnacle rocks. I wondered if my mother had thought of this place while she was at home, dying in that little room.

I followed a road up around the corner of the island that led steeply into deserted fields. There were no real houses here, only remnants of stone huts. I could hear the ocean, and I followed the sound, crunching up through the dry grass until I started wheezing.

103

I thought there was a ringing in my ears, but it started to sound like music, and as I came over the last hill, I saw a boy sitting in the grass, blowing on a tin instrument. The boy turned around; it was Liam.

"Howaya, Gráinne," he said. He didn't seem surprised to see me—more like he'd been waiting for me. I remembered Clíona saying he was happy I was back. Maybe he had a crush on me, I thought, so I smiled at him and sat down. His hair had fallen out of its Sunday combing, into a dark blanket above his eyes. He was cute, not as beautiful as Stephen, but close. I felt that old anticipation well up. Something familiar to focus on.

We were at the top of the island; at the edge the land shot down in steep cliffs to the water below. My hair was so short it was no comfort in the cold, and I felt dizzy. Liam got down on his stomach and motioned for me to do the same. We leaned our heads over the edge. The black slices of the cliff went so far down, it was hard to capture the depth. The only way I knew how high we were was by looking at the seagulls, some of which looked like pieces of lint floating far below.

"You wouldn't want to walk up this way at night, without someone who knows the island," Liam said. "You'd walk right off the edge of the world." Our arms were touching now, and I looked at him, thinking this view was all his ploy to make a pass at me.

"Aren't you watching?" he said, so I looked back down. The seagulls, hundreds of them, weren't flying so much as spreading their wings and letting the wind carry them.

Liam sat up and watched me, his elbows propped on his bent knees. I shifted my position so he wasn't looking at the worst side of my hair.

"Do you not remember me?" he said. His eyes were so blue they looked drawn in with layers of thick pastels.

"No," I said, plucking at a rock that was covered with something like sharp, light green hair. "Do you remember me?" He looked serious, then broke into a wide smile.

"Ah, no," he said. He was teasing. "Sure, why would I? We were only babies."

"So why would I remember you?" I asked.

"No girl ever forgets me," he said.

"You wish," I said.

He blushed and threw a clump of dry grass at me. "Do you want to hear a tune?" he said.

"Are you going to sing?" I said sarcastically.

"Ah, I could now, but not during our first reunion, I'd be too shy." He picked his whistle out of his pocket. It had six holes and a blue plastic mouthpiece. He blew into it, playing some notes, then started a song. He was really good; his fingers blurred they were going so fast. The tune sounded sad, and fluttery. I liked the look of his mouth, and waited for him to finish playing, and kiss me.

"That's 'The Cliffs of Moher,' " he said when he was finished. "The place is in Clare, but the song reminds me of this. The gulls." He gestured toward the cliff's edge, and played some more. The music was like the way those gulls let themselves be blown up down and around with the wind.

"Where did you learn to play that?" I said. Liam wiped the mouthpiece on his sleeve and pushed the whistle back in his pocket.

"My father taught me," he said. "He plays fiddle with the lads in the pub. Sometimes they let me in on a session, in the afternoons. When I'm eighteen they'll let me play the night hours. I play the flute in the sessions, sometimes the guitar."

"You're pretty good," I said. He stood up, brushing grass from his legs.

"Everyone's good at something," he said. I hoped he would ask me what I was good at, so I could say "kissing," and grab him. My mother would have done something that bold in an instant. I wondered whether his mouth would have that heat, like Stephen's, and whether he would step away at the last minute.

"Will I show you the island?" he said instead.

"Oh," I said. I looked back toward the harbor. "How do you get out there?" I said.

"Granuaile's castle?" he said. "I should have known you'd want to go there; you're named for the pirate queen." I stood up and tried to look ready for an adventure, though secretly I was afraid we'd have to swim there.

We walked back to the pier and Liam untied one of the large black rowboats with a high pointed front and thin oars.

"You can't walk out unless the tide's low," Liam said. "So we'll take my Da's curragh. Da's out in the trawler now, but years back everyone fished in these. They'd harpoon sunfish, big as whales, and drag them in to shore."

I couldn't imagine being far out to sea in such a little boat. It looked thick, layered with tar, but vulnerable. I heard my mother's scold, how it was ridiculous for me to be afraid of the water after all the time she'd spent teaching me how to swim.

We rowed across the harbor toward the jutting finger of land where Granuaile's castle stood alone. Liam was stronger than he looked; his arms pulled the oars through the water like it was air. The harbor streamed by my side like a highway. He pulled us up into a sandy cove and I climbed clumsily out of the boat.

We walked up a grassy hill, potholed with nooks of sand. The castle rose slowly up ahead of us, gray stone walls reaching up with no roof. Inside was a huge room carpeted with grass. Stairways were carved into the walls and led to narrow pathways all around the top of the castle. There were openings in the stone, slits just wide enough to peer out with one eye. At the front, which I had seen from the ferry, part of the wall had fallen away, leaving a gap looking down on a slide of sharp rocks and the crashing waves of the open sea outside the harbor. To the right, a grassy stairway led to another room, where tiny white flowers pushed up between the pebbles of the floor.

"This was Granuaile's bedroom," Liam said. "One of her children was born here, and while she was in labor, the castle was attacked. Her men kept interrupting her, asking for instructions on how to handle it. Gráinne gave birth to the boy, then marched down to the fighting, roaring about the eejits who couldn't do without her for ten minutes." Liam laughed. "Fearless, that one," he said.

She who inspires terror, I thought, like my mother had always wanted me to be.

Liam sat down by an indent in the wall that looked like it had once been a fireplace. The stone above it was slightly lighter than the rest, and when I looked closer I saw that it was a carving. The upper half of a naked woman, her breasts pointy and severe, her head bowed so that her hair covered most of her face. Her eyelids peeked out, lowered in what looked like sadness. Her bottom half had fallen away; severed by the rough inside of stone.

"That's a mermaid," Liam said. "There's lots of these old carvings on the island. I wasn't let to look at them as a boy, on account of what Nana called their 'pornographic bosoms.' The lads and I used to sneak around, peeking and poking at all the stone tits on the island."

"Couldn't you find any real ones?" I said. I meant it to be flirtatious, but he took it as a geography question.

"Ah, there's real mermaids here as well. There have been for ages. Some of the island surnames, like mine and your Da's, are supposed to be those of the descendants of captured merrows."

"Oh, come on," I said. How naive did he think I was?

"That's the story. My surname, MacNamara, means 'son of the sea' in Irish. The mermaids, they swim into caves like, and sing with sad voices, trying to draw in the lonely men. If a man follows, the mermaid grabs him and takes him down under the water, has her way with him, and drowns the eejit. 'Tis bad luck for a fisherman to see a mermaid, for it means he'll drown if he's not captured first.

"But sometimes, the odd cute man can capture one of the creatures. Mermaids wear this enchanted red cap, the 'cohullen driuth,' and if you nick it, their fins turn to legs and they can't return to the sea until they get it back. That's how come the MacNamaras and the O'Flahertys are said to come from a union with a mermaid. Your man somewhere along the family tree snatched her up as his bride and she had his children before she could escape. There's some that say she took one of her children under the sea with her, turned the girl into a baby mermaid who never grew any older."

"That was cruel of her," I said, still suspicious but drawn in.

"Ah, sure, she loved her husband as well. But the pull of the sea was too great and she had to go back eventually."

"You don't really believe that," I said, and Liam shrugged.

"Doesn't matter if I do or I don't. There's no harm in it. 'Tis just a story, sure."

"Have you ever seen a mermaid?" I said.

"Ah, no. But I thought your Mum was one."

"My mother?" I said. "You remember my mother?"

"The odd bit of her, yeah." Liam was blushing now. "My Da used to tell me the stories in the cradle, and I remember your Mum being at Nana's house. She talked funny, I thought, and I wasn't allowed to the beach with her because she swam naked. She had all that red hair, and the eyes like seaweed, and she'd always be looking out over the water like she missed something. It was silly, I know, but I was only the wee boy. Then she vanished, and the relations were whispering, and my Da says I cried and cried because I thought she'd taken you under the water with her." Liam snapped his mouth shut, like he'd just remembered I was listening.

"I thought you didn't remember me," I said. He plucked a white flower out of the floor, twirling it in his dirty fingers.

"I don't, not much so," he said. He wasn't looking at me. "I just remember missing you."

I pictured my mother, with her hair the way it used to be, trapped in a world where she talked funny, and myself as a little girl, dragged screaming under the sea.

"I wish I could remember you," I said. I was tired of everyone telling me stories of a life I couldn't recall.

Liam looked up and smiled, shifted so he was kneeling by the window in the wall. When he motioned for me to join him, I was conscious of my own breathing and I licked my lips. Kneeling, we were the perfect height to see the ocean through the slit in the stone. Without looking at me, Liam took my hand, not entwining fingers like most boys, but like a child, gripping my palm and wrapping his fingers over the space above my thumb. His hand was dry and warm and it felt natural, not like the kind of pass that would send me into panicked expectation. A smell came hurtling back to me, smoke and salt and damp, and the warm grip of a hand, tiny and plump like my own. Liam let go, but I had remembered.

"We're still friends," he said. "We're just after a gap is all."

I watched the tide recede and thought of Stephen's hands sliding my fingers down cool ivory keys.

What does it mean, I wanted to ask Liam, *This is my body, it will be given up for you*? Why does it make me think of Stephen, of kissing, of marooned blood clots, and my mother's hair like abandoned nests in the wastebasket?

Liam was saying something about Seamus and Clíona, and my mother leaving the island.

"They were brokenhearted, the both of them. Nana just made herself busier, you know. Seamus did as well, but for years he had this desperate look about him. He used to meet the ferry in the evenings, said he was just getting his post, but everyone knew he was wishing to see you and Grace on the quay. Then, about a year after you'd gone, he disappeared for months. Folks were hoping he'd followed after you both, but he came home alone and didn't talk about where he'd been."

"He doesn't even want to see me," I said. "He left a note saying he can't face me."

"Ah, I doubt that's the whole truth of it," Liam said.

"What is, then?" I asked.

"I don't know," he said.

Which Seamus is my father? I thought. The Seamus staring out to sea, waiting for me? Or the neat-handwriting Seamus who ran away?

When we rowed out again it was dark, and the moon was huge and textured, glinting a road of light across the water. Liam paddled around the side of the harbor, so he could bring the curragh to a cove closer to the hotel. The water was still, but there was that same far-off moan of wind which rose and fell in a rhythm, and now it reminded me of seagulls below cliffs.

"Do you hear that, Gráinne?" Liam said, when the moan rose to its highest pitch, echoing over the water. "It's the mermaids. They're singing."

CHAPTER 14

Grace

After the Willoughbys' party, school days and family dinners were chores Michael and Grace had to get through until nighttime, when they could meet at the swimmers' cabin. Grace was exhausted during the day and infused with energy at night. She could not pay attention in class, and her first report card was so bad, Clíona wouldn't shut up about it for weeks.

"It's not unintelligent you are, so you must be plain stupid bringing home these marks. Nothing but education is going to get you the fancy life you're looking for."

Grace smiled to herself. School no longer mattered. Love was the immediate and lasting thing. Michael kept his grades up with barely any effort and in November he received an early acceptance notice from Harvard. He told Grace before anyone else.

"I'll get an apartment instead of a dorm and you can stay with me every weekend," he said. She was delighted, already imagining what the freedom of their own place would be like.

The swimmers' cabin was hidden from the house by trees, and once everyone was in bed they could sneak out, light a fire in the wood-burning stove, and make love until they collapsed. The wood would crackle with gunshot pops while they thumped on the day-bed, startling them and making them cling tighter. For the rest of Grace's life, the smell of burning logs would make her think of sex. As would the sound of the sea.

They went on like this, undetected, all winter long. Clíona had not been as watchful as usual, for she had started dating a man named Jacob Alper. Grace saw him when he came to the house to pick her mother up, but she didn't bother looking closely at him. Grace hadn't much interest or faith in her mother's taste in men. She couldn't imagine where the two had met, unless it was at the su-permarket—which seemed pitifully middle-aged to her. She was just glad to have her mother out of the way on weekends.

In the spring, when the grounds man brought the motorboat out, Grace became excited at the prospect of swimming again. No more days cooped up in a classroom or that tense house. She could immerse herself in the ocean, where she was alone and in charge. This was what she was thinking about in her room when she heard the crash of pottery from downstairs, then what sounded like Mrs. Willoughby screaming. This was not out of the ordinary, so Grace just kept looking out her window. After some more thuds, she saw Mr. Willoughby stomping across the driveway. He got in his car and drove away with a violent screech of tires. Clíona came up to the attic, shutting the door behind her.

"What now?" Grace snapped. Clíona was flushed and breathless from running up the stairs.

"Your woman is upset," she said. "Your woman" was how she always referred to Mrs. Willoughby.

"What else is new?" Grace said.

"She's just after saying something that disturbs me. So I'm asking you is it true." Grace rolled her eyes. Clíona continued. "Has Mr. Willoughby ever . . . did your man touch you somewhere inappropriate?"

"Mr. *Willoughby?*" Grace sputtered.

"Your woman seems to think you're bedding her husband. Sure, she's mad, but I wanted to make certain he'd made no advances on you," Clíona said.

"Of course not." Grace tried not to laugh.

Clíona paused, looking relieved, and sat down on Grace's bed. "Have you gotten yourself in any trouble?" she asked, in a voice that was kind, for her.

"No."

"Sure, if you did, you'd know well you could talk to your mother about it." Clíona looked uncomfortable.

This was not a role Clíona was good at, Grace thought—the supportive mother. "Everything's fine, Mom."

"I just wanted you to know that," Clíona said. "That you can come to me."

"Sure. I'll keep it in mind." Grace swallowed her sarcasm. The last person she would ever want to confide in was her mother. Clíona wouldn't understand. Grace was young and in love and planning for the future, while Clíona was stuck in the past. Grace wouldn't allow herself to be pulled into her mother's muck.

That night she waited over an hour for Michael at the swimmers' cabin. When he arrived he didn't even close the door behind him.

"I can't stay," he said quickly. "We have to cool it for a while. Mom's breathing down my neck."

"She thinks I'm sleeping with your *Dad,*" Grace said, and Michael nodded.

"I know," he said. "She's nuts. But she's right to suspect something. Dad's sleeping around and you're sleeping with me. She's bound to figure it out if we're not careful."

"So what if she does?" Grace said. "We're leaving in the fall anyway."

Michael looked at her strangely. "Your Mom could lose her job," he said. "And then where would you live next year?"

Grace had been fantasizing that Michael would end up taking her to Harvard with him, but she'd never mentioned it. A bit of fear tingled in her throat, but she swallowed it and smiled.

"I can be discreet," she said. "I'll be the picture of virginity."

"I wouldn't go that far," Michael said, kissing her. He grunted happily when she pushed her tongue in his mouth. She put her arms around his neck, hoping he would be easily convinced to stay. He broke away.

"Mom's waiting," he said. "She thinks I'm making her tea." And he left.

Michael avoided her for over two weeks. When he wasn't at school, he was sitting with his mother, who'd taken to bed with one of her imaginary illnesses. Grace moped around the house, avoiding everyone. Mr. Willoughby wouldn't look at her if he came across her path accidentally, and Mrs. Willoughby muttered "slut" or "tramp" if Grace passed by her open bedroom door. Grace spent most of her time in the attic, trying unsuccessfully to catch up on the schoolwork she'd been putting off. She failed three of her five final exams anyway. At night she'd take long walks on the beach to avoid Clíona's worried stare.

On the last day of school, Grace stayed home with a sore throat. Clíona was shopping, and only Grace and Mrs. Willoughby were in the house. Grace was told to listen for the woman's bedside bell.

She dozed half the morning and woke to a faint, persistent ringing. She stumbled down the attic steps and over to Mrs. Willoughby's room.

"Yes?" she said in the doorway. Mrs. Willoughby was sitting in her rocking chair, rude pink blush smeared on her cheeks, an afghan draped on her lap. She looked ancient, though she wasn't even forty.

"Where have you been for the last twenty minutes while I've been clattering this damn bell?"

"I was napping," Grace said. "I have a cold, you know."

"Lying slut," Mrs. Willoughby growled. "You were off fucking my husband in the grass someplace."

"I wouldn't look twice at your husband," Grace said, turning to leave.

"Michael told me; it's no use hiding it now," Mrs. Willoughby said. Grace turned back.

"Told you what?" she said.

"Told me about your cheap affair with my husband. I suppose you must suck him off. Men go for that sort of thing."

Grace felt dizzy. "You're lying. Michael wouldn't say that. He loves me."

Mrs. Willoughby grinned. "Oh, really?" she said. "Is that what he told you? What a cruel trick to play on the servant's girl."

Grace straightened her shoulders and marched up to the chair.

"Fuck you, lady," Grace said. Mrs. Willoughby put a hand to her mouth, pretending to be shocked. "If your husband finds you repulsive it's because you are and it's got nothing to do with me," Grace said. Any trace of sympathy she'd ever felt for this woman was gone. "You're pathetic. Your husband thinks so and so does Michael. Someday they're both going to dump you."

The look on Mrs. Willoughby's face made Grace blush. It was as if the woman had just been told she was dying. It occurred to Grace for the first time that Mrs. Willoughby really believed that they were all out to get her, unfairly. That she was a martyr. And of course she would, because Michael, Clíona, everyone let her think so. Grace had just shattered something, and she could almost see the shards slicing through what was left of Mrs. Willoughby's mind.

"Get out!" Mrs. Willoughby screamed, standing up and knocking the rocking chair backward. Grace scurried. When she closed the door behind her she heard something break against it. On her way down the stairs she heard more slams and crashes. It sounded like the woman was trashing her room; it wouldn't be the first time.

Grace wasn't going to stick around for when Mrs. Willoughby emerged.

She left through the back door and went down to the beach. She stripped to her underpants and dove off the dock. The water was brilliantly cold, but she kept her face toward the sun and swam fast until her muscles warmed. As she relaxed into the familiar rhythm, she began to feel bad for having said those things to Mrs. Willoughby. Grace knew what it felt like to be hated by your own family. Didn't Clíona constantly disapprove of her? No wonder Mrs. Willoughby made so many scenes. Grace would do it herself, if she thought it would get her anything.

She'd been swimming about twenty minutes when she heard the motor start up. She stopped to tread water and looked in the direction of the dock. The motorboat was coming at her full speed, Mrs. Willoughby at the engine, her hair flying madly behind her. In the instant before she was afraid, Grace was surprised that Mrs. Willoughby looked so excited—almost as if she were happy for the first time in years.

The next few minutes Grace would barely remember. She knew she dove to avoid the bow of the boat, which was rushing at her head. Then something grabbed her by the hair and held her down so she couldn't come up for air. She pulled on it and there was a rumble under the sea, which must have been Mrs. Willoughby falling in. Grace swam without looking back, her legs tingling with fright at the thought of something grabbing and pulling her under. When she got to shore, she turned and saw the boat charging empty out to sea. She was sure Mrs. Willoughby was swimming in after her, so she ran, her arms crossed over her naked breasts, up to the house door, which she bolted behind her. She went to her attic room and climbed soaking-wet into her bed, hiding like a child under the covers. She was crying, wanting her mother. What would she do when Mrs. Willoughby came up after her?

When she didn't hear anyone come in the house, she tried to

get up. The walls breathed in and out around her and she shook violently from the cold. She lay back down to clear her head.

Her mother was leaning over her.

"Grace?" she said. "What are you still doing in bed? Where's your woman? I can't find her anywhere." Grace started crying. "Did she ring for you at all?" Clíona said. Grace shook her head. Clíona smoothed the fringe from her daughter's forehead.

"Jesus, child, you're roasting." She pulled down the sheets. "Why haven't you any clothes on?"

"I was cold," Grace said, realizing too late that this made no sense.

"You're dosed. Get these flannels on you. I'll call the doctor." Clíona stood up.

"Mom," Grace said, "don't leave me, please. Stay here, okay?" Clíona looked suspicious at first, but her face softened.

"All right, love," she said gently. "You'll be well enough in a day or two." She sat with her daughter until she fell back to sleep.

Grace came down with pneumonia. While she was still in a fevered delirium, Clíona told her that Mrs. Willoughby had drowned. Grace cried like a baby, but couldn't say why she was crying.

"Hesh," Clíona said, fixing the bedclothes and avoiding Grace's eyes. "No tears now."

For two weeks Grace stayed in her attic bedroom. No one asked her any questions, and only her mother came to see her. Grace was terrified that someone would find out and think she murdered the woman. She remembered the clothes she'd left on the dock, but a few days later found them washed, ironed, and folded in her dresser. She told herself it was possible she'd grabbed them running back to the house, but she couldn't remember.

She asked her mother about Michael, wanting him to come up and see her.

"He's in a bad way, that boy," Clíona said sadly. "It's desperate. He blames himself, I think. He asked after you, but I wouldn't think he'll be up anytime soon. He's off on his own mostly."

Grace would have snuck down to see him, but Clíona was sleeping on a cot in the attic, to nurse her or keep an eye on her—Grace wasn't sure which. She wanted to see Michael's face, to make sure he hadn't realized this was all her fault. She wanted to tell him that it would be all right, that as soon as she was better they could run away. That they still had each other.

When she was feeling better and she did see him, it was only briefly, in the house, always with someone else there. He avoided looking at her but she told herself that was for his father's benefit.

Grace desperately wanted someone to comfort her. They all thought Mrs. Willoughby had committed suicide, but Grace felt like a murderer, even if murder hadn't been her intention.

She was afraid to approach her mother and didn't even consider talking to Michael about it. She went to the church, because she knew priests weren't allowed to repeat anything, and she chose the confessional of a priest she didn't know well, but who'd always seemed kind and wimpy. He was Irish, and Clíona had raved about him. In the dark cubicle, Grace could hear the guilty thumping of her heart. She crossed herself when the priest pulled the screen aside, revealing his graph-covered shadow.

"Bless me, Father, for I have sinned," Grace recited. "It has been . . . a long time since my last confession."

"Try to come every week, dear," the priest said. "What sins have you?" Grace paused. She couldn't just rattle them off like lying and talking back to her elders.

"I think I'm responsible for a woman dying, Father."

The priest shifted slightly forward. "In what way?" he said.

"Well, she tried to attack me, in the water, and I got away but she drowned. I didn't know she was drowning, I thought she was still coming after me."

"I see." The priest paused. Grace held her breath. What would be the penance for murder? She could be saying Hail Marys for years. "It doesn't sound like you're responsible for this woman's death. It was a tragic accident," the priest said.

Grace exhaled, relieved. She was beginning to see the benefit of confession. She could leave all her mistakes in that little box, and the priest could dispose of them for her. Like shedding her clothes and entering the water.

"Have you any other sins?" the priest said.

"Um," Grace said. She tried to remember what she was supposed to think of as sins. Dishonoring her mother was a good one, but mostly she avoided Clíona and she didn't think that counted. She had used to say "impure thoughts"—a phrase the nuns had taught her that had seemed to cover just about anything.

"What age are you?" the priest asked when her pause grew too long.

"Fifteen," Grace said.

"Have you respect for the body God gave you?" he said.

"Yes," Grace said proudly, thinking of swimming.

The priest made a rusty sound in his throat. "What I mean is, are you still a virgin?"

Grace blushed. She hadn't thought to mention that, though now that he had, she knew she was in trouble. She considered lying, but lying to a priest was probably a bigger sin than sex.

"No, Father." She thought she heard him sigh.

"Did someone force you?" he said.

"Of course not."

"How many boys have you let do this to you?"

"Oh, just one, Father."

"You shouldn't give in to the temptations of the flesh," the priest said. "I'll ask you to sever all relations with this boy and meditate on your soul."

Grace hadn't expected this. Penance had never been something she couldn't kneel down and rattle off.

"I can't do that, Father. I love him."

The priest made a disgusted noise in his throat. "Your love for God should take precedence." The comforting tone he'd had for her murder confession was gone. He spoke quickly, spitting the words. "Any relations with a man are a sin unless you are married in the eyes of God. I cannot grant you absolution, unless you cease such behavior. I suggest you go home and think it over." He blessed her and closed the screen quickly.

Grace sat in the dark closet until she felt she could no longer breathe. Then she left the church, the eyes of all who were kneeling for penance accusing her.

That night, Clíona moved out of the attic, and Grace wrote "tog room" on a sheet of notebook paper and slipped it under Michael's door. She went out to the swimmers' cabin, the sandy ground beneath her feet foreign and unsteady. She curled up on the daybed and waited for Michael.

The words of the priest echoed in her head. She'd heard of people being refused absolution; the children had been warned of it in Catechism school. Grace had thought it only happened to truly evil people, but apparently it was easier to be damned than she'd ever imagined. If she died tonight, she'd go straight to Hell.

She dozed, on and off, dreamed of Mrs. Willoughby with pits where her eyes were, seaweed strangling her neck. Occasionally, Grace would wake with a start, believing she'd heard the latch on the door, but there was no one. Finally she slept soundly and rose at dawn with a thought that froze her: *He never came.*

CHAPTER 15

Clíona

It's still my belief that if I'd gotten Grace home earlier, when she was still the wee child, she'd be living in Ireland today. Even if she'd moved back to the States later in life, it would have been as an Irish woman choosing to emigrate as I did. But I stayed in America too long; Grace became an American girl. I got stuck there, you know that sort of way. I couldn't come home until I'd made some money, and then I had the child and Inis Murúch was not the place for single mothers at that time. (Sure, now it's different. Barbara, the girl who works in Marcus's shop behind the pub, is expecting, and she with no husband and, I suspect, no notion of who the father is. In my day children were taken away from such girls, raised in orphanages like criminals or exported to the States for adoption. Which is why my relations, Marcus included, believe I was widowed. I wasn't going to risk the wrath of this small Catholic community.) And of course, once Mrs. Willoughby fell ill, I couldn't just up and leave those children. They needed me, much as I needed them. There were no jobs for me to return to in Ireland so secure as that one.

For a short while I thought I might marry in America, when your man Jacob Alper was courting me. He was a Jewish man, not the sort you'd meet on my island. My father would've died from the shock of it had he known, but it never came to the point I had to tell him. If he'd been willing to listen I could have told him how much the Jews are like the Irish. Sure, you'd have thought we'd come from the same family when Jacob and I got chatting. But my father was an old one, and not much interested in expanding his world.

Jacob was the closest I ever came to my childish ideal of love. Not that I don't love Marcus; he's my husband, and never a rough word has passed between us. But Jacob was passionate. I still blush when I think of the things I let that man do, things I'd never tell anyone about, especially Grace, who used to ask. My first experience with sex had been disastrous, and my life with Marcus has been more business than pleasure. Jacob stirred something up in me, sinful as it was. I dream of him occasionally, even now, and I wake up terrified that I might have talked in my sleep. But Marcus could keep snoring through a war, God love him.

I can remember lying naked in Jacob's apartment, with nothing to hide me because we'd kicked off the bedclothes, and I didn't care one bit. We would spend most of our dates there, making love more times in succession than I thought possible, until the hour came for him to drive me home.

I was not shy with Jacob, not even in the beginning. I was a different woman altogether. He wanted to look at every inch of me, and I let him and explored his body as well. I'm ashamed to say I can barely remember him clothed. But I can still see the smooth protrusions of his hips and the line of soft hair that ran up his stomach and bloomed into ringlets across his chest. He used to like me to lie with my arms above my head, while he kissed me on every spot he could find. More than once, when I gave up and grabbed hold of him in the process, he'd whisper to me that I was sexy. And it's the only time I ever was—sexy, I mean—to myself as well as someone else.

I gave up my guilt for a time then. I'd a daughter after all, and no chance of having another, nor any reason to pretend I was pure. When it was over, I was in part relieved to go to Confession and leave it behind me. I fell under the power of lust like most do, but I got out of it, sure. Not that I regret it, I can't somehow. But it can cloud your mind, all that passion, just the same as it lightens your body. Just look what happened to my namesake, Clíodhna. Drowned in the sea of her own desire. Sure, it's only a myth, but sometimes myths have more truth in them than life.

Marcus came into the picture when Jacob and I had been to-gether just over ten months. When Marcus wrote to me that first time, just after Mrs. Willoughby's accident, it was to ask permission to call during his trip to Boston. I'd known him as a boy; his father owned the hotel, and all the island girls considered Marcus a good catch. I had taken no notice of him at the time, as I'd had my nursing aspirations. Brigid O'Connor was the lucky one snatched him up, and she'd five children by him before she died. Her oldest, Mary Louise, was minding them as best she could, but I'd had it in a letter from my father that Marcus intended to remarry once his year's mourning was up. I hadn't thought your man had looked twice at me, but he admits now he fancied me as a girl. Says I was too stuck-up to notice him, which may be the truth. I had a high opinion of myself before I got out in the world.

So along comes Marcus with flowers, and sweets from Ireland, and a gift of Aran gloves for Grace. He stayed in Boston for a month, calling every other evening, before he asked for my hand. I made my decision quick and didn't look back. I broke it off with Jacob, who fought me a bit, but gave up when he saw how determined I was. I know what that daughter of mine thought, sure. Thought I settled for Marcus she did, for the security of the hotel and all.

It wasn't that so. Marcus is a lovely man, not a burden I saddled myself with. And simply enough, I wanted to return home. I'd no future in Boston; Michael was off to university and the girls were half grown. Jacob, passionate as he was, was a writer and not a family man. He loved me, sure, but was not ready for a commitment. You make decisions in life, I tried to tell Grace, you make compromises. I'd not loads of opportunities knocking at my door, no college education, and a rebellious teenager by my side. Marcus gave me my home back. He got a mother for his children and a partner in the hotel. There are marriages based on less—and they aren't as happy as ours.

Grace refused to see it from my position. (I wonder if she'd be so superior now. Sure, I haven't seen her in twelve years, but I'd be surprised if she spent much of that time without some man at her side. She'd have been with someone, if not for money and security, then surely for some other benefit.) She'd gone a little off her head after Mrs. Willoughby's death, and my announcing our move to Ireland didn't help the situation. Ill with pneumonia then, she'd kept the black mood long after she was healthy again, which made me suspect there was more to Mrs. Willoughby's accident than the others thought. Not that Grace was responsible, of course, but she knew more than she was saying. I found her clothing by the dock that day, though I never mentioned it, and neither did she. I don't know that I'd want to have the whole story, truth be told. Grace had a mysterious side to her that I was better off staying away from.

I'm not as dim as she thought, either. I knew something was going on with her and Michael, but it stopped after the accident, that was clear enough. I never asked how far it went, and I didn't find out until it was too late. I blame myself in a way, so wrapped up in Jacob I was, I didn't see the signs early enough. But sure, I couldn't have stopped her. If there's one thing I know about children, having one of my own and five steps, it's you can't teach them to avoid your mistakes. The harder you try the more they take after you. I try not to think about what I'd have saved Grace, had I known that fact a wee bit earlier.

Grace's behavior when she found out we were leaving for Ireland was desperate. Even I didn't know she could take things so far. With Michael avoiding her as he was, she learned quick enough that he wasn't going to be her knight in shining armor. What possessed her to go to Jacob I don't know, but I suppose he was her only choice, barring Mr. Willoughby, who I admit would have been even worse.

Grace disappeared when I was packing for our trip home. I was frantic. I'd the police looking for her, and Michael riding around in his father's car half the night. Not a word for two days, until Jacob rang to say I should come pick her up. I was the confused one, but I'd Michael give me a lift over there.

Jacob let me into his flat, and there was my daughter, pissed to Heaven and collapsed on your man's bed—the same bed I'd been sneaking off to. God, that was hard to take. Jacob brought me into the kitchen and whispered what had happened.

The girl had tried to tempt him. He gave me no details but assured me she had been determined.

"I'd watch her, Clee," he said. "For a fifteen-year-old she knows what she's doing."

"You didn't—" I started, but he backed away.

"I'm not a pervert, for Christ's sake. That's one messed up girl you've got. She doesn't want to go to Ireland and she'll risk prostituting herself to avoid it."

"We're going all the same," I said.

"You won't change your mind?" he said. I don't think I broke the man's heart, but I remember that moment and how he looked at me and touched me, right on that spot below my earlobe that he knew was my weak place, and I still believe he loved me. Love may be enough for a less practical-minded woman than myself, but I'd made my decision. Seduction wasn't going to change it.

"Will you help me get the girl down to the car?" I said. He was polite enough after that, and it was the last I saw of him. I had it from Maeve that he became quite the popular author in the States later on.

Michael was the abashed-looking one on that lift home, but I'll say he didn't do right by her in the end; never even said good-bye, to my knowledge. He was just a boy, and Grace should have known better than to think he'd take care of her. And she couldn't see the guilt he felt after his mother's death, how he punished himself and Grace because of it. I felt sorry for her, though, understanding the betrayal of men myself, and so I never wrote to Michael. It was a shame, seeing as I once loved him like my own son.

It hurt me sure, it did, that Grace despised Ireland. Here I was, home to the place I'd longed after for seventeen years, longed after for my daughter's sake as well, and she couldn't get away quick enough. Maybe I was too hard on her, expected too much. I could have let her stay with my sister in Boston, though Maeve would have needed convincing, as Grace was a handful. But I truly believed it was best for her to come with me, sure every girl needs her mother. I didn't want my daughter farmed out so she never knew her true home. Of course, now I see she was farmed out to the Willoughbys' along with me. I didn't give her a proper home until she was too far gone to recognize it.

I try not to waste time crying over things I can't change. If we all knew then what we know now, the world'd be a perfect place.

God in heaven, I'll never forget the look of my child's face on that airplane. Like a prisoner being taken to the lockup, she was. I was nervous enough, flying for the first time, and there was poor Marcus bending himself backward trying to cheer us both up, though Grace was fierce rude to him. If I'd known how much worse she'd get, I'd have cherished that plane trip as a bonding family moment.

Once we got to Inis Murúch, I'd my hands full. Marcus's youngest, Tommy, was still in nappies, and Stephanie wasn't school-age yet. The twins, Conor and Marc Jr., were going on twelve and prone

to dangerous mischief if I didn't keep my eye on them. There was
the hotel to organize, while Marcus ran the pub. Mary Louise was
a great help to me, she was, and we got on grand, so much so that
Grace might have been jealous had she minded me at all. It was
summer when we arrived and Grace was rarely inside. Spent her
time swimming, naked at night, which started the gossip, but I forced
her to wear togs in the day. She made no attempt to be friendly to
the island girls, not even Mary Louise, who could have been like
her older sister. Grace moped on her own and wrote letters to Michael, but she never got any post back. I gave her the space to work
it out, thinking that once school started up she'd snap out of her
mood. I watched her closely though, looking for signs of the drinking that had led her to Jacob's bed. She never took it up seriously.
A great relief, because I know the taste for drink is an easy thing for
an Irish child to learn.

Grace shared her bedroom with Mary Louise and Stephanie in
the beginning, the twins in the loft room and Tommy with Marcus
and myself. We'd one toilet for the lot of us, and it was a job to get
Grace to learn to hurry her washing. She'd been spoiled with her
own toilet at the Willoughbys'.

The night Grace was ill, I thought first she was stubborn and
taking her time as she usually did. Stephanie was whining outside
the toilet with her legs crossed, and Mary Louise was banging on
the door.

"What's the trouble now?" I said, when I'd come up after the
noise. I knocked on the door and called to Grace. "There's the rest
of the family needing the facilities, your highness."

"Leave me alone," came her muffled voice from the door crack.
I knew something wasn't right. I sent Mary Louise and Stephanie to
use the hotel toilet, and tried to get Grace to let me in.

"Fuck off, Mom," she yelled in response. She was crying, I could
hear the gulps and sniffles, and she was flushing the bowl every other
minute.

"Grace, stop this now. Let me in. Are you ill?"

She cursed so furiously, I backed away from the door and went downstairs. Marcus was in from the pub, Mary Louise had got him.

"What's wrong with the girl?" he said.

I asked him to take the children to my cousin Maggie's for the night. He did so, leaving me to handle it. He's happy enough to let me deal with crises, Marcus is. Grace was always beyond his understanding, though he was kind to her.

I waited in the hallway outside the toilet until half-twelve, when Grace finally opened the door. She'd a bundle of towels and the bath mat with her, and she shuffled to the stairs before she saw me watching. Her face was streaked with dirty tears, her eyes swollen and veiny.

"What is it, Grace? What's happened?" I put my hand on her arm but she backed away. The towels were soaked in dark, clotted blood.

"Jesus Christ in Heaven," I whispered, crossing myself. "What have you done?" At first I thought she'd hurt herself, slit her wrists like. She started crying again.

"I couldn't stop it," she said. "It's not my fault."

"Are you after miscarrying?" I said. "Were you pregnant?" She only cried, but it was obvious enough. "Hush, now, you'll be all right, Grace. Stop your crying."

The blood had seeped into the lino cracks in the bathroom. I took the soiled towels from her, thinking it was a wonder she was still standing, after losing so much blood.

"Are you dizzy?" I said. She was ghost-white, and her eyes wouldn't focus on me. I wanted to shake her. Why hadn't she come to me? I was her mother, yet she'd never treated me as anything but a nuisance, a stranger. Like a maid.

I gave her a sanitary towel and made her drink some tea. She was still bleeding, and my mind kept going back to the day she was born, and all I'd lost with her: the blood, my womb, and the life I'd planned for myself.

I'd Marcus wake up Eamon, the ferry owner, so we could take

Grace to the hospital. I had her wear my wedding ring, told the doctor she was married. A mistake, I know now; I didn't mean her to think I was ashamed of her. After all, hadn't I gotten myself in the same trouble once? But I was worried they'd report her to child services, and take her away from me otherwise. As it was, the doctor just thought we were ignorant islanders, letting our daughter marry so young. He fixed her up though, told us there was no reason she couldn't try again in the future. A relief of sorts, but not as he thought it. Marcus didn't say much through the whole thing, though I suppose he had moments of doubt about my ability to raise children. I was having them myself. What sort of mother was I, with this secretive, promiscuous daughter who seemed on a path to destroying herself? Dear God, I prayed at the time, why must she repeat all I have done to shame myself? I wanted to talk to her, comfort her, but she wouldn't even look at me.

Tell me what to do for you, I would have said, had she any interest in listening. It was physical, this pain I felt for her, like it was myself who had miscarried. I should have done something, everything, differently. I hadn't loved her until too late, hadn't taken her home to Ireland until she didn't know it to look at it. Her pain was my doing and I could feel it sure as she did. Worst of all, she'd never believe me to tell it.

I brought her home and tried to start again. But she locked me out and I'd no clue how to break in. She failed her first term at school, got dropped back a year, and failed that as well. She was in such a bad way that Marcus and I talked of sending her to hospital. She quit school and rarely left the house, except for days when she wandered the island and we found her sleeping in a cove, her head pillowed in seaweed. She lost weight rapidly, two stone in less than a year. Like a corpse, she was, those wet green eyes in the white bone of her face. I didn't know what to do for her; she was talked up all over the island, and Marcus's children suffered for it. Mary Louise was always the one to fight the gossip. No one would talk shite about her family, step or otherwise. She was so like Grace once was, it saddened me.

It was Seamus O'Flaherty saved Grace, saved us all, he did. He was twenty-five years of age then, just home with his Da after finishing his graduate studies in Dublin. He called to our house, being a friend to Marcus and remembering me from his wee days. He'd grown into a fine man, kind and smart and funny as his father. He was fishing in the days then and writing articles for the Galway newspapers in his spare time. I told him as much as was appropriate about Grace and asked him as a favor would he come see her occasionally.

Grace, thank God, took to him. He walked the island with her in the evenings, and she gained a stone, got the color back in her face. She was still a bit ghostlike in her manner, but one day I even heard her laugh as they came in the front door. That was a great day, the sweetest sound I'd heard in a year. Seamus started tutoring her in her subjects so she could return to school.

I don't mind what she said later, Grace fancied that man more than she ever had Michael. And if it wasn't for Seamus, I still believe, I would have lost her. Suicide, though it's not discussed, is not unheard of on our little island.

Though I lost Grace eventually, sure I did. She made herself dead to me. God help me, I'd no idea how to be that girl's mother. I look at Gráinne now and think Grace got it right. Sure, she lied to the girl, but Gráinne knew she was loved in spite of it. She'll always know. They were friends as well as relations, those two. More than I can say about my mother and myself. And Grace and I, though no one intended it, ended up the worst of enemies.

I can't walk this island at night, not once, without seeing my daughter looming up ahead, out of my reach. I couldn't give Grace a father or a home or even the assurance that I loved her. But Gráinne, please God, can get all of it. Everything I've been saving and hoarding like a miserly woman in my heart, all these long years.

CHAPTER 16

Gráinne

I had to wait until my grandmother and Marcus were asleep, until I hadn't heard a sound for over an hour, so by the time I got down to the telephone it was almost midnight. I picked up the receiver before I realized I didn't know how to dial home from so far away. I tried zero but no operator came on. There was a phone book in the drawer of the end table, and I found out in the blue section that I needed to dial the country code first. The phone rang seven times before Stephen picked up. I imagined it ringing in the cottage even though I'd dialed our apartment.

"It's me," I said to Stephen's tired hello. I made my voice as low as I could get it without whispering. "It's Gráinne."

There was a click and a pause, and for a second I thought he'd hung up.

"Gráinne," he said, then he sighed. "What's wrong?"

"Nothing," I said. I'd thought he'd sound happy to hear from me. I'd imagined snuggling the phone as he whispered: *I miss you, Gráinne. So much more than I thought I would.*

"There's an echo," he said next. "Can you hear that?"

"An echo?" I said, looking quickly around the dark room. "No."

"I can hear everything you say twice," Stephen said. "It's annoying. How are you?"

"I'm fine," I said.

"Fine, fine." He giggled. Giggling wasn't like him. "A boy called here for you tonight. He sounded really disappointed when I told him you'd moved to Ireland."

"I didn't *move*," I snapped. Another click, another pause.

"Is something the matter?" he said. "Did you meet your father?"

"Not exactly," I said. I moved the receiver away from my mouth, so he wouldn't hear me trying not to cry.

"Oh, Gráinne," he said softly, and that started the tears plopping down my nose. "What happened?"

"I want to come home," I said. *Home-home*, was what he must have heard, the echo sounding twice as desperate as my voice.

"You've only been gone for two days," he said.

"I don't care, I want to come home."

"What do you want me to do?" he said.

Please don't sound so exasperated, I thought. "Let me," I said. "Let me come stay at home until I figure out what to do."

"Gráinne," he sighed. "You can't stay here. I'm moving."

"Moving?" I squeaked.

He explained something about a teaching job and how hard it was being in the apartment, but I was hardly listening. I was thinking of the heat that had come from his mouth, of how I'd pulled it in toward me, and almost, almost captured him.

"I think you're better off with your family," he said.

"Why did you kiss me, then?" I said before I could stop myself.

"If you don't even want me there, why did you kiss me?" It felt dangerous, saying that out loud.

"Gráinne," he said firmly, in the voice of an adult scolding a child. "I never kissed you."

"Liar," I whispered.

"It was an accident," he said. "We were both upset. I can't say I know how you feel because I don't—you've just lost your mother. But I do know that I'm not what you need. Are you listening, Gráinne? I can't be what you need."

Suddenly, I saw how he must see me. Heard my voice through his ears. A naive girl with a crush on him. A nuisance. An echo of my mother but nothing near her reality. I saw myself standing by that bonfire, saw how I must have looked like I'd been waiting for him. When he wasn't what I'd been waiting for at all.

"This is going to cost your grandmother a fortune," Stephen said.

I nodded, pretending to be agreeable, as though he could see me.

"Gráinne?" he said. "I'll write to you when I get settled, okay?"

I drew a breath, and spoke loudly, clearly, so my voice would not be lost in the echo.

"No, you won't," I said, and hung up. For a while I stared at the phone in the dark. It looked odd, foreign; I'd heard it ringing earlier that day in short, doubled sounds rather than long single rings. They were desperate, impatient sounds that reminded me, in their urgency, of the phone I hadn't wanted to answer.

"Gráinne," Clíona said, "if you don't eat something, you'll be getting sick."

I was at the breakfast table with her again. I couldn't stand the thought that I'd be stuck at this same table for years.

"I don't care," I said. I wanted to get sick. So sick they'd all be sorry: Stephen, my father, all of them.

"Will you have juice, at least?" she said. I took a sip of the orange juice to shut her up. I pushed back my chair and tried to leave the kitchen.

"Where do you think you're going?" she said.

"For a walk," I snapped. "Is that allowed?"

"A walk?" Clíona laughed. "It's pissing rain out there." I hadn't noticed until she said it.

"Mary Louise could use some help at the hotel," Clíona said. "If you've a lack of things to do."

I shrugged. Anything was better than staying in that house. Clíona watched me like I was a prisoner, like at any moment I might bolt and she would have to wrestle me down. She guarded me, and my father wouldn't even come to glimpse at me.

"What happened," I said to her. "What happened between my parents that my Dad doesn't even want to meet me?"

She handed me a rain slicker. "Don't think so much," she said. "Your father will come around. If it's meant to be, it's meant to be and there's no use in agonizing over the why of it all."

"That's the stupidest thing I've ever heard," I said.

She clenched her jaw and tried to smile at me.

"Get going now," she said. "I told Mary Louise you'd call over to her."

For an hour I helped Mary Louise change the beds in the upstairs rooms. It was more like someone's house than a hotel: the furniture was creaky and the sheets weren't germless white hotel sheets, but floral-patterned and slightly worn. In every bedroom there was a picture of Jesus, holding his hands up to his immense, exposed heart, which was glowing and strangled with thorns. The heart looked like a lumpy jellyfish caught up in seaweed.

Mary Louise didn't say much at first, but she was watching me. Not with the prison-warden expression of my grandmother; Mary Louise just looked at me like she was curious.

"Why are you staring at me?" I said, finally. "I bet you think I look like my father."

She smiled. "Heard a lot of that, have you?" she said. "Actually, you put me in mind of your mother. You've Seamus's coloring, but your Mum's there in the way you carry yourself."

No one had ever told me that. Stephen almost told me once, but he'd stopped himself.

"Were you friends with my mother?" I said. Mary Louise didn't seem like her type, at least on the outside. She looked like a housewife plumping those pillows. My mother had never plumped a pillow in her life.

"Well, sisters more than friends," Mary Louise said. "I was fond of your Mum, but she was never really happy here and not open to friendship, you know that sort of way. I think it was hard for her, being dumped into our family so suddenly." She snapped the clean sheet open and motioned for me to hold the other end. "She must have felt somewhat the way you feel now."

I didn't answer that. I didn't want this woman's sympathy.

"What about my father?" I said. "Was she happy with my father?" Mary Louise smiled and shook her head, like she'd just had a vivid flash of my parents together. I was jealous that she could do that.

"I've never seen any two people so in love as your Mum and Da," she said. "It looked almost desperate. It was plain as day to everyone but themselves how much they fancied each other."

"What's that supposed to mean?" I said. That didn't sound like my mother. She'd always known when a man liked her and exactly how much.

"Well I myself have never been so in love that it scared me," Mary Louise said. "Not that I don't love my husband—I do. But I'm not the sort who feels desperate love—you know? That's what your mother and Seamus had. I think they were both so scared of how much they loved each other that they couldn't see clearly enough to know it was reciprocated. I used to watch them watching each other. It was plain on their faces—love and not a little bit of fear. It's not the sort of love that makes you comfortable."

Mary Louise stuffed a comforter into a clean flannel cover. She reminded me of my mother—not what she talked about, but the way she said it. No hedging.

"You know," I said, "everyone keeps telling me what a great guy my father is. But my mother left him and I'll bet she had a reason. Besides, he doesn't even want to see me."

Mary Louise buttoned the comforter in swiftly and smoothed it across the bed. "The reasons people have for leaving other people are more complicated than whether or not they love them," she said. "I don't think there's anyone but your Mum who understands it completely, and we can't ask her now. And your Da wants to see you, he does. I've known him my whole life, and believe me, he wants to see you more than anything in this world."

"What's he waiting for then?" I said. "If he wanted to see me, he'd be here." I heard an echo in my head: *If she wanted to see me she'd have left the door open.*

"Like I said, Gráinne. Love and fear are not comfortable bed-fellows." She tossed me the bundle of dirty sheets and winked.

This was how I used to feel with my mother, I thought. Like I could ask any question and get an honest answer. Now it was my mother I needed answers about.

Mary Louise was looking out the window toward the road that led up behind the hotel.

"That's your Da's house there," she said, pointing to a white cottage with red window ledges. "That's where the three of you lived. We don't lock our doors on this island."

She didn't say any more, just led me along to the next bedroom.

I walked up around the back of the hill, so Clíona wouldn't see me on the road.

My father's house was a small cottage, one-story like the rest on the island, fenced in with tree limbs connected by barbed wire. In the yard there were a few chickens and a rooster who eyed me suspiciously. I turned the door knob with both hands so it opened with a quiet snap.

Once inside, I couldn't see beyond the white echoes of sun in my eyeballs. There was an odor like my grandmother's house: turf, coal, and yeast, and underneath that the man-smell, socks, shaving lotion, and salty thick skin, which I recognized from home.

The white spots in my eyes dissolved and I looked around the room. It was a living room and kitchen combined, with a fireplace at one end underneath a picture of Jesus and his jellyfish heart. There were books everywhere, stacked in ladder piles next to the couch and on the coffee table. On the left wall two open doors revealed a bathroom and a small room which was dominated by a bed heavy with quilts and wool blankets. My father's room. Once my mother and father's room. They must have made love in that bed, with abandon at first, then quietly when I was a baby sleeping nearby.

Looking at that bed, I remembered my mother's muffled, musical moans, which I had listened for, through many men and years, late at night. By the time it was Stephen who pulled those sounds from her, I was imagining myself pressed beneath him, and those magic, uncontrollable noises in my own throat.

On the wall with the fireplace there was another door, which I opened slowly, half-expecting to see someone—my father, my mother, myself—on the other side.

It clearly had been my room. Under the window was a toddler-sized bed with detachable safety rails and a quilt with bright patchwork fish swimming along the edges. The center patch was a mermaid pieced together in various shades of blue and green. She had no facial features, just a pearly-white satin disk beneath her sea-green hair. There was an old changing table painted in a chipping white and a bin of toys: Legos, wool-stitched dolls, storybooks, and a collection of shells and sea glass.

I didn't remember any of these things and, for an instant, doubted my assumption that it was my room. Maybe my father had a new child that no one had told me about. But the toys were arranged too neatly, there were no diapers on the changing table shelves, and when I pulled back the quilt the sheets underneath smelled stale.

The other half of the room was an office. There was a desk wedged against the wall, with a computer and more books, plus typed pages fanned across so the desktop was barely visible. Newspaper clippings and photographs were pasted on the wall all the way up to the ceiling, and I walked closer so I could read them. The articles were all by my father and some were very old, the paper jaundiced and wrinkled. Interviews with celebrities I didn't recognize and politicians I'd never heard of. A story about a missing teenage girl, in a place called Wicklow, who had last been seen hitching her way home from work. A series of interviews with hunger strikers in a prison in Northern Ireland. I paused on this one. I couldn't understand all the references, but they were IRA members—I'd heard about those—who wanted to be treated differently because they were political prisoners instead of just plain criminals. The article was from 1981, a year after I was born. Some of the men died after starving themselves for months, waiting for a recognition that never came. I wondered if they had enjoyed their hunger, if they had felt like they were accomplishing something, if they had imagined their stomachs consuming their bodies and their memories from the inside out. I wondered if they had really wanted to die.

Along the right edge of the group of articles was a vertical line of photos—some of me as a baby and some of my mother looking like she was trying not to smile but couldn't help herself. In the lowermost corner there was an oversized black-and-white of a young girl in a sandbox. She was playing with a tea set, pouring pretend tea into a miniature cup and laughing, half her face hidden by dark curls. It took me a minute to realize it was me. But it couldn't be; this girl was at least four or five. How could my father have a picture of me two years after we'd left him? Unless my mother had sent it.

I knew that sandbox. It was where I used to go after school with my baby-sitter until my mother picked me up on her way home from work. She'd had a boyfriend then who was a photographer—one of those boyfriends I later remembered and she didn't. He'd taken a lot of pictures of me—I can still see the camera at his eye. He might have taken this picture and my mother might have sealed it in an envelope and mailed it across the world.

Maybe she had stayed secretly in touch with my father. Maybe she had written letters about me, sent pictures of me at ten when I won the state spelling bee, at thirteen when I'd gone to my first boy-girl dance. The idea of this was stranger than the idea of her never contacting him. If she shared me with him then why had she never done the same for me?

The photo blurred and my eyes stung with salty tears. I should have been angry at my mother, but I wasn't. What I was thinking in my baby room, looking at my father's daily view, was this: If I could have my mother back, if I could make it so she had never been eaten by those tumors, I would not ask about my father this time. I wouldn't ask about any of it. I'd take what she wanted me to have and nothing more. Because if I had to lose her to get this—an empty house, ancient pictures, and an echo of a father hiding away from me—then it wasn't worth it.

I ran out of the house and almost fell over Liam, who was sitting on the front stoop.

"What are you doing here?" I said. I think I yelled, because he flinched, though he didn't back away.

"My Mum said you'd be here," he said. "I just came to look after you."

"I don't need you guarding me, too," I said.

"I'm not guarding you, silly," he said. "I'm inviting you for tea. Mum has it ready for us."

"Why can't you just leave me alone?" I snapped.

Liam looked at me strangely, not hurt as I'd intended him to be but curious, as though I'd said something in a foreign language.

"Because we're friends," he said. "I want you to feel at home."

"This isn't my home," I said. I was crying again.

Liam scrounged in his pocket and pulled out a wrinkled handkerchief. He folded a clean corner and wiped my face quickly, unembarrassed, like he was some uncle of mine and he'd done it a million times before.

"It is if you want it to be," he said.

I don't know whether it was what he said or the feel of his fingers steadying my chin, but something made me exhausted. I didn't want to fight him. I didn't want to have to fight anyone.

"I'm sick and tired of tea," I said to him, and he laughed and walked me up the road to his family's house.

CHAPTER 17

Grace

She wakes Stephen when she rips the bedcovers from his side. He sits up quickly, with the attention of someone who barely sleeps, who's always listening. Grace is stuffing the comforter and sheets between her legs, like she is trying to plug herself up.

"What is it?" Stephen says, trying to pull her fingers from the wrinkled covers.

"Seamus," she says. At first, Stephen thinks she's said "shameless." "Seamus, I'm losing the baby. It's Gráinne, she's bleeding out of me. Stop her, Seamus. Please!" She is crying, her legs tight around the clumps of sheets.

"It's Stephen, Grace. I'm here. Gráinne's asleep in the other room. Remember?"

"Didn't you hear me?" she yells. "Do something, you fuck. I'm having a miscarriage."

"Grace, you're not having a miscarriage. You're not pregnant. Please, honey, wake up."

Grace looks at him and it is Stephen, crying; she has frightened him again.

"Is Gráinne all right?" she says, and he shrugs, then nods. He looks knackered, she thinks. Hasn't he been sleeping? She lets go of the bedding, allowing him to smooth it back over her. She remembers now. She's not having a miscarriage. It is she who is dying, not Gráinne.

"It's freezing in here," she says. "Why is the bed all wet?"

Stephen feels the bed around her, finding nothing. "It's not," he says.

"It is so," Grace sighs. No one ever notices this but she. "This house has gone damp." She can smell the mildew in the duvet. "Can I have a mint?" she asks. She's been vomiting all morning, and her throat is sore and bitter. Stephen gives her a Tic Tac. She was expecting a Silvermint, large, white, and round, with the texture of baby aspirin. These are what Seamus used to give her, when she was pregnant with Gráinne.

She forces herself out of bed, holding her breath at the wallop of pain. In the dark kitchen, she finds a note tacked to the refrigerator from her daughter.

> *A mermaid found a swimming lad,*
> *Picked him for her own,*
> *Pressed her body to his body,*
> *Laughed; and plunging down*
> *Forgot in cruel happiness*
> *That even lovers drown.*

Grace is sure that Gráinne still dreams of drowning. She doesn't know that she comes from an island both nourished and cursed by the sea; where people disappeared yearly, dragged under the rough waters by jealous mermaids. But something inside her must remember.

Grace wishes she could wake Gráinne up, hold on to her as she used to do in the water while teaching her to swim. Just enough above the surface so she felt safe. But Grace is drowning herself, her lungs and mouth full of liquid pain. She might not be able to hold on tight enough, and Gráinne would be pulled under. She leaves her daughter a note about the grocery shopping and limps back to her bedroom.

Stephen goes to the bathroom to get her medicine. She tries to think quick of what it is she wants to say, because once she gets that shot, it won't come out right.

"I'd like to know what she was thinking," Grace says, when Stephen comes forward with needle and vial.

"Who, Gráinne?" he says.

"No, my mother. I'd like to know what she was thinking." She has to concentrate on every word, because the pain is ripping them away from her.

"When, sweetie? When do you mean?"

"Always," Grace says as the needle plunges. She's sinking now.

"I think I got it wrong," she says. Stephen crawls in beside her. "I think I got it backwards."

"What's that?" He's stroking her hair. Has he done that before? There was another man who did that, but they're all bleeding into this one beside her.

"I thought I was the strong one," she says.

Stephen kisses her ear, breathes warm, damp air over her face. "You are. You're the strong one, Grace."

The night she miscarried, the blood-soaked towels made her think of Jesus, the slice in his side, the maroon rivulets following the lines of his palms. *That blood was shed for you*, the Sisters had said when she was a girl. *Jesus bled so you don't have to.* Had she actually believed that once?

"No," she says. She's losing her grip. She sees a man's moon-white hand, holding her palm against a textured stone wall. She has the sense of her mother carrying her, which can't be right because she hardly remembers her mother ever touching her. Only it's Gráinne holding her up above the cold water, and she wants to say: Put me down, I'm bigger than you! Then Seamus is back, lying beside her in the bed, holding on so tight she can barely breath—and still, she knows if she wriggles away and escapes to the ocean, her body will ooze out from the inside, blood and pulp and bone, until there is nothing left of her human shell.

CHAPTER 18

Grace

In the five years that Grace lived on Inis Murúch, no matter what the season, she was always cold. The weather was not a normal cold like the freezing wind of Boston she was used to, but a wet cold that ate its way through everything she used to cover herself. Everything she had, oiled wool cardigans, long johns, layers of socks, and the three blankets on her bed, all of it was slightly moist. It was as though she'd gone swimming fully clothed and was eternally caught in the sluggy hour between being soaked and fully dry. Damp.

All the islanders spoke of it, it was a fact of life. "My house has gone fierce damp," they would say. Yet it didn't seem to bother them. No one but Grace huddled by the turf fire or laid their underclothes on the cast-iron stove for the morning. It seemed as if she was constantly shivering, waterlogged, while the rest of the family remained comfortable. Only when she was swimming did Grace feel warm. If she immersed herself in the freezing ocean, her muscles came alive, and heat crackled like a coal fire in her middle. It was the in-between she couldn't stand, the damp that refused to dry. It followed her like a curse, like the memory of running soaked and freezing from the water, while Mrs. Willoughby drowned behind her.

She hated it here. Hated the island, which she knew every inch of because she could only walk forty minutes in any direction before coming to the barrier of the sea. She hated Marcus, the ignorant pig her mother had married, and his children, who were like dim, grinning dolls. Their eyes, duplicate disks of the same blue shade, reminded her constantly that she was not one of them. She despised the islanders, all of whom she seemed to be related to. They were like a colony of inbred, nosy aliens who spoke without moving their mouths in a secret, throaty language. The food was greasy, the milk tasted strange. The sky was either hurling horizontal rain, or just recovering from a shower, or threatening another downpour any second. Old, smelly men snaked their arms around her waist and told her they loved her and wanted to take her for moonlight walks. It didn't matter that they were her great-uncles or her cousins twice removed. Everything and everyone around her made her cringe and want to bite, spit, and scream. I hate you, she wanted to say to the Anties clucking about her grades and her shortened skirts. I hate you, to her baby stepbrother Tommy, who wailed whenever Grace looked at him. Most of all, Grace hated her mother for dragging her here, then ignoring her in favor of her new, blue-eyed family.

Grace missed Michael. On good days, she wrote to him, clinging to the hope that he would write back two words: Come home. On bad days she was humiliated, unable to wash away the smell of her sex, which she now thought was disgusting, fungal. She dreamed that Michael was growing inside her stomach, attached to her organs with bubbled vines of seaweed. She threw up in the mornings, after lunch, and sometimes during dinner. It didn't occur to her that she was pregnant. Her periods had never been regular. That's what she thought it was—one of her occasional periods—when the blood started.

It was in the bedroom she shared with the blue-eyed girls, Stephanie and Mary Louise. Stephanie was only four, one of those invisible, introverted children who are easy to ignore. But Mary Louise was irritating. Clíona liked Mary Louise because she was responsible and pleasant; Grace despised her for the same reasons.

That night, Mary Louise was reorganizing her records while Grace lay on her damp bed, looking at the yellow water stain on the ceiling. There was a cramp in her lower abdomen, squeezing and releasing slowly like a blood pressure cuff.

"What sort of music do you fancy?" Mary Louise said. Grace wouldn't look at her.

"Why?" she snapped.

"Ah, I'm only curious," Mary Louise said. "I thought maybe we'd like some of the same." Grace sat up, pulling her cold fingers into the sleeves of her nightgown.

"What makes you think we have anything in common?" she said. Mary Louise only smiled.

"Aren't we sisters now?" she said. "We've that in common, sure."

"Whatever that means," Grace said. She stood up. Mary Louise looked at her and blushed.

"You've a visitor," she said, gesturing at the back of Grace's nightgown. Grace looked and saw a red-brown stain on the floral print.

"Fuck," she said, and the cramp squeezed again. She felt a burp of thick fluid against her underwear.

"Do you need a sanitary towel?" Mary Louise said, but Grace ignored her and went to the bathroom.

For the next hour her insides slopped out, filling the toilet and soaking six towels with red jellyfish flesh. Nothing would stop it. One clot was so large she thought sure it contained one of her organs, that eventually, everything else inside her would follow. She ignored her stepsisters' knocks and pleas for the bathroom, and later swore angrily at her mother's curt voice through the keyhole. She didn't come out until the bleeding had lessened, and she was dizzy. Clíona was the one who told her she'd miscarried, when she saw the towels.

"I couldn't stop it," Grace cried. She wanted her mother to touch her then. Needed her for forgiveness, comfort. Someone to mop up the crud that seeped out of her, and make her well again.

But her mother was unreachable. Her reaction was only shame mixed with annoyance. Like she couldn't be bothered. To her, Grace was like the remains on the towels: a child she'd never wanted. She looked on Grace with those hooded black eyes and said only: "Stop your crying now." And suddenly, Grace was alone. Her mother took her to the doctor, made her wear a wedding ring. In the hospital waiting room, Grace imagined she saw emotion in her mother's face. Something like fear or maybe guilt. It was gone in an instant, and later Grace forgot it. It wasn't what she had wished to see anyway.

The winter after her miscarriage, Grace felt nothing, no connection to life other than the damp cold that kept her moving. When she thought of it later, it was as the year of her death. Emptiness without peace, time moving on without purpose. She was emotionless on the outside but infected with a fear that grew like a hard tumor in her abdomen. She didn't eat or sleep. When it was day she couldn't remember it ever being dark; at night it was as though she'd gone years without the sun. Her mother and the blue-eyed family were invisible—or maybe it was Grace who was invisible and they normal, living. She tried to drown herself every time she entered the water, but her swimmer's body wouldn't allow it. It always went up for air no matter how hard she fought. She hadn't the strength to die any more than she had the strength to live. At times she felt possessed, like her dead jellyfish baby was clamped onto her soul, dragging her down into a grave where the dirt caved in from the sides, filling her mouth, nose, and eyes with a sickly sweet plug.

When she first saw Seamus O'Flaherty, it was as if the thick gauze covering her world had been ripped just enough to let him show through. He was the only person she'd looked at in a year who had sharp, definite outlines, features, and skin color. He was something to focus on. His black hair curled and glittered around his ears and neck; his face beamed white, as if the moon were just beneath his skin; his dark eyes were a warm liquid texture that seemed to shift within itself, capturing and retreating from the light. He smiled at her and her insides cracked, the clotted fear squeezed aside, making room.

She couldn't speak to him. She wanted to, but was afraid when she opened her mouth that all her words would meld into a primitive moan. Language had left her, and the sounds she had in her throat were too ugly to let out. He must have been warned by her mother, because he didn't ask her to speak. He spoke for both of them and did it in a way that made the whole situation seem normal.

He brought her to the beaches and told her the stories of Inis Murúch. He spoke of the mischievous mermaids, whom the island people thought were sinful, corrupting men with lust and seduction. His voice was like no one else's; it savored every word and rose like waves at the end of a sentence.

" 'Tis said that the merrows sing in their sad beautiful voices with the hopes of capturing lonely fishermen," he told her. "They seduce the man beneath the waves and make love to him, which of course drowns the poor eejit. Then the merrow keeps the man's soul in a cage in her parlor beneath the sea."

In the coves, Seamus made Grace listen to the singing of the mermaids, the moan she believed was wind, which was much like the painful, wordless sound that echoed inside her chest.

"When I was only a wee boy," Seamus said, "my Nana told me the story of Muirgen, the dark beauty seduced from her home beneath the water. You see, if a mermaid falls in love, well, then your man has the power to carry her to shore, where her split tail transforms into legs. Muirgen fell in love with my great-great-grandfather, Pádraig, and they married and had nine human children.

It is said they were very happy for a time, and devoted to one another. But the pull of the sea was too great, and one morning Pádraig and the children woke and found her gone, her one dress hanging like a shed skin on the hearth. Pádraig never saw his wife again, but they say the children glimpsed her in their dreams, leaning her dripping black hair over their bed." Seamus laughed and the music of him echoed in the cliff walls. He looked at the dark water and she heard the rhythmic frothing of waves on sand.

" 'Tis supposed to be bad luck for a fisherman to see a mermaid, for it means he will drown that very day. But when I was born, my Nana told Da that I would bring luck to him, because I had the look of Muirgen about me, and the mermaids would spare me from their seductive curse. That is why I still go to sea with my father, though I've my own dreams. He likes to think he needs me, especially since I'm his only child and mother died while having me. I don't mind so much, sure. I love the water."

Sometimes, Seamus spoke to her in Irish, which sounded like a sad, powerful chant. Like language that could raise corpses, bring the most dangerous of the mermaids from the sea. Like the untranslatable monologue simmering in Grace's brain.

She thought he wasn't real, this man. She couldn't take hold of him and watch his reaction. He was only a voice, a glowing face, flawless skin on the back of a neck. He seemed to float slightly above the earth when he walked, and his face was so bright it made her blink. He was like an angel, she thought. Like the father–angel she had imagined when she was a girl.

On Saint John's Eve, the night before the summer solstice, Seamus took her to the bonfires. The islanders had been piling them for weeks, competing to see who could build the largest. They used furniture, tractor tires, driftwood, old fence palings. There were no large trees on the island, only gnarly bushes blown low by the wind. They made do, the islanders, throwing in anything that would burn. The bonfires, when lit, were as large as houses. They cracked loudly, shifting and spitting red pills into the air. The sound made Grace ache for Michael and she tried to walk closer to the flames, but Seamus stopped her. She thought they might warm her, but only her face burned with the heat, the rest of her remained damp. Fingers of fire squealed, reaching out toward her from the center. Seamus pulled her along from fire to fire, her face growing moist again in between them. The sunset lingered for hours, daylight still clinging at ten-thirty, and Grace imagined that eventually the island would be void of darkness, the sun exposing her twenty-four hours a day.

When the sun was finally swallowed, Seamus took her across the harbor in a curragh, the moon shining from behind him like a halo. They went to the castle, walking in their bare feet across the grass carpet. He told her about the adventures of the pirate queen Granuaile, who had ruled the west of Ireland in pagan times. Grace remembered these stories from her mother, but she could not tell him that. He took her to the pirate queen's bedroom, showed her the mermaid carved above the fireplace. The merrow's tail split halfway down into two sharply curved fins, and her hair fell over her face in curly ropes of stone. Seamus took Grace's hand and touched it to the mermaid's pointy breasts. He told her to make the sign of the cross, and she did, automatically as she'd done at Mass for so many years. Seamus recited along with her motions: "In the name of the Father, the Son, and the Holy Ghost, Amen."

"That will heal you," he said. He smoothed the curls away from Grace's face, tucking them behind her ear. "So they say. It can't hurt, anyways."

"I'm so cold," she said, and her voice vibrated like pain in her throat. "I can't stop it. I'm always, always cold." Seamus sat on the ground, his back against the mermaid's tail. He pulled her in like a baby to his lap. His shirt wasn't damp, but warm and dry against her face. He blew fiery air onto her fingers, rubbing them with his own warm hands. She thought it was unnatural, the amount of heat that was coming from his body. Not even during sex had Michael felt like this. Seamus was roasting, like the innermost coals of that bonfire. She drew heat in greedily, until she was dry clear through, and still he seemed hotter than when she'd started.

When he brought her home that night, Seamus stopped at the door, sweeping her back clean with the frayed end of his scarf.

"Try not to look like I had you supine in the grass, would you?" he said. Grace laughed. Her laughter, she thought, was like the feeling after vomiting, when your throat hurts and your mouth tastes of bile, but you know the sickness is out of you, and once you've brushed your teeth, it will fade into memory.

CHAPTER 19

Gráinne

For the rest of August I waited, on a shrunken, empty stomach, for my father to come.

"It's any day now, he'll be on that boat," Clíona said. I watched the ferry in the morning as it took the islanders and the mail away, and in the evening, when it brought the mail in and the islanders home.

In between, I taught Liam how to swim. He'd told me he didn't know how when we were at the cove, where he wouldn't go in over his waist.

"Don't you go fishing with your Dad?" I said to him.

He looked out-of-place and nervous in the water, even though he was confident in the curragh.

"Aye," Liam said. "He can't swim either."

"How can you live on an island and not know how to swim?"

I said. Liam shrugged. His chest was blue and goose-pimpled above the water.

"Seamus is the one fisherman I know can swim," Liam said. "Besides him, your mother was the only islander went in the water for pleasure. And the tourists in the summer."

"So you're surrounded by beaches, and nobody swims?" I said. "What a waste."

"We don't see it like that, sure," Liam said. "The water's our livelihood, not a playground." I was treading water, and Liam backed away whenever I splashed a bit.

"What if you're out in your curragh and it tips over?" I asked.

"I'd drown, I suppose. I never thought about it."

"Well, if I teach you how to swim you won't. I was afraid of drowning until my mother forced me to learn." That was a lie, of course. I rarely went in water where I couldn't touch bottom. "I'll show you," I said. "It'll be fun."

Liam agreed, but he didn't look too enthusiastic.

The first day I showed him how to tread water, which he couldn't do well. He kept sinking, then panicking, and standing up with a splash. I tried to remember how my mother had taught me. I made him float on his back in shallow water, with me holding my hands beneath him so he wouldn't feel scared. He took that better.

"I like the way it sounds with my ears below the waves," he said. "I can hear the whole ocean." It was nice, holding him up. It reminded me of Stephen showing me piano—an excuse to get closer, anyway. Though Liam never acted like I was making a pass, or like he was planning any moves on me. It was infuriating, really. I'd never had to wait so long for a boy to want me.

I made him hold his breath and sit with me under the water. I held his hand and watched him. He kept his eyes shut and his cheeks puffed out. His hair floated like soft black seaweed toward the surface. This is how a mermaid would see him, I thought, if she seduced him into the water. He squeezed my fingers when he needed to go up for air.

At the end of a week, Liam could dog-paddle clumsily, but he swam underwater with the grace of a fish. I think he was happy I'd taught him, though Clíona and Mary Louise thought we were both crazy. He even got a little cocky, and started charging me under the water and flipping me off my feet. I didn't mind, because it was like flirting, and we raced and wrestled after his lessons. The sunny weather was holding on, and we'd lay out on the warm rocks to dry. Sometimes, I couldn't remember ever being so content, closing my eyes and falling asleep to the sound of Liam breathing. Other days, I was going out of my mind. We were half-naked on a deserted beach and all Liam seemed to think about was drying off and getting back for supper.

"Liam," I said to him, one hot afternoon on the rocks. He had his eyes closed, and beads of water had dried into salty patches on his cheeks.

"Yeah?" he mumbled, shading his eyes to look at me.

"Do you like me?" I said. I felt stupid, but he had reduced me to bluntness. Liam smiled and closed his eyes again.

"I do, sure," he said.

"Like a cousin, though, or a sister?" I probed. "Or something else?"

"As a friend, I'd say." Liam opened one eye. "I think you're good-looking as well, if it's a compliment you're fishing for." I tried not to smile.

"I'm not fishing," I said.

"All right so," Liam said, closing his eyes again.

"Are you a virgin?" I asked. Liam sat up.

"Why is that your business?" he said. He wasn't looking at me, but turning his T-shirt right side out.

"It's not," I said, lying back down so my hip bones were visible through my suit. "I'm just curious."

"Well I am, if you must know," he said, putting his shirt on. "But it's by choice. I've had my opportunities, sure." I believed him. There were a lot of girls on the island who had eyes for Liam, and by the way they talked I knew they weren't prudes. Plus, all the island boys assumed Liam was sleeping with me. Whenever we walked on the road together, someone would jeer: "MacNamara's off to get his hole before tea."

"Don't you want to do it?" I asked. I thought all boys wanted sex, and a lot of it.

"Ah, sure, someday," Liam said. "I'm waiting, though, till it's right. I'd want to love the girl."

"You're a romantic," I teased. Liam shrugged, blushing.

"I wouldn't think you're a virgin," he said.

"Why not?" I said, and Liam just raised his eyebrows. "Well, I am."

"So we think the same then," Liam said.

"Not really," I said. I didn't think I was waiting for love, just for a boy who kissed right. Who didn't ruin the moment. Stephen, had he actually kept kissing me that night, would have been perfect. I would have slept with him in an instant.

"Well, I'm in no hurry, anyways," Liam said. He stood up. "Will we go for tea?" I put my sweatshirt and shorts on over my suit, wishing he wouldn't watch me now. Liam had an ideal that I didn't live up to, and I'd already started thinking that he might live up to mine.

We walked back to the hotel without talking, and rather than look at Liam, I focused on my hunger. I licked the salt from my lips and told myself: This is all I will ever need.

When the package came in the mail, I recognized Stephen's writing instantly. I took it from the table and went up to my room, feeling Clíona's eyes on my back.

Inside the box was a tiny pink envelope with my name on it. Stephen had forgotten to add the accent over the *a.* It was my mother's stationery; someone at work had given it to her in last Christmas's grab bag. She'd never used it.

Dear Grainne,

    I packed up the apartment and gave most of your mother's things to Goodwill like she asked me to do. These are some items which I thought you might want to keep.

                            —Stephen

    P.S. If you came back here, you wouldn't be happy. It's your mother you miss, not me.

I tossed the letter on the bed. He hadn't even left me his new address.

There was a manila folder in the box, and when I opened it, I saw the typed quotes I had left for my mother at the cottage. There were at least thirty pages—I couldn't remember having left so many. There were also all the birthday cards I'd given her since I was five, the letters I wrote the summer I went to sleep-over camp, and a thick stack of my childish paintings. I hadn't realized she'd kept any of this stuff. My mother wasn't the hoarding type—anything beyond necessity she tossed in the trash.

I pulled out the string of rosary beads that had been in my mother's hands during the wake. You could see the hollows between the miniature Jesus' ribs. I could only associate this with my mother dead—why would Stephen think I would want it? I dropped it into my bedside table drawer, out of sight.

At the bottom of the box, wrapped in tissue paper, was my mother's skintight red velvet miniskirt. Her man-hunting skirt. She wore it to clubs and on first dates. She'd had it on the first night she brought Stephen home. I knew why he'd sent it to me: I'd been begging her to lend me that skirt for two years, but she'd never relented. "Not my magic skirt," she'd always said.

I held the brushed fabric up to my face and inhaled. I smelled the cardboard box and old finger-paint from my drawings. Faintly, she was still in the velvet: stale smoke, salty sex.

I took off my jeans and underpants and slipped the cool velvet up my thighs. When I walked, the soft elasticized lining pulled gently at my pubic hair. It didn't fit as tightly as it was supposed to, but it was short enough; I was taller and thinner than the last time I'd secretly tried it on. When she was in the hospital, having her breast removed.

I wondered if my father had ever seen this skirt. I briefly entertained the fantasy of going after him, wearing the skirt to Dublin and showing up at his office. When he saw me he would think of a time when he had slid the skirt down my mother's legs and brushed his fingers back up her naked thighs.

Or he would tell me to leave, get out of his sight, never come back. Like Stephen had.

If Liam wasn't going to kiss me, I'd find someone else to do it. Not an island boy, because I could see it would be easy for my reputation to get back to Clíona. She was not like my mother, and I didn't think she'd want to chat with me about sex.

The night of the August full moon, there was a group of boys from Cork staying in the hotel. I was allowed to go to Marcus's pub, because Liam was playing his flute with the musicians his father usually led. Liam's father wasn't home yet; he was still out at sea and not due home until October.

I wore my mother's skirt with a black tank top that hugged my now tiny breasts. My ribs were becoming more visible; there was a furrow of hunger running below each one.

The musicians played at a corner table without amplifiers or microphones. There was a thin man with a fiddle; a woman, who said she was a cousin of Clíona's, with a tiny squeeze box; a couple of men with tin whistles; and a huge, smiling man with sideburns that grew in across his cheekbones, who paddled a drum Liam said was called a "bodhrán." Liam's flute was not silver like I'd expected, but smooth black wood with finger holes instead of levers. The music sounded like all the instruments were chasing one another around in a complicated dance. One or two at a time, islanders got up to stomp on the wood floor until the sounds of their feet blended with the rhythm of the instruments. Everyone was laughing and teasing one another. There was a lot of laughing on this island, I'd noticed, and people were always winking, like the entire population shared some private joke. Some of the older women had the deep wrinkles like Clíona's gouging their faces. I thought of my mother's obsession with moisturizer, the way she used to check for wrinkles under the harsh bathroom light. The wrinkles on these island women weren't ugly, though. They looked as though they wore maps of their lives on their faces.

I was allowed to sit next to Liam, though Marcus watched to see that no one ordered me anything but Diet Coke. John Patrick, the bodhrán player, kept sneaking me sips of his hot whiskey. It was sweet and fiery in my throat, and I drank half of his three glasses.

The boys from Cork were going through rounds of Guinness as quick as they could order them. One of them, the cutest one, kept looking at me when he went up to the bar. His hair was too short, but his features were delicate, like Stephen's, and he looked about nineteen; he had stubble on his cheeks and chin. I watched him without blushing, made sure he saw me holding the whiskey glass. *Man-hunting*, I heard my mother say. He came over to the table with a Guinness for himself and a hot whiskey for me. I set it beside me on the bench so Marcus couldn't see it from the bar.

"How' you?" he said. His accent was thick and different, more all over the place than the islanders'. "Great seisiún, lads," he said to the musicians, and sat on a stool in front of me. Liam looked at him suspiciously, but kept playing. I hoped he was jealous.

"I'm Kieran," he said, and he shook my hand. "And you're the loveliest thing in this godforsaken pub." I smiled.

"Gráinne," I said. "Thank you."

"You're from America, are you?" he said. Everyone knew I was an outsider the minute I said more than my name.

"Yes," I said. "Boston."

"How'd you get a name like Gráinne, so?" he said. He was weaving a little on his stool.

"I was born here," I said.

"Ah, so you're Irish, then," he smiled. "You're just after losing your accent."

"If you say so," I said, but I smiled back at him.

"Will you go for a walk on the beach with me there, Irish Gráinne?" Kieran said. I felt Liam twitch beside me.

"All right," I said.

"That's grand," Kieran said, standing up and chugging down the rest of his beer. I put my jacket on and Liam stopped playing.

"He's only asking you because you're an American," Liam whispered. "He thinks you're easy." I leaned down to him. His lips were swollen and wet from the flute playing.

"I *am* easy," I said. I didn't like the sound of that. The whiskey was getting to me. Liam blushed, though, and turned away, so I followed Kieran's path through the crowded pub.

We walked down the sand toward a bonfire, which was blowing high and sideways with the wind. Kieran was stumbling a bit, and I didn't feel so steady either. It was a relief to sit down.

He didn't waste any time; he kissed me before I'd even looked at him. Too much tongue and bad breath, but I laid down with him anyway. He had his hand up my shirt and was squeezing one of my breasts through my bra. He didn't move to the other one, and I had a brief drunken panic that I only had one breast, that the other was missing, the flesh stitched up in its place. I started to feel nauseous. I rolled so I was half on top of him, and took charge of the kissing. He seemed to like that, and for a few minutes I convinced myself it wasn't so bad. I was even a little excited and wet. I considered unzipping his jeans, but he had his hand up my skirt first. He gasped when he felt that I had no underwear on. He pinned me back beneath him and plunged what felt like all of his fingers inside me. That hurt, and what little attraction I'd had disappeared with the pain. I pulled his hand away. I could smell myself, along with the scent of fire, sea, and Guinness.

"Ah, come on," Kieran soothed, trying again.

"Stop," I said, pushing him. I sat up, pulling the velvet back over my thighs. I thought suddenly of the mermaid's enchanted red cap which Liam had told me about. If a man snatched it, she was doomed.

"What's wrong with you?" He said it meanly, and I half considered lying down and letting him, to avoid the confrontation.

"I don't want to, okay?" I said.

"Ah, why not?" He grabbed my breast, that same one, and tried to kiss me.

"Cut it out," I said. "I don't even like you." And I didn't. What was I doing with this guy? I wanted to be inside the warm pub; I wanted Stephen to be here.

"Could you not have told me that before?" Kieran said, standing up. He kicked sand at my back. "You fucking tease." He went back to the pub. I sat by the fire, trying not to cry. Magic skirt and all, I would never be a sexy woman like my mother. It wasn't possible to be a seductress and a tease at the same time.

I got up, flicked the sand from my backside, and went back to the pub. I saw Kieran by the bar, saying something to his friends. Probably about me, because they laughed. I went into the grubby bathroom, lit a cigarette, and inhaled, watching myself in the mirror. "Gráinne," I whispered. It should have been my mother's name, not mine.

I left the bathroom and sat down next to Liam, who had his flute in his lap. He was glaring at Kieran's group. He'd probably heard them talking about me.

One of the men was singing, and everyone in the pub was politely quiet, listening to him. I recognized the song—it was the one my mother used to sing, when she broke up with a boyfriend, the one she'd typed up for me on her last night. *Go and leave me if you wish to. . . .* I wanted to tell Liam, who was listening to it like it was any old tune. Only Stephen would have understood, would have heard the words and seen my mother flirting, then blood clots and distant notes tacked up in a deserted kitchen. I could never have explained it to anyone else.

Liam took my hand under the table. Like he had at Granuaile's castle, squeezing my palm softly and smiling. We stayed like that, holding hidden hands, until Liam was asked to play again.

CHAPTER 20

Grace

Seamus wasn't easily seduced. Once Grace came back to herself, the memory of Michael only a sting, she began to wonder what it would be like to make love to Seamus. Heat would be a part of it, she knew. She wanted new hands to touch her, wanted a body she wasn't familiar with to explore. With all the confidence that had tempted Michael, she now turned to Seamus. He seemed immune, at first, then like he enjoyed proving that she couldn't get to him.

He'd had sex before, she knew by the unsurprised look he gave when he first saw her naked. They'd gone swimming, and she'd let her bikini top float away. He only looked at her for a moment, maybe appreciative, but certainly not enthralled. He fished the bikini top out of an island of seaweed.

"Did you lose that?" he asked, and when he handed it to her, she felt stupid as well as angry. It occurred to her that sex with

Michael had been more like playing doctor, two kids poking and giggling at private parts. She hadn't thought so at the time, but now Seamus, who was nine years older, treated her like a child.

He seemed altogether unimpressed by her body. Once, when he was tutoring her in her little bedroom, the door left open at Clíona's insistence, Grace had leaned back on the bed, letting her skirt fold up above her thighs. He glanced up from the Seamus Heaney poem he was reading, and looked at her like she'd grown a tail.

"Have you got a brain in that leg of yours?" he said, and Grace lifted her knees, checking. "Apparently not," he said. He tossed the book at her, and the corner of it bruised her thigh. "Read some of that aloud now," he said. "And tell me what you'll write for an essay."

Grace sighed and sat up properly on the bed. She read with exaggerated annoyance, imitating an Irish accent.

"Give me that," Seamus yelled, but he was smiling. "It's blasphemous, that rendering."

Sometimes, he forgot himself, and touched her, on the back of the neck when she had her hair up, or on her hip, gently guiding her along the dark island roads. The brief contact left her greedy, and she moved into him, hoping he would kiss her. He never did, just backed away like it was an accident. He would be careful then, and she'd have to wait a few days before he forgot and reached for her again.

One night the family was gathered at the pub, celebrating Mary Louise's engagement to Owen MacNamara, a fiddle-playing fisherman whom Grace thought was too handsome for her prudish stepsister. Grace was watching Seamus order a round of Guinness at the bar; he was laughing at something Marcus had said. She didn't notice that Mary Louise was at her side until she spoke up.

"You fancy him, don't you?" Mary Louise said. Grace sipped her Coke, crunching the ice loudly.

"I don't know what you're talking about," she said. Mary Louise smiled that wide, annoying smile.

"I know what it means when a girl looks at a fellow the way you're looking at Seamus O'Flaherty," Mary Louise said.

"There's not much else to look at," Grace said. "The rest of the men in this place are as ugly as your fiancé."

Mary Louise only laughed. When Grace was being mean, Mary Louise seemed to think she was trying to be funny.

"Don't worry," Mary Louise said. "I can keep my sister's secrets." She squeezed Grace's arm and walked off to her table before Grace had the chance to shake her off.

Later, when Seamus was leaving, in a cloud of cigarette smoke and hearty singing, he took hold of Grace's arm. His lips grazed like dry, heated feathers just to the side of her mouth, and he whispered something she didn't hear. Then he was walking away. She should have put an arm around him, pulled him in closer, asked him to repeat what he'd said. But it all happened too fast and she was distracted by the drunken idiots dancing on the corner table. She was encouraged, though. Surely he would do it again. But he didn't, not even the next time he was drinking at the pub, where she was hanging around, anxious and thirsty. He bought her a Coke and sent her home.

Now that Grace was feeling better, Clíona was pushing her to go back to school. Grace returned to classes for winter term, but quit again after the teacher, Mr. MacSweeney, whacked her across the knuckles with a ruler.

"You can't just drop out of school because the master smacks you," Clíona said. "If I know you, you asked for it."

"I told him to fuck off," Grace said.

"Jesus in Heaven! Are you mad?" Clíona said. "You'll go back tomorrow and use that smart mouth of yours to apologize."

"How can you send me to a school where they beat you up?" Grace said.

"Listen to you. You've no bones broken. He didn't beat you,

just gave you the thwack you deserved. I got them when I was a girl, and I've given you a few in my time as well."

"Not since I hit you back," Grace said. Clíona was silent. They'd had a fight when Grace was thirteen; Clíona had smacked her cheek for swearing, and Grace had punched her mother in the mouth. It had turned into a wrestling match, broken up by Michael. Clíona hadn't touched her since that day.

"How do you expect to get an education so?" Clíona said. "Mr. MacSweeney's the only teacher on the island."

"I'll study with Seamus," Grace said. "I hate that school. We have to pray between courses. They have no right to make me pray in public school."

"You're not in America now, Miss Know-It-All."

"I will be," Grace threatened. She stomped up the stairs, slamming her door and waking Tommy from his nap.

Clíona insisted that if she wasn't in school, she work at the hotel. Grace only agreed because she'd make some money—maybe not enough to escape right away, but it was a start. She went around with Mary Louise in the mornings, changing bed linens and cleaning toilets. She made jokes about the stains on the sheets but Mary Louise ignored her.

"Mary Louise, there's a condom in the bin here. Want to see what they look like?"

"Ah, cut it out, would you?" Mary Louise said, blushing. "We've five more rooms to do before lunchtime." She was a pathetic prude, Mary Louise—Grace was sure she hadn't even had sex with Owen yet. She was the type to wait until her wedding night.

Clíona worked all day, ordering everyone around. No detail escaped her. The beds had to be made up so tight, the guests would have to rip the sheets apart just to get into them. The paperwork had to be flawless. One day, she yelled at Grace just for poor penmanship.

"Look here, girl. What's this booking for—Conroy or Connor? I can't read it if you write it with the wrong hand."

"I wrote it with my right hand," Grace said. "What difference does it make? Everyone's name sounds the same anyway."

"Are you looking to get sacked?" Clíona asked. Grace slammed the reservation book shut, just missing her mother's fingers.

"Stop pretending like you're my boss," she said. "We both know you're just a servant. You were a slave at the Willoughbys' and you're the same to Marcus."

"You bold thing," Clíona said, taking the book away from her. "I'd a job that bought you the things you needed, remember. And I'm part owner of this hotel—Marcus and I are fifty-fifty. I'm no doctor, sure, neither are you. Dropping out of school and just after lifting your skirt to catch that rich boy in America. . . . I'd watch who you call a slave from now on, cause I've a few choice names for you if you push me."

"If you hate me so much, why don't you just send me home to Boston," Grace yelled back.

"You won't be going anywhere before you're eighteen," Clíona said. "And I don't hate you." Her voice dropped a bit, and she looked away.

"Yeah, well I hate you," Grace said. "And I hate this place, and next year you'll wish you were nicer when you realize you'll never see me again." If Grace hadn't known better, she'd have thought her mother looked hurt. She would have liked that. But Clíona closed her eyes and opened them, glaring at Grace with dark indifference.

"I think you'd be better off working at the shop," Clíona said. "Where you can't get under my feet all day."

"Fuck that," Grace said. "I'm not going to waste my life in your husband's crappy little shop. Or should I call him your master?" She walked away, leaving Clíona with her mouth poised to respond.

At Christmastime, there was a dance in the island hall. Seamus walked Grace down, but was soon surrounded by Anties, who were praising him for his first article in *The Irish Times*. It had been published that morning, and Marcus had ordered extra copies for the shop, so Seamus's family could collect them. Grace, a little tipsy from the poteen an uncle had slipped her in her lemonade, stood in the nook by the doorway flirting with four of the island boys. Not one of them compared to Seamus, but they were attentive. They teased her and dropped their eyes to her breasts when she laughed. Brendan was the one she focused on because he wasn't at all related to her family, but a cousin to Seamus. He was thick-chested and callused, his complexion almost rashy it was so red, his lips full and kissable. Grace leaned into him, and he kept one hand, hidden from the others, heavy on her back. She was really hoping Seamus might see them, but he was buried in relations at the other end of the hall. When the other boys left to drink beer in the car park, Brendan took Grace's hand. She let him think he was luring her outside.

He pinned her against the cold concrete wall on the dark side of the building; he kissed like a cow and pinched her breasts. He had no idea what he was doing, but she let him go on for a while. She pressed her palm against the crowded fly of his jeans.

"Jesus!" he said, grinding against her hand. He kissed her so hard their teeth banged together, sending a ringing through Grace's temples. Then Brendan was propelled backward, his mouth still open, and for an instant Grace thought she'd shoved him.

"What the fuck do you think you're up to?" It was Seamus, holding Brendan by the collar of his jacket. "And your mother right inside these walls."

"Ah, Shamie, leave us be," Brendan whined. He was hunching over, trying to hide his erection.

"If I ever catch you with her again, I'll break your chopper in two," Seamus said. He pushed Brendan toward the hall door. "Get your hole someplace else." Brendan jogged along, giggling now, and disappeared around the corner.

"Who do you think you are," Grace said. "My father?" She was thrilled at the possibility that he was jealous.

"Looks like you need one," Seamus said. He stood at a distance from her, his arms crossed.

"I know what I'm doing," Grace said.

"Sure, that's what I'm afraid of," Seamus said. "Come on in now."

"You're acting jealous, Shamie," Grace said, stepping forward so her breasts pushed into his arms. He stepped back.

"Stop that, would you?" he said. He was in the light from the doorway now, looking furious. "What's wrong with you? You don't even fancy that boy, you're only using him, and you don't seem to care that he's using you as well."

Grace shrugged. "What do you know about anything?" she said. If he wasn't jealous, why didn't he mind his own business?

"I know a ride won't get you what you want," Seamus said.

"Maybe all I want is a ride," Grace said. Seamus stuffed his clenched fists deep in his pockets.

"High aspirations," he said, and he walked back inside. Grace went in briefly to look for Brendan, but he was dancing with an island girl. Clíona motioned for Grace to join her and Marcus at the bar, but Grace pretended she hadn't noticed, and left, walking back to the hotel alone.

Grace turned eighteen in April, and on her birthday a storm attacked the island with sharp hail and moaning wind. Clíona made a special family dinner and a cake, and the children all feigned enthusiasm, wearing the paper hats they kept in the closet for their own birthdays. Mary Louise gave Grace a pair of fake pearl earrings, which Grace thanked her for but knew she'd never wear. Marcus offered her a job at the pub, which Grace refused so passionately he ended up leaving the dinner table to smoke by the fire. When Clíona brought the cake out, with candles like a forest fire melting the frosting, the children sang quietly and out of tune. Grace wished she'd never see any of them again, and blew out the flames.

"It's hard to believe my baby girl is eighteen," Clíona said, looking suspiciously sentimental. She tried to smile at her daughter, but Grace looked away, plunging a knife into the cake. Clíona started the dinner dishes, leaving the children to stuff in as much dessert as they could while she wasn't watching. Grace came into the kitchen with the stray glasses, plopping them into Clíona's dishwater.

"Did Seamus not say he would come?" Clíona asked. She'd adopted a sweet tone for the day, which Grace hated more than her normal nagging.

"He did," Grace said, shrugging. "It doesn't matter."

"That's not like him," Clíona said.

Grace tossed the butter dish in the refrigerator so it clanked loudly. "Would you leave it alone?" she snapped.

"Don't take that tone with me," Clíona threatened.

"Pardon me," Grace chirped. "Would you fuck off, Mother dear?"

"Can you not be civil on your birthday at least?" Clíona asked. "I'm only trying to make it nice for you."

"You only did all this because you know I'm going to leave soon," Grace said. "And you're jealous."

"Jealous?" Clíona laughed. "I'm content where I am. You've not even money for the ferry, so I don't envy you trying to go anywhere." The knock at the door stopped Grace from answering. Clíona wiped her hands on a towel and went out of the room. It was Eamon, looking like a wet dog, bringing a rush of wind and a few hailstones in with him.

"Princess Grace," Clíona called, laughing. "Your chariot awaits you." She offered to take Eamon's dripping hat. "How're keeping, Eamon?"

"I won't be staying, Clee," Eamon said. "We need Marcus on the boat. Paddy and Seamus haven't come in yet and they took the curragh out this morning."

"They're right eejits going out before a storm," Marcus said. He threw his cigarette in the fire and got up to put his coat on. Grace and the children were crowded at the kitchen doorway, quiet so they wouldn't be sent from the room.

"Ah, you know Paddy," Eamon said. "He thinks if he's with his boy nothing can drown him."

"You kids get upstairs now," Clíona said, and they groaned but trudged up, the twins with hunks of cake in their trouser pockets. Grace stayed behind.

"Seamus will be all right," Grace said to Eamon, with an assured tone. He took it as a question.

"Don't worry yourself, girl," he said. "The O'Flahertys have got the mermaids on their side, in the odd case God isn't watching."

"Mind that talk," Clíona said, pushing Marcus out the door. "Mind yourselves as well." She kissed her husband's cheek roughly. Grace watched the men from the window, two figures swallowed in a bullet-spray of rain.

Grace slept after hours of waiting, and dreamed of a dark-haired mermaid under a storm of water, her breasts mapped with green veins. She'd trapped Seamus and was kissing him, blowing water into his lungs. She had his penis gripped in her webbed fingers, and when he ejaculated black foam, she let him go. He sank, dead and plump with water, toward the rocky bottom.

Grace woke and heard voices in the sitting room. From the stairway she saw Seamus laid out on the sofa, Clíona tucking blankets around his bare chest. Marcus, Eamon, and two other men were standing, dripping on the carpet, behind her.

"Why did you not take him to hospital?" Clíona was saying. "He'll have hypothermia after being in that water."

"We couldn't risk going to Galway in this storm," Marcus said. "Besides, feel him yourself. He's not even cold, sure, he's not." Clíona pressed her palms against Seamus's head, hands, and feet.

"Jesus in Heaven," she said, covering him up again. "This boy's blessed by angels if any of us are."

"More than his father, sure," Eamon said, and the lot of them crossed themselves.

"Is he dead?" Grace said, and they all turned to her. She walked to the sofa, looking at Seamus's moon-white face against the blankets.

"He's all right, child," Clíona said. She touched Grace's arm briefly, then took her hand away to fuss with her own bathrobe.

"I mean his father," Grace said. "Is he dead?"

"Shush," Clíona said, and the men backed into the kitchen for their tea. "The sea took him, yes."

Grace sat down on the floor and watched Seamus breathing.

"Poor Shamie," Clíona said softly. "He's no family now." She went to put on the kettle for the men.

Grace slid her arm under the blankets and took Seamus's hand. It was as hot as ever, and she stayed there, gripping it, until he woke up and saw her.

Grace volunteered to mind Tommy at home during Paddy O'Flaherty's memorial Mass. She didn't want to be there, the one outsider in a family of mourners. Seamus's grief was like Michael's—it made her a stranger. She couldn't help wondering if he would turn to her now, as Michael had after his father's affair, and let her take advantage of it. He'd better hurry, she thought, because she was leaving. She was determined to remake herself, into a being independent from any race or family. Like Granuaile, who took her father's and husband's kingdoms and made them into her own.

Grace had been taking money from the hotel register, twenty pounds a day, whenever she dropped by to relieve her mother for lunch. Her own version of piracy. In another month, she'd have enough for a plane ticket to Boston, which would be the starting point. Anything was possible, she believed, once she was away from this island.

When she went to Seamus's house late that night it was to take his grief and turn it into lust. She felt sorry for him, she knew how much he loved his father, but sympathy made her feel useless. She preferred manipulation.

But when she arrived, he was not surprised, nor did he act like he was giving in. He'd been expecting her, and undressed her by candlelight in his room, as though he'd done it a dozen times before. Grace felt shy, for the first time she could remember. She hesitated from taking his clothes off, so he did it himself.

"It's not my first time," Grace said, warning him.

"I know," said Seamus, and he didn't stop. He swept her hair back from her collarbone and took a long look down her body.

"Why now?" Grace said, fishing for assurance. "What were you waiting for?" She couldn't decide between the excitement of him looking at her and the disappointment that she wasn't initiating it. "Wait!" she felt like yelling. She wished she could rewind to the beginning and rip his clothes off.

"I wanted you to love me," Seamus said, his hands in her hair. He didn't seem broken or even like he was giving anything up. It was quite a confession, Grace thought, to voice so casually.

"I do love you," she said, happy to assert something. He kissed her, his mouth like warm tea on her tongue, and her legs rippled like water weeds.

"No, you don't," he whispered, easing her back on the bed. His body over her was blue-white, his muscles like shadows in a full moon. He held her hands up by the pillows, keeping his eyes level with hers, and he watched her, not blinking, as he slid between her legs. He stayed motionless until she couldn't stand it, her insides screaming. She lifted him off the bed with her hips. He moved slowly then, slower than Michael had ever managed, and every feeling he raked out of her was delayed, stretched over a torturous space of time. She pulled at his back, but she still felt like he wasn't close enough. She wanted more of him, his whole body, inside her.

"You were there," he whispered. She arched her neck, trying not to gasp.

"What?"

"You were there, in the water. When my father was pulled down. I lost hold of him and dove, and you were there—waiting for me."

"I wasn't," Grace said. Her orgasm was backtracking, building up stronger just when she thought it had finished. His face hovered above her like a wet moon. She kissed him, filling his mouth with her tongue, and her whimpering echoed in his throat.

When it was over, the slickness on their bellies already beginning to congeal and pinch like sunburn, she noticed the hot tears on her face and thought they had fallen from him. But she looked, and he wasn't the one crying.

CHAPTER 21

Clíona

I'm thinking about Gráinne—as I do all day every day—when Liam brings her into the hotel, sopping wet and blood running over her eye.

"What's happened?" I say, rushing out from behind the desk. I put my handkerchief over a gash in her forehead.

"She slipped on the rocks when we were swimming," Liam says. He's shakier than she is, though he's trying to look as if he's holding her up.

"It's nothing," Gráinne says, but she looks surprised to see my hanky soaked with blood.

I bring her into the house and ring Bernie, the island nurse, but her daughter tells me she's on the mainland for the day, so I take out the first aid kit and clean the wound, which is deep enough to need stitches. Gráinne looks frightened when I thread the needle.

"You can't do that," she says. "I need to go to a hospital."

"Nonsense," I say, preparing a syringe with a local anesthetic. "I've stitched that boy beside you in three places. I know what I'm doing." Gráinne doesn't look as though she believes me, but Liam tries to reassure her. He shows her the faint scars on his leg and the one under his overgrown bang.

"Nana's as good as any doctor," he says.

"And less expensive," I say.

"What if it gets infected?" she says.

"Stop your whining," I say. "I wouldn't let that pretty head of yours go septic." Once she's gotten the local, she keeps straining her eyes up, checking on me.

"Am I hurting you?" I say.

"No," she says, grudgingly, as if she'd prefer this without the painkiller, if it meant she could be mad at me.

I stitch the wound up small and neat, so she won't have a big mark on her forehead. It's up by her hairline, and once that shearing of hers grows in, the scar will be hidden well enough.

"Why do *you* know how to do this?" she says. I ignore her superior tone.

"I help the nurse on the odd day," I say. "I wanted to go into medicine myself once, and I've never lost interest in it, I suppose."

"If you wanted to be a nurse, how'd you end up a maid and a hotel clerk?" Gráinne snaps.

"I had your mother younger than I'd planned," I say. I show her the neat black line in the hand mirror. It will bruise up soon, but the blood's gone. I start bandaging her forehead.

"My mother thought you had no ambition," Gráinne says— softly though, as if she knows how bad it sounds.

"Did she tell you that?" I say.

"Once," Gráinne says. "When I asked about you." Liam's passing me the sticking plasters, looking uncomfortable, as if he's afraid of intruding.

"Your mother didn't think much of how I turned out, it's true," I say.

"Didn't you tell her, though," Gráinne says, "that you wanted to be more?" I'm finished, so I turn away from her, gather up the papers and the bloody gauze.

"I'm not ashamed of who I am, Gráinne," I say. "And I didn't tell Grace any such thing, because I never wanted her to think she'd held me back. That wouldn't have been fair to her." What would happen if I told Gráinne everything? That I'd started out a bad mother, that I'd hated that fierce little baby for stealing my chance in life.

"Maybe if you'd told her the truth, she would have liked you better," Gráinne says fiercely.

"There's more to it than that, sure," I say.

"What?" Gráinne yells. "What more?"

"Not now, Gráinne," I say. She storms off, sending her chair crashing on the lino, thumping up the stairs and slamming the door so hard the pots rattle on their hooks in the kitchen. All this banging around, it's like living with my daughter again.

Liam looks at me apologetically.

"I guess it's confusing," he says. "When you don't know the whole story."

"Yes," I say. "It most definitely is." I don't know the whole story myself, and what I do know, I'd not have the easiest time explaining.

It is at night, now, when Marcus is sleeping, that I practice what I would say to Gráinne if I could:

I made mistakes, compromises followed.

The best intentions sometimes have the worst outcome.

Life's defining moments never come at a person singly, but rush at you two or three at a time.

If I could have laid my life out one crisis at a time, I am sure I could have handled them all. As it happened, though, I always missed something. It was in this way that I lost my daughter, not all at once, but step by step through the years.

It was just after Seamus's father died that my own father was struck with the illness he never recovered from. Since he had stopped fishing five years before, Da had lived a quiet life. He insisted on staying alone in the house where he was born, even though I thought he'd be more comfortable with Marcus and myself. During the days he tended the sheep and cattle, and at five o'clock every evening, he put on his waistcoat and went to the pub. He sat at the corner of the bar with the three men he'd fished with for fifty years, drinking Guinness slowly until his eyes clouded; then he walked home alone over the dark pitted roads. Da's was the lonely life of most older island men, but he didn't think himself lonely. He thought himself patient; he was waiting in the only way he knew how. Waiting for the day when he would join my mother.

We never found out for sure what was wrong with my father, because he refused to see the doctor. I myself suspected kidney failure, and at first I was angry because I knew he could prolong his life with dialysis. My father was old-fashioned and fatalistic; if it was his time to go so be it, he wouldn't be pumped along by a machine. (I myself have been accused of fatalism—by my daughter and by Gráinne. I often say if a thing is meant to be it will happen by the grace of God, though I'm not sure I believe that. Sometimes I think my faith is more of a habit than a reality.)

As it happened, while Grace and Seamus were falling in love, I was spending all my time nursing my dying father. At first he resented me; it is hard to keep your pride when your own daughter assists in all your bodily functions. But as he grew weaker he seemed to want me there. He liked me to sit at his bedside while he was sleeping.

My father was always an affectionate man; when I was a child it was his hands that comforted me in fever, his lap that I snuggled in before going off to bed. His body was the warm, solid body of a fisherman; his hands so thick with skin he could slide a knife a quarter of an inch into his thumb before drawing blood. Yet he was gentle. My mother's body was soft, at least it looked soft, but she never touched us. Her breasts and stomach were not a place I thought to bury my head, but an armor that protected her from my touch.

One afternoon while I was sitting by my father, reading to him from a book of Patrick Kavanagh's poetry, he opened his eyes and looked at me with a peculiar expression. I could tell he wasn't about to ask me to help him to the toilet or make him a cup of tea.

"What is it, Da?" I said, closing the book.

"You put me in mind of your mother," he said, and I was taken aback. He rarely mentioned her; I think he missed her as much then as the day she died and it pained him to speak of it.

"It's Maeve who takes after Mum," I said. Maeve had her gold hair and amber eyes which had always gotten the men's attention.

"It's not your head I'm thinking of," my father said. "She's there in your manner. Your voice. The way you read that poetry."

Am I so cold? I thought. That was my mother's manner, frosty, and her voice had been the harsh angry music of a woman who hated her life.

"Mum had the Northern accent, Da," I said. I thought maybe his mind was failing.

"It's not the accent," he said, frustrated. He let it go, scowling and turning his face away.

I shouldn't have argued with him, I knew his intention was to compliment me. He saw my mother differently than I had. After all those years of believing my mother a cold, unforgiving woman, it frightened me to hear myself likened to her. For the first time I had the notion that my father had seen my real mother, and I her façade, rather than the other way around. Perhaps I had merely misunderstood her, just as I believed that Grace misunderstood me.

My father died twenty-three years after his wife, and yet it was my mother I grieved at his funeral. I grieved that I had not known her, that she had died before I was a mother, before I had a chance to understand that no one is the mother she plans to be.

It was this grief that caused me to do what I did to my own daughter. I'll have to tell Gráinne eventually—I know that well enough. She'll find out when she meets her father and she's better off hearing it from me. It's my own fault, all of it. Grace leaving, Gráinne growing up without a father. I trapped my daughter here, like a fish in a net, and once she got away she never came back. I can't say I blame her. Marcus says I shouldn't blame myself, but I can't just let it be. You have children, you're responsible for them forever, is the way I see it.

I can't say I didn't expect that romance between my daughter and Seamus, I was only too preoccupied to recognize it. I would have preferred it happen later, but Grace was a beautiful girl and Seamus not immune to beauty. He was honorable enough in his intentions, if not in his actions. He loved her with all his heart, he did. Loved her with more than that, as she turned out pregnant and she barely eighteen. My baby girl, following my mistakes like a road map. Of course, she couldn't find a better man than Seamus to get in trouble with. He never hesitated about marrying her, knew what he wanted, sure. It was Grace who made everything more complicated than it already was.

She came to me one morning when Marcus was not in the house.

"I'm going to have an abortion," she said.

And I saw her, in that moment, lost to me.

"You'll get that filth out of your head this instant," I said. Even she was taken aback by my tone. "You'll marry Seamus. I'll not let you ruin your life and your soul along with it."

"I don't want to marry Seamus. I'm moving back to Boston, I can get an abortion there."

"Shut your mouth," I yelled. "You'll not get off this island until you've married that man and had this baby. You made this mistake, now you'll handle it like a Christian woman, or God help me, I'll handle it for you."

She accused me of hypocrisy, which of course was true enough.

I am a woman who's made her share of mistakes. I can't say abortion would have been any worse than resenting your own baby. This isn't a Catholic position, I know, but a reflection of how my faith changed over the years, though I've kept up appearances. I did not always find God as pragmatic as I'd have liked.

But this was what I was thinking: This child will change things. Grace would grow up, a new baby would bring us closer together. And it's not as though she didn't love Seamus, that was plain as day. She only wanted to do the opposite of everything I wanted for her.

I was as good as my word. Eamon was instructed to call Marcus did Grace try to get on the ferry. She gave in after a week of trying, and one failed attempt at stealing an islander's boat. Seamus caught her in the harbor, going round in circles.

She married him. He gave her a sweet carving on the day, one he'd made himself, of Granuaile in her curragh; he knew my daughter, he did, better than she thought. And he adored her more than Michael Willoughby ever had.

Grace could have been happy with Seamus, had she let herself. But I forced her to marry him and she was determined to get me back for it, and her husband in the process. I can't say I'm sorry, for if she'd had that abortion, Gráinne wouldn't be alive, and that girl, I know, was everything to Grace. She was a good mother, no matter what decisions she made later.

I'm not proud of what I did. But I did it out of love. I did not want to die with Grace thinking me cold and unfeeling. Of course, it was Grace who died, died without me, half a world away. Died thinking exactly what I believed of my mother. Died, possibly, not thinking of me at all, but thinking herself alone, as she always had, from the time she was born and I did not know how to love her.

God help me, I was a mother, and more than once I foolishly thought I'd done the right thing. I'd take the blame, all of it, heaped like coals on my head, if I could just have her back awhile. Back from the beginning. Newborn and flat-faced, rashy and wailing with colic. I'd cherish every scream. She'd be the best-loved baby since Jesus Christ Himself.

CHAPTER 22

Grace

Grace stole Jack Keane's boat in a desperate panic, though she didn't know how to navigate it, and the fog was too thick to even see the mainland. All she could think of was escaping her mother. That expressionless face ruling her life. She was terrified that if she stayed on this island, that would be her own face someday: callused and wrinkled by sea winds, impenetrable.

She accidentally locked the rudder in turn position and the boat went out of control, spinning her in circles. She was stuck, fated to go back again to where she'd started. Pregnant. Desperately in love. Trapped.

Stupid, was what Seamus called her, when he'd grabbed on to the circling boat from his curragh.

"How could you be so stupid, Grace?" he said. "You could have been lost at sea, drowned. Surely death can't be more desirable than marrying me."

He brought her to the empty hotel lounge to dry out by the fire. He wrapped her in a wool blanket and held her in his lap, stroking her damp hair. Grace cried, silently, though she clung to his body as if it were the hot water bottle she took to bed at night.

"I don't want to have a baby," she said. "I'm only eighteen. I don't know *how* to have a baby." Seamus rocked her, shushing.

"It's my fault," he said. "I should have been more careful. It will be all right. You'll be a brilliant mother, you'll see." Grace moaned at this, crying harder.

"If you know it's a mistake, why won't you let me get rid of it?" she said.

Seamus stiffened. "I can't let you kill our baby," he said. Then he softened, and kissed her temples gently. "Ah, Grace," he whispered, "why do you not want to marry me? I love you to distraction. Sure, I'll be good to you, always."

Grace shook her head vehemently, scattering salty drops from her cheeks.

"Don't you love me?" Seamus said. She buried her face in his shoulder.

She did love him, or she thought so, if this mixture of longing and terror was love. She couldn't get enough of him, and she was sure he knew it. Despite her feeling that she wasn't in charge, she had gone back to his house almost every night after that first one, needing to feel him inside her. She sobbed with every orgasm, called out his name until he had to cover her mouth so the neighbors wouldn't hear. She only had to look at him and her insides liquefied and ran away like tears of wax. During sex with Michael—though she'd enjoyed it—she had always kept thinking, planning, taking notes and storing them for later on. With Seamus she ceased to think. It felt like swimming: as with her body and the water, her body and his were all that mattered. But also, she thought sometimes, being with Seamus was like drowning.

She was afraid of him. Of the way he looked at her in bed sometimes, mean, serious, as if he were plotting against her. He had never hurt her, he was gentle in every way, but still she felt like she'd been captured. Seamus had once told her that his father believed that mermaids kept the souls of drowned sailors in cages beneath the sea. He joked that his father was there now, being let out only thrice daily for his meals among the colony of sea-people. Grace felt like one of those souls, in a sensuous, loving cage, but a cage nonetheless; she would never get off this island if she married Seamus. He loved Inis Murúch. He wouldn't even move to Dublin despite the fact that he was writing for *The Irish Times*. Grace would end up an island wife like her mother or Mary Louise, sitting around pots of tea, talking about their husbands as though they were unruly little boys.

"This isn't my home," Grace said to Seamus, not answering his question. He sighed.

"It can be, Grace," he said. "If you want it to be."

"No," she said, but quietly now.

"Just give me some time, Grace. We'll have the baby and I'll make you happy, you'll see."

She married him because the fear of losing him was as strong as the fear of giving herself up. Because she'd never felt this way about anyone and was afraid she never would again. Because he had swallowed a part of her which she could not get back: her liquid center which she could not leave without.

She married him because she hoarded a secret hope that someday things would reverse, and she would be able to take him away with her.

Grace threw up in the bathroom while her wedding guests were set-dancing, the hotel function room rank with the smell of body odor and stout. She knelt with her forehead against the cold tiled wall, willing her stomach to settle down. She hadn't been sick as often this time. Mary Louise was also pregnant and fiercely ill the first half of every day. Grace had heard the island women saying that so much sickness meant she was carrying a boy. Michael's baby, which had slopped out of Grace in the bathroom, must have been a boy, she thought. And this one, Seamus's, would be a girl.

When her nausea had passed, Grace sat on the closed toilet seat, not ready to face her wedding party yet. She heard a group of girls come into the bathroom, smelled the spray of perfume and the face powder. Mary Louise was with them; they were all giggling and teasing one another. Grace lifted her feet and held her knees so they wouldn't see her under the door.

"Ah, we saw you dancing with Francie Raftery, Margaret," Mary Louise said. "It's love, I suspect."

"Not a fucking chance," Margaret shrieked. "He'd his hands groping through the back buttons of my dress. Mind my back, girls, have I got paw prints on the silk?" The group of them whooped. "It's good craic, anyways, the party," Margaret said. "Not half as good as your wedding, Mary Louise. This one's spoiled by that bitch of a bride."

"Mind what you say about my sister," Mary Louise said quietly. She tried to change the subject back to Francie, but Margaret, who sounded drunk, wouldn't let her.

"What are you, a saint?" Margaret bellowed. "I wouldn't call that tart my sister for anything. Stealing Seamus O'Flaherty from all us deserving girls on the island. Everyone knows she trapped him. And now she'll be having her baby just after you have yours, Mary Louise. She has to keep all the attention for herself, that one."

"Ah, shut up, would you?" Mary Louise said, louder now. "Don't blame my sister just because Seamus never looked twice at you, Margaret." Grace heard Mary Louise's heels stomping out of the bathroom.

"Don't mind her, Margaret," a girl said. "She's not herself."

"I feel sorry for her is all," Margaret said. Someone peed in the stall next to Grace, and they all left her alone again.

Grace wasn't surprised at them. She was aware that the whole island knew she was pregnant. Clíona had told her she should be grateful that Father Paddy had accelerated the counseling so they could marry quick. The counseling had consisted of pamphlets on God and Holy Matrimony. "If you have relations with your husband on a Saturday night," it said, "you will not be able to receive the sacrament on the Sunday."

(At Mass that week, Seamus had leaned over and whispered to Grace, "Mind the couples who don't go up for communion." She'd ignored him. Everything about this religion of hers seemed ridiculous. Blind people reciting prayers that were never answered. She wished there were some other way to marry Seamus, but the priest was their only option.)

Grace didn't care what people said about her, but she was surprised at Mary Louise's defending her. Surprised and furious. She should have kicked open the stall door and punched that Margaret in the lip. She didn't need Mary Louise sticking up for her, nor Seamus, nor Clíona. She didn't need any of them, and someday she'd make them all realize it.

When she returned to the party, Seamus was waiting anxiously for her. He took her hand, grazed his hot lips against her cheek, and said she looked pale.

"Do you feel all right, Mrs. O'Flaherty?" he smiled. She took her hand away.

At the church, when Father Paddy had told him to kiss the bride, Seamus had looked at her with such intensity, she'd forgotten she was angry at him, forgotten she was trapped. For an instant, he was everything she wanted and she was grateful as his warm kiss enveloped her. Then she opened her eyes and saw Clíona's grim relief, and wanted to rip the lace and satin off her ribs and run screaming from the church.

For their honeymoon, Seamus took Grace to Florence, where they stayed in a hotel overlooking the river, and spent their days in the museums, or drinking too much cappuccino. They made love every evening until Seamus was exhausted, then Grace watched him sleeping and listened to the hum of the dark city from the window. Grace liked Florence; it was dry and warm all day and night, and she soaked the sun in greedily. The Italian men were gorgeous, and paid her as much attention as Seamus allowed.

One afternoon while Seamus was napping, she slipped out and wandered the *mercato*, smiling at the men who tried to sell her "beautiful things for a lovely woman." She purchased a silk scarf the color of seaweed from a man wheeling a cart, who said the fabric matched her eyes. She went to a small museum which held four of Michelangelo's sculptures, staring for a long while at the Madonna and Child. The Virgin Mary's carved face had a mixture of euphoria, terror, and grief as she looked at the baby, an oversized thing with a grown man's self-absorbed face. Is that how I will feel? Grace thought, massaging her abdomen. Will I love my child and hate it at the same time? She didn't want to feel for her daughter the conflicting emotions she had for Seamus. She was also determined not to be like Clíona, making her daughter miserable while clucking that she did it out of love. She would name her daughter Gráinne, so she'd be strong. No one, not even Grace herself, would be able to smother her.

On the way back to the hotel, Grace met Seamus, who was walking briskly across the bridge.

"Where have you been?" he said angrily. She crossed her arms, backing away from him.

"Why is that your business?" she said. Seamus paused, then laughed, hugging her.

"I'm sorry," he whispered. She saw the man who had sold her the scarf, watching them. She didn't return Seamus's embrace.

"I thought you'd left me," Seamus said, holding her tighter. "I don't want to be like this, Grace. Tell me you won't leave me." It was because he sounded so vulnerable, and because the man with the scarves winked at her, that Grace put her arms around Seamus and smiled into his chest.

"Don't be silly," she said. "I love you."

★   ★   ★

Mary Louise gave birth to a boy, Liam, on October 29, with the island midwife and Clíona looking on. Grace, whom Mary Louise had asked to be there, sat outside the bedroom, squeezing Seamus's hand every time Mary Louise screamed.

"I want you to take me to the Galway hospital," Grace whispered to Seamus. Her baby was due at Christmas. "Where they can give me drugs." Seamus smiled.

"What happened to natural childbirth?" he said.

"Fuck that," Grace said. They could hear Mary Louise cursing Owen from the bedroom, and Owen murmuring for her to breathe.

When it was over, and the house filled up with visitors, Mary Louise wanted Grace to be the first one to hold Liam. Since Grace had gotten married, Mary Louise had been smothering her with sisterly affection. Grace had put up with it only because she'd been bored; there was nothing for a pregnant woman to do on the little island. But she told herself, whenever she pretended to listen to Mary Louise's chatter, that she would never end up like her stepsister. Trapped in a life that had been mapped out by the previous generations on the island. Where men were catered to like babies who couldn't fend for themselves, and women were expected to do everything and ask for nothing.

Grace took the bundled baby and scowled at it.

"You *would* have a boy," she said. Mary Louise laughed.

"Whatever you do, forget about the breathing business," Mary Louise said. "I just about murdered Owen at the end, puffing in my face the way he was, thinking he was being useful. He should have stayed pacing in the sitting room where he belongs."

They could hear Owen talking to Seamus in the other room.

"It's not so bad," Owen said. "Just keep her breathing and try not to hyperventilate."

Mary Louise rolled her eyes. "Hurry up and have your wee one, Grace," she said. "If it's a girl, she can marry my Liam."

Grace handed the baby back quickly. There was no chance her

daughter would marry an island boy—all the island men went from their mothers' laps to their wives', expecting to be spoiled. Except Seamus, who'd grown up without a mother and learned to take care of himself.

"Ah, no, he's hungry," Mary Louise said, looking terrified as the baby began to cry.

"How can you tell?" Grace said.

"Look at his mouth, he's opening and closing it like a hooked fish," Mary Louise said. "Quick, Grace, run and get your woman so she can show me what to do. And send the men to the pub. They'll just get under our feet here."

Grace's labor pains began on the morning of Christmas Eve. At first, they felt so much like the cramps that had come with her miscarriage, she woke Seamus up, crying.

"I think the baby's dying," she said. "Stop it, Seamus, the baby's falling out."

He called Mary Louise and Clíona, who calmed Grace down and convinced her that everything was normal. Seamus had Eamon bring them to the mainland on the ferry, even though it was snowing and the sea was rough. In the gas-stink of the cabin, Grace clung to Seamus's body, as though she were drowning. With each pain she wanted to dive overboard, where the cold sea would numb her middle. She would push Seamus away for an instant, then grab him again.

"I'm here," Seamus whispered, his hot breath swimming in her ear. "You're all right, Grace. I'm here."

At the Galway hospital, something went wrong. Grace did what the nurses told her, endured Seamus's silly breathing and coaching at her side. But the baby would not come. When the doctor came in he told her that the baby was backwards; they'd have to do a cesarean.

They wheeled her through cold hallways toward the operating room. Seamus jogged alongside and tried to keep hold of her hand.

Grace was thinking of her mother. Hadn't this happened to her? "Blood and scalpels" was how Clíona had always described it, as if Grace's birth had been more like a tragic accident than a blessed event.

"Am I dying?" she whispered to Seamus, and he shook his head roughly, though he was paler than she'd ever seen him.

"Don't speak of it," he said. "I will not let you die, you can be sure of that."

Then he was gone and she was spread out under spotlights, a masked woman covering her mouth and nose with a pear-shaped instrument. Grace felt her tongue soak up a sharp, poisonous air and she sunk, as if in thick water, feeling at the last moment as though she did not know how to swim.

When she woke up after the surgery, for an instant she thought it had all been a nightmare, and that she was back in Scituate, fifteen years old and waking up next to Michael. But Seamus was there.

"You're all right, Grace," he said. "We have a baby girl."

Together they studied the bandage on her stomach, peeling it away to look at the row of black stitches, like insect legs growing from her skin.

"Is that all?" she said, and Seamus kissed her. There was a dull pain in the muscles of her stomach, which fired up when she tried to move.

The nurse came in with Gráinne wrapped in a fuzzy pink blanket. Grace was terrified. What would she possibly do with this thing? But she softened when she saw the pink face, and she put her lips against the girl's tiny, perfect nose.

"I'm sorry I ever thought of giving you up," she whispered, so Seamus couldn't hear her.

Later, Clíona came in, smiling and carrying a vase of roses.

"How's she coming with the feeding?" Clíona said.

"She's perfect," Grace said. "Took to it right away. I think she

190

likes me." Seamus sat down on the side of the bed, putting his arm around Grace.

"Of course she does," he said, kissing her.

"She'll be a good baby, I suspect," Clíona said, squinting at the three of them. "You were a handful yourself."

Grace frowned, snuggling Gráinne closer. "So you've told me," she snapped.

"Ah, you were a joy nonetheless," Clíona added, blushing. Seamus squeezed Grace's arm. He leaned down to the baby and whispered something in Irish.

"What's that?" Grace said.

"Just a lullaby my father used to sing me," Seamus said.

"Can't you sing it in English?" Grace snapped, and Seamus laughed.

"I've never tried," he said.

Clíona went off to pester the nurses. Grace gave the baby her breast, and felt dizzy and aroused as Gráinne suckled. The baby was as warm as Seamus.

"Isn't she beautiful?" Grace whispered, and Seamus moved in closer.

"She is," he said. He put his hot mouth to Grace's ear. "I'm proud of you," he whispered.

Grace had a fierce urge to kiss him, but she wriggled away.

"You're holding me too tight," she said.

CHAPTER 23

Gráinne

September came with rain and cold wind and no word from my father. Clíona told me I'd be going to the island school with Liam. I didn't want to fall into the familiar routine of school clothes (here they wore uniforms), homework, and gym classes. If I went to school it would be like living here.

"You're fifteen years of age—you belong in school and that's final," Clíona said to me. She didn't look angry, but cold, like she was trying to remain strong and emotionless.

"What's the use in going to that dinky school when I'm leaving soon anyway?" I yelled back. I must have sounded really mean, because Clíona flinched and looked suddenly miserable.

"All right, Gráinne," she said and she turned away from me. It was too easy. I hesitated in the kitchen, but she seemed to have forgotten me; she looked out the window at the rain on the harbor and for an instant, from her expression, I thought someone must be drowning out there.

"I'm not going," I said again, mainly to see if she was listening to me.

"I heard you," Clíona said, running water over the dishes. "Do as you like." I left the kitchen, thumping up the stairs to my room.

For all her talk of wanting to be my family, she certainly wasn't acting like one. Even my mother, who had let me get away with almost anything, would have made me go to school. I was beginning to think that Clíona didn't want me here at all.

Liam had no time for me once school started. He was in class most of the day and at night he was swamped with homework. He was preparing for some big test—the Junior Cert, he called it—and he had more subjects than I'd ever had in school.

"You islanders certainly take education seriously," I said to him one afternoon. "For a bunch of fishermen."

Liam got mad. "We're not ignorant hicks, you know," he said. "We've one of the best public school systems in Europe."

"It was just a joke, Liam," I said. "You don't have to snap at me."

"Americans think the Irish are stupid and backward," Liam said.

"No, they don't," I said, but he just raised his eyebrows. "Well I don't," I added. "I'm sorry."

"Never mind," Liam muttered, trying to smile at me. "I'll see you at Sunday dinner, all right? I have to study now."

The days without Liam were so lonely, I almost regretted my decision about school. I walked the island until my legs felt bloodless and weak. I wrote ten different letters to Stephen, but they all sounded childish and whiny, so I tore them up. I wanted to sound like a woman, wanted Stephen to imagine my body the way it was at the beginning of the summer and long for me to come back. I knew I wasn't attractive now, I was a corpse with a screaming scar over my eye. When I saw myself in the mirror I looked like I was dying—trapped and starving, waiting for my father to come by sea and save me. I still stood on the quay in the evenings, as my father had once watched for me, though it was beginning to look like he would never come.

Sometimes, I woke up in the middle of the night terrified. In the dark, I would try to conjure up my mother's face, but it never came out right. Her features would be mixed up with Clíona's, or Mary Louise's. I'd started having dreams and memories of being a little girl, the first ones of my life that my mother wasn't in. When Clíona was bandaging my forehead, she'd been so close I could smell her yeasty skin, and I'd remembered sitting in her lap when I was little. We were on the beach, and she was showing me how to blow on a gold pinwheel, making it spin and shimmer in the sunlight. I couldn't get my mouth quite right, and I kept checking her pursed lips and trying to imitate them. In the memory, she was not the same stern, secretive woman. I called her Nana.

I had flashbacks of a man, his face white like the moon in his dark hair, singing to me. The song wasn't in English, but I could remember that I'd understood it, though I couldn't translate it now. And I could see myself with Liam, playing under the table in the pub, grownup legs and feet like a fence holding us in, the smell of cigarettes and my mother's musical laughter filtering down. The memories kept me from sleeping, and came with a sick fear that boiled in my hungry stomach.

One day while I was walking, the rain started in fat, hard drops, so I ducked into the church to wait for it to end. The weather here could change so quickly; not a cloud in the sky and then downpour. Sometimes there were even sun-showers—when the rain fell from midair and the sun shone simultaneously. The sun-showers depressed me; it was like the sky was lying.

The church was empty and I walked up the right-hand aisle softly, to keep my steps from echoing. The benches all had plaques on them, dedicated to dead people. The last names were familiar: MacNamara, O'Malley, O'Flaherty. It was strange to think I was related in some way to almost all of them. I'd been to Mass every

Sunday with Clíona but had never looked at this side of the church. We always sat on the left side, under the stained glass window that showed a mother and baby. Our bench had Clíona's mother's and father's names on it.

I liked going to Mass. I didn't understand it and didn't think of God like I was probably supposed to, but after a few times it was all familiar. I knew every word now, every gesture, and it was comforting, like reciting memorized poems in my head. When the priest laid out the bread and wine he always did it in the same order: he removed the draped cloths from front to back, folded them precisely, uncovered the goblets, and set everything in front of him like there was a map on the table to guide him. It made me think of helping my mother set the dinner table. Of the careful deception I now performed at every meal, moving my food around and slipping it into my napkin.

"Hello, Gráinne," a voice said, startling me from behind. It was Father Paddy, not in his Mass gown or even in black, but wearing fisherman's rubber overalls and boots. I felt silly, like I'd been caught trespassing.

"It was raining—" I started to explain, but he waved me off.

"You're always welcome here," he said. "I do not mean to disturb you."

"Oh, I wasn't doing anything," I said. I didn't want him to think I'd been praying or something; he might ask me questions about prayers I wouldn't be able to answer.

"It's a nice place to come when you've thinking to do," Father Paddy said.

"I guess so," I murmured.

"Your father comes here," he said, looking up at the stained glass windows. "These two were his favorite panels when he was a boy."

I followed the priest's eyes to the giant, dimly lit patterns. Each of the windows was divided into separate squares with people pieced together like miniature quilts.

"The one to the left is the Seven Deadly Sins," Father Paddy said. "And next to it, the Seven Virtues. Do you know them yourself?"

"No," I said, though I vaguely remember my mother referring sarcastically to such a thing.

"That first figure on top—the man with the puffed-out chest—that's Pride. Then the fat man drinking—Gluttony. It's Anger that the arguing couple there represent. The lazy-looking fellow in the center is Sloth; the man looking over the fence, Envy. That skinny fellow with the large purse is the miser; he represents Avarice. Then you see the sinful lovers—Lust. The bottom panel is the devil raking all the sinners into Hell." Father Paddy smiled and winked at me. "I wouldn't dwell on that part."

I couldn't tell if he was teasing me or not. My mother, when I was hard to get out of bed in the morning, used to bang on her teacup with a spoon and yell: "Sloth is one of the Deadly Sins!" I thought she'd made it up. After her first dates we had a ritual. "Love or Lust, Mom?" I'd say, and she'd smile, the edges of her mouth raw from too much kissing. "Lust," she'd say. The first time she'd gone out with Stephen she'd said, "Lust, with potential." We certainly didn't consider Lust a sin. My mother didn't even believe in sins, or religion at all.

Yet my mother once knew how all this church stuff worked, the stories and prayers, everything I didn't understand myself.

"Here's the Seven Virtues in this window," Father Paddy went on. "Helping the needy, then clothing the naked, tending the sick—your grandmother is a lovely example of that virtue. Then visiting prisoners—can you see the tiny face peering out the cell bars? Along the bottom: feeding the hungry, comforting the fatherless, and the laying out of the dead. All of which leads you to Saint Peter at the gates of Heaven."

The hungry stained glass figure looked like my mother had in her purple robe—her neck so thin it made her head look heavy and fragile. The fatherless figure was a glass child. I supposed that would be me. Why was fatherless so much worse than motherless? I didn't see anything so virtuous about laying out a dead person; that was easy enough. It was tending the sick that was the hard one. I'd watched Stephen do it, from the other side of a sliding glass door.

"What are the fishes for?" I asked. There was one carved under each window, all of them bent like they were swimming.

"The fish represents Christ," Father Paddy said.

"What about mermaids?" I asked, and he looked like he was trying not to laugh.

"I'm afraid it is not my jurisdiction, the mermaid," he said. "You're better off asking your father that."

"Um, Father?" I said, knowing that was what I was supposed to call him, but feeling ridiculous.

"Yes?"

"You know that part of Mass where you hold up the cups and say: 'This is my body, it will be given up for you'?"

"I'm familiar with the phrase, yes." He smiled.

"What does that mean, exactly?"

"Ah," the priest said, linking his hands behind his back like he did sometimes during Mass. "Jesus knew he was going to die. That is why he gathered the Last Supper before his crucifixion. He gave himself up in his death—he suffered so we would not have to."

"Well it didn't work," I said. "Because people suffer anyway."

"I'm not speaking of day-to-day suffering," Father Paddy said, "but the suffering of death without redemption."

"Oh," I said. "So if you're Catholic, that's what you believe? That Jesus gets you into Heaven?"

"That's the bare bones of it anyway," he said. "Also that Jesus gives us a model of how to live a virtuous life."

"That's what Clíona believes, and my father?" I said.

"Aye. They're good Catholics, all your family."

"My mother wasn't," I said.

"Well I did not know what your mother believed, Gráinne. I'm sorry to say that I did not know her well."

"I don't know if I believe it either," I said. I glared at him, daring him to be angry with me. But he smiled.

"I don't think you're supposed to know what you believe in at fifteen," he said. "I imagine that's why it's so difficult."

I believe in my mother, I wanted to say, but I kept quiet. I believed in who I was when I was with her. But now I'm not sure of anything.

The stained glass windows brightened suddenly, casting a pattern of blue and red on Father Paddy's shiny scalp.

"It stopped raining," I said. "I have to go now."

"Come see me if you're needing to talk, Gráinne," he said. "I run off at the mouth a bit, but I'm a good listener as well."

"Okay," I said, but I didn't really think I'd be back. He could answer questions about windows and prayers but he couldn't tell me what I needed to know. Like who I was and why I was here. Or why my father, the only one who could answer my questions, would not come to see me.

I left the church and headed for the beach, the warm sun only emphasizing how damp and cold my clothes were.

Mom, I said to myself before I thought about it, *can't I come home now?* As if I were only away at camp, proving to her that I could be brave and independent, and that once it was over she would reward me by taking back her place at my side.

My body was changing again. One morning, while I was putting on my new, smaller bra, the underwired cups slid up over my chest and dangled beneath my collarbone. I had no breasts left. Only shrunken plum-sized protrusions beneath my nipples. Like most of the flesh had been lopped off and my nipples stitched back on. It was not only my flesh that was giving way; my blood seemed to be going, too. When I walked, my fingers and toes turned purple with death-white splotches. "Bad circulation," Clíona said to me, looking worried. I wore so many layers I was sure she couldn't tell that I had practically no body beneath them. I imagined that eventually my clothes would cave in on themselves, drop to the ground like a witch's cloak, and I would vanish completely.

By the time Liam's sixteenth birthday came in late October, I was having dizzy spells, and Clíona was talking of sending me to the doctor. I put her off, faking a cold. She no longer really believed I was eating, but kept putting plates of food in front of me anyway. The neighbor's dog learned to wait outside our door at dinnertime, and I would sneak her whatever I'd managed to mash into my napkin.

Clíona planned a joint birthday party for me and Liam, even though my birthday wasn't until Christmas Eve, because she said we'd always celebrated together as babies. Mary Louise thought Liam's father, Owen, might make it home for the party; he had radioed they were on their way home. For some reason, this made me as nervous as Liam was excited. He came to the quay with me in the evenings, to watch for the trawler.

The morning of the party, I woke to what sounded like waves crashing over the roof of the house. When I looked outside, I saw it was the wind, whipping rain and swaying the power lines on the island. Our electricity was out, which meant no hot showers, but Clíona made the dinner and cake on the gas range in the hotel.

Mary Louise pulled me aside in the house kitchen, to give me my birthday card in private. Inside she had written the address of *The Irish Times* in Dublin and a phone number.

"You'll be able to reach your father with that," she said. I didn't answer. I already had the number of the paper; I'd looked it up in the hotel phone book. I'd almost called my father a few times, but something kept me from going through with it. Once I'd gotten as far as the *Irish Times* receptionist, but lost my voice when she'd said: "Extension, please."

"Gráinne," Mary Louise said softly. I couldn't look at her. "Waiting doesn't always get you what you want. Sometimes, it's the waiting on a thing that causes it to pass you by."

"Tell that to my father," I said, shoving her card in my jeans pocket.

"I'm telling it to you," she said. "In Ireland, Gráinne," she whispered, "you're best not depending on the man to make the first move." She walked out to join the family.

Liam and I blew out the candles together. I didn't answer when Clíona asked what I'd wished for. *Family*, was what my mind had automatically called out, though the table was full of so-called relatives. To me, "family" was only another word for my mother.

When Clíona was slicing the cake, Eamon came into the hotel, dripping water and looking battered from the wind. He said that Owen's boat had lost radio contact.

"Don't worry, now," Eamon said. "I'm just letting you know Owen won't make it for the party. I suspect they're holed up somewhere, sitting out the storm."

Mary Louise decided to go back to her house to wait by the radio. Liam said I could come, but Clíona tried to stop me.

"There's nothing you can do there except get under your aunt's feet," she said. "Stay here, I want to talk to you."

"Leave me alone," I said, pulling away from her. "I'm going to wait for Liam's father."

I fell asleep on Mary Louise's couch. When I woke in the middle of the night, I saw Liam sitting up in a chair by the fire. He was raking the coal, his face glowing orange and moist.

"Liam," I whispered. He didn't look at me. "Are you scared?" He wiped his cheek with his sweater sleeve and shoveled more chunks of coal on the flames. The fire exploded and spat upward. Tiny black slivers pinged against the grate.

"Go back to sleep, Gráinne," he said.

I drifted off and dreamed I was in a curragh on stormy seas. I flung myself overboard, and a mermaid was waiting for me. I grabbed on to her neck and rested my cheek against her soft, floating hair. She swam toward warmth and light, which I thought at first was at the surface, then realized, as the water filled my lungs, was the bottom of the sea.

At dawn Liam woke me to say he could see the trawler pulling in to the harbor. We ran down to the quay, the rain soft and misty, the smell of low tide seeping into my skin. There was a group of islanders already there waiting with Clíona, Marcus, and Mary Louise. When the blue trawler pulled up to the quay steps, women ran forward to meet their husbands. I stayed back, watching.

Liam was tying the ropes onto a column, to steady the boat. The fishermen came up one at a time, looking tired and sea-worn. They all looked like island men, the ruddy faces, similar noses, and untrimmed beards. Women took them into their arms, and with each reunion, I looked at the next man for Liam's father, whom I'd only seen pictures of. Two more men came up the stairs. A pause in the line and then one last fisherman. They were all so wet and bundled, I could have missed him, so I looked at each man again. He wasn't with them.

"He's not there," I said, a lump like dense fog in my throat. I heard voices in my head, mixed together in one long, mournful noise that sounded like the windblown singing of mermaids.

"Clíona," Marcus said, touching her shoulder and gesturing down the pier. She looked up and her face went hard and pale. I turned and looked myself. Mary Louise was standing at the edge of the quay, swaying in the wind, her dress flapping wetly behind her. The fishermen were standing to one side, appealing to her to step back. Her mouth was wide open, and I realized that the sound in my head was actually her, screaming.

"Dear God in Heaven," Clíona said, crossing herself, "the sea's taken Owen." She left me then, and walked down the pier. She pulled Mary Louise back from the lip, held her steady with her large hands on my aunt's little shoulders. She said something to Mary Louise that I couldn't hear. But it made my aunt stand a bit straighter, and her screaming stopped, and faded out over the water.

In the pale morning light, with Mary Louise's undone hair, it almost looked like my mother Clíona was holding. My mother and my grandmother, grief flowing out of one and strength coming in from the other. I wanted to join them. But it wasn't my mother, it was Liam's. And Liam's father, Owen, who played the fiddle, whom I hadn't seen since I was three years old and couldn't even remember, was dead.

I watched Liam, who took his mother's arm and helped Clíona guide her away from the boat. His face looked blank, but I knew he must be terrified, and I was surprised to see him walking so calmly. He was fatherless. I expected him to bolt off, run away from it all, vanishing into the fog. But he got in an islander's car with his mother, and before I knew it, it was me that was running, the rain like needles against my eyes, sprinting blindly away from the voices that called my name out like a song.

CHAPTER 24

Grace

"Do you hear that, Gráinne?" Grace whispered. She knelt down to where her daughter was digging in the sand. "It's the mermaids, they're singing."

The little girl rose from her squatting position, putting a hand on her mother's shoulder to steady herself. She stretched her neck, listening in the way that Grace loved—as if she were using her entire body to capture the sound.

"Mer-mays," Gráinne repeated, her coal-colored eyes widening.

"They're ladies, sweetie," Grace said. "Ladies who live in the sea."

"Mer-laylees," Gráinne said. She cocked her head in the direction of the singing wind. "Plitty."

"Yes, it's pretty," Grace said. She brushed the violet-black curls from Gráinne's forehead.

Gráinne squatted again, returned to shoveling sand. She took her time, lifting each shovelful slowly and patting its contents into a neat pile. Grace watched her. Her little girl was so careful, so graceful in her movements. She surveyed every situation before plunging in. She liked to taste things, touch them, before accepting them. She smelled her own fingers periodically throughout the day, to see what invisible layers they had collected. She was rarely frustrated, never impatient, even at two years old. Grace envied her.

From the first moment she had held Gráinne, Grace had not wanted to put her down. The baby's sweet, warm skin was unlike any body Grace had ever known. That first year she had wanted to keep Gráinne to herself, but she couldn't go anywhere without nosy, peering island faces. Mary Louise kept calling in with Liam, or jogging along with the carriage to catch up with Grace on the road. Whenever Grace met island women, they'd pick up the baby without invitation.

"Is that Seamus's girl?" Mrs. Keane would say. "My, she's getting big. She's the image of her father—Grace, I don't see a sign of you." Grace got into the habit of whispering into Gráinne's baby ears everything she couldn't say to others.

"How it's possible that Mrs. Keane can be uglier than her husband, I do not know. Next time she holds you, Gráinne, spit up on her." The baby's eyes sparkled, and followed Grace's voice.

"She worships you," Seamus always said, but Grace was jealous at how much the baby adored him. When he spoke to her in Irish, Gráinne laughed and gurgled as if they were conversing. It was like their secret language, and Grace hated it.

"I'll teach it to you, too," Seamus said, but Grace ignored him.

"Your father's a sexy man, Gráinne, but he's manipulative," she said, and the girl smiled.

"Why do you say things like that?" Seamus said, angry. "You'll confuse her."

"I tell her everything I think," Grace said.

"And that's what you think of me?" Seamus said, handing her the baby.

Grace kissed him. "Only sometimes," she said.

Gráinne kept Grace warm in the daytime—a clean, powder warmth that Grace breathed in hungrily. At night, it was Seamus who heated her, from the musky fire within his chest, and made her believe, in that moment before dreaming, that her body would die without him.

Seamus only left her when he was given a newspaper assignment he could not resist. He made most of their meager living on his father's fishing boat, but would not give up the journalism, no matter how Grace begged him. She didn't like his being away, for it was when he wasn't next to her that she imagined leaving him.

He was often sent to the North, where there was fighting, to interview paramilitaries and men in prison starving themselves in protest. When he returned from these trips, his mind stayed away. For days he would be distant, he wouldn't seem to see Grace, he would mutter and curse to himself, or bury his face in Gráinne's hair, looking miserable. It was the only time Grace ever felt she had no effect on him, and this frightened her.

"Why do you have to go there?" Grace said once, as he was packing his camera bag. "It's dangerous. What if you get shot?"

"I'm a journalist," Seamus said. "Someone has to listen to these people and tell their story."

"Why does it have to be you?"

"I'm Irish, Grace. This is my country—my countrymen who are digesting their own organs in jail. We have our freedom, you and Gráinne and I. They don't. The least I can do is help them demand it."

Grace did not feel she had her freedom. When Seamus was not there, his island was her jail. She hated his love for his country, wanted him to love her as much as he did those anonymous, violent men. She wanted him to give up everything for her, the way she imagined she had for him. She was afraid, when he left her alone, that she might disappear. That she might make herself disappear.

On the nights Seamus was home, he and Gráinne had a bedtime ritual. He would tuck her in, sing to her, and when she started to fight her sleepiness, he would put a hand on her forehead.

"Can I close my eyes?" Gráinne would say in her charming new voice.

"Yes," Seamus would say. "Close your eyes."

"What if I open them?" Gráinne would yawn.

"I'll still be here," Seamus would say.

Grace always listened to them with guilt flooding through her. When Grace closed her eyes, she imagined opening them in a place far away from Inis Murúch.

Grace began to go to the pub with Mary Louise when Seamus was away. Owen and the other musicians would play for the summer tourists, and the crowds made the island seem almost exciting. Grace and Mary Louise would put their toddlers together in a carriage, and the two slept peacefully through the noise. Grace would drink hot whiskeys until the room blurred with excitement and possibility. She would run her fingers through her hair and return the appreciative glances of new men.

Toward the end of one night, Grace was sitting in a corner booth, flirting with a young Norwegian man. He kept his hand on her thigh while he wooed her in broken English, gazing at her with ice-blue eyes. Mary Louise interrupted them, telling Grace that Gráinne was looking to be fed. The man excused himself, scurrying off at the mention of a child. Grace went over to the carriage, but the kids were still asleep.

"What's the idea?" Grace said to her stepsister.

"Would you tell me what you think you're doing with that man?" Mary Louise said. "What will Seamus think?"

"I was only talking," Grace said. "And Seamus isn't here. Who's going to tell him, you?"

"The first person he sees when he gets off the boat will tell him," Mary Louise whispered.

"I'll talk to whoever I want," Grace said. "It's nobody's business."

Mary Louise sighed and patted Grace's arm. Grace could tell by the look on her face that her stepsister thought Grace was only being friendly. She wanted to smack her. Mary Louise was the stupidest woman alive.

"I wouldn't want people to get the wrong idea, is all," Mary Louise said. Gráinne woke up then and called for her mother. Grace picked her up.

"I'm mapping out escape routes," Grace whispered to her. Gráinne laughed and repeated her, her babyish voice rising and falling in waves like her father's.

In August, when the nights were warm, Seamus and Grace would leave their daughter with Clíona and walk to a secluded beach on the western end of the island, to watch the sunset. If she closed her eyes, and blocked out the bleating sheep, Grace could almost pretend they were somewhere else, and that behind them there was so much more than that little island. She remembered back to when the dark blanket had fallen over her mind and she had thought that getting Seamus would be the answer to everything.

Once they stayed beneath the sheltering cliffs until after dark, building a fire from driftwood and a broken fence. Grace stood looking out at the dark sea, listening to the waves sizzling up after her. Seamus wrapped his arms around her from behind, pressing his fiery chest against her back.

"How is it that you're so warm?" Grace said, craning her neck back so he could kiss her.

"It's not me that's warm." Seamus laughed. "It's that you're always cold."

"Maybe," Grace murmured.

"Do you know why the mermaid fell in love with my great-great-grandfather?" he said.

"Good kisser?" Grace said. Seamus smiled into her hair.

"Because his body was the warmest thing she could find outside of the sea."

His voice was like cords pulling everything inside her toward him. She turned around, kissed him so deeply that he whimpered far back in his throat.

"Tell me you're happy," he whispered, and she nodded automatically. "If I let go," Seamus said, "would you dive back to your home beneath the sea?"

Grace leaned her head into his chest. "I don't know," she said. "Could I take you with me?"

"Sure, I'd go anywhere with you," Seamus said, locking his fingers behind her so she couldn't wriggle away.

"But we don't," Grace said. "We never go anywhere."

"I'll take you to Dublin next week," Seamus said.

"That's not what I meant at all," Grace said.

Seamus kissed her earlobe, and her body lit up like a raked fire. "You haven't given it enough time," he said. "You're getting happier every day, I can see it. Wait awhile."

Grace wanted to say she could be on this island for centuries and never be happy, but Seamus was kissing her, filling her with a heat that swallowed her words.

He took off their clothes and made a blanket on the sand, pulled her down and made love to her slowly, and for so long that Grace was delirious. She thought she heard the singing of the mermaids in the coves, a sensuous chant calling to her in the same rhythm as Seamus's sliding hips. But when he clamped his mouth on hers, she realized she'd been moaning, so loudly that her voice echoed in the cliff walls.

The next time he was in Belfast, Seamus sent her a letter. Inside was a poem, copied out in his neat, almost feminine script.

I went out to the hazel wood,
Because a fire was in my head,
And cut and peeled a hazel wand,
And hooked a berry to a thread;
And when white moths were on the wing,
And moth-like stars were flickering out,
I dropped the berry in a stream
And caught a little silver trout.

When I had laid it on the floor
I went to blow the fire aflame,
But something rustled on the floor,
And someone called me by my name:
It had become a glimmering girl
With apple blossom in her hair
Who called me by my name and ran
And faded through the brightening air.

Though I am old with wandering
Through hollow lands and hilly lands,
I will find out where she has gone,
And kiss her lips and take her hands;
And walk among long dappled grass,
And pluck till time and times are done
The silver apples of the moon,
The golden apples of the sun.

"He'll follow us, Gráinne," Grace said, folding the paper carefully. Gráinne was playing with the miniature tea set Clíona had given her for her second birthday. "Wherever we need to go, he'll follow us."

"*I* know that," Gráinne said, pouring invisible tea into a special cup, the one she'd just recently begun to save for the mermaid.

CHAPTER 25

Gráinne

The sea had not taken Owen MacNamara's body, but swallowed it
and spat it back up with the life gone. The men on the boat had
found his broken form on the rocks of an uninhabited island, as if
sea creatures had ravaged it then tossed it away. They delivered him
to the mainland so the undertaker could prepare the remains for the
funeral. I overheard all this in the whispered conferences of Clíona
and Marcus, who assumed I was sleeping. Clíona sounded almost
like she was crying, though it wasn't like her. Two days after the
storm, every islander who could walk stood on the quay, waiting
for the ferry to deliver Owen's coffin.

As the boat rounded the harbor entrance by Granuaile's castle,
the church bells began to gong, so loudly the ground vibrated beneath our feet. The men, looking stern and pale, lifted the coffin
from the boat and carried it up to Liam's house. There was an open

viewing, where Mary Louise and her children sat to one side, and the islanders stopped to kneel by Owen's swollen, rubbery face. There were monstrous flower arrangements with blue ribbons that said *Da, Beloved Husband*, and *Captain*, and three candles lit in a semicircle around his head. I listened in awe as the islanders said things to Mary Louise and Liam that no one had dared say to me. People hadn't talked about my mother at her funeral, except to say stupid things like how full and lovely her face looked, considering. I remembered, watching Liam nod to mourners, how I'd snapped at a woman from my mother's work.

"They stuffed her cheeks with cotton," I'd said. She'd stuttered and turned to Stephen, to get away from me.

In Liam's house, there was drinking and laughter in the kitchen, and men telling funny stories about Owen. The women cried openly and clutched at Mary Louise.

"You're all alone now, God love you," they said to her. It was true, of course, but I was amazed that people were saying such things out loud. Mary Louise only nodded and gave a comforting smile. People kept reminding Liam that he was now the man of the house.

"You'll have to take his place in the pub as well," Marcus said. "Your father was a great one for the craic, boy." I thought it was mean to remind Liam what he was missing, but he thanked them. Imagine if my mother's funeral had been like this, I thought. People commenting on her bad wig, reminding me I was an orphan, saying "I heard she never even said good-bye to her own child."

I couldn't think of anything bold to say, but when I took Liam's hand, I tried to squeeze in meaning, to hold it the way he'd always held mine. He didn't seem to notice, but moved on to the next hand in line.

"Why are the mirrors covered?" I asked Clíona, when she came and stood beside me.

"Ah, it's just an old superstition," she whispered. "Some believe if you look into the mirror just after a death, it's the spirit's face you'll be seeing instead of your own."

I remembered cutting my hair in front of that cottage mirror. How I'd said my name again and again, making myself a stranger. I would have given anything to see my mother's face looking back at me.

"Is that a Catholic thing?" I asked Clíona, and she laughed. I couldn't get used to all this laughing during a funeral.

"Ah, no, Gráinne," she said. "We Irish are devout Catholics, but we're fanatic pagans as well." Liam's grandfather, who had been sitting quiet and frail on a chair just behind me, giggled.

After the funeral service, the islanders walked in a line behind the pallbearers, up the long hill to the graveyard. I'd never been sure which or how many of the island children were Liam's siblings, but now I could distinguish five of them with Mary Louise, all boys, looking like those identical dolls that come out of one another— becoming smaller and smaller in the same black suits. Liam helped carry the coffin and he was as tall as the other men, though thinner.

At the grave, Father Paddy said a prayer that started: *Yea, though I walk through the valley of the shadow of death, I shall fear no evil, for thou art with me.*

The priest had said that at my mother's funeral. I realized now that the prayer was supposed to be in the voice of the dead person. At my mother's grave, I had thought it was me walking through the shadow of death. And I was afraid, because my mother was not there.

The rest of Father Paddy's words drowned in my ears; I could only hear a pulsing—a wavering, muffled sound, as though I were listening under water.

The men put the coffin in the ground, covered it with dirt, then a layer of stones and shells.

"How long is Da gonna be in there?" Liam's smallest brother asked, which made people who had stopped crying start up again. They wailed as loudly and unabashedly as they had been laughing before. Mary Louise picked the boy up and whispered in his ear.

They would all be able to come back here, I thought, on anniversaries and whenever they missed him; they would plant flowers and an engraved stone. My mother was in a stoneless grave south of Boston. I wouldn't remember which grave it was even if I got back there. I would never be able to show it to my father.

Clíona put her hand on my shoulder and tried to pass me a handkerchief. I stepped away and wiped my eyes, looking at the tears on my palms. With the sun burning my vision, the sliding drops looked like blood.

The next morning, I packed a bag with clean underwear, the carving of Granuaile, and my passport, in case I had to prove to my father who I was. I wore my mother's claddagh engagement ring on my index finger. When Clíona left to check in hotel guests, I snuck down to the kitchen and took forty pounds from the grocery jar. I'd woken up hot and fuzzy-headed, so I gulped down four aspirin from the bottle next to the oven. I left through the kitchen door so Clíona would not see me from the hotel.

When I reached the ferry, it was Eamon's son who helped me on. I was relieved; he'd just moved home from the mainland and didn't really know me, so wouldn't ask questions. I sat on a crate with my back against the damp wood of the cabin. Just before we were scheduled to leave, an American family got on. I recognized them from the hotel: a husband and wife about my mother's age, and an awkward, moody-looking girl of ten.

When we pulled away from the quay, Eamon came out of the cabin and sat down beside me. I half expected him to scold me, but he was calmly cutting an apple with his pocketknife, eating each sliver before he cut another.

"Is it going to see your father, you are?" he said, when the apple was half gone.

"No," I said, too quickly. "I'm just doing errands for Clíona."

Eamon nodded, licking spatters of apple juice from his mustache. "You'll want to take the train from Galway," he said. "If you put a pleasant face on you, those Americans there'll give you a lift to the station."

He stood up then, went over to the couple and said something I couldn't hear, and the mother smiled at me, nodding in agreement. Eamon walked past my side toward the cabin.

"Thank you," I said, suddenly on the verge of tears. Why was this man, whom I'd never said one nice word to, helping me? He winked and handed me the last slice of fruit before disappearing inside. I tossed the apple, which had browned quickly in the air, into the rushing gray water below.

The American mother came over to me, swaying on the rocky floorboards.

"I understand you're an islander," she said. "We're visiting from Boston, in the United States."

I almost snapped at her, almost told her where I was really from. But, for some reason, I changed my voice, and the music of Clíona came out of my mouth.

"I am," I said. "Did you enjoy your holiday?" I was even convincing to myself.

The mother was awfully interested in me. She asked me stupid questions: Did I go to school? Did I speak Gaelic? Had I ever seen a mermaid? She spoke very loudly, emphasizing her words, and I thought it was because of the sound of the engine and the wind. But when we docked in town, she kept yelling, as though I were deaf, or didn't speak English. We walked up the main street to their rental car, her husband dragging the suitcase on wheels.

"Here, I'll put your bag in the trunk," he said to me. I had forgotten it was called a trunk—on the island, they called it "the boot." He stuffed my backpack in with a pile of green plastic tourist bags.

"I want my Irish girl," his daughter demanded, and he dug for a minute, then pulled out a boxed doll.

"I feel like we've spent the entire week shopping," he said to me, and winked. I rolled my eyes, in conspiracy with him, a reaction that came to me automatically. My mother's boyfriends, Stephen included, used to do that all the time—whisper to me about what they thought were strange feminine habits: excessive shopping, canisters of cotton balls in the bathroom, rolled napkins in silver rings at the dinner table. As if they thought, because I was only a girl and not a woman, that I would find it as foreign as they did. I'd always played along, because it was one thing I could share with them that even my mother couldn't.

We climbed in the car; I had to sit in the back with the daughter and another pile of purchases. The girl hadn't said one word to me yet.

"Show her your doll, honey," the mother said, shifting to face us from the passenger seat. The daughter reluctantly turned the plastic-filmed box, displaying a doll with bright red hair, green eyes, and a green velvet dress with a claddagh stitched into the chest. It was strangely familiar, like someone had made a doll version of my mother, or Mary Louise.

"Her name's Meghan," the daughter said. She moved the box down and the doll's eyes closed, so she looked like she was laid out in a tiny, plastic-covered coffin.

"Do you leave her in the box so she won't get ruined?" I said. The daughter smiled, and nodded at me. "I used to do that, as well," I said in my new accent.

"What's your name?" she asked, warming to me.

"Gráinne," I said, hearing my mother's voice.

"Like the lady in the castle?" the girl said. "The queen pirate?"

"Aye," I said. "It's her I was named for."

"What a lovely name," the mother said. "Are you actually a descendant of that queen?"

"They say so, yes," I said, though no one had ever mentioned such a thing to me.

"How nice to know so much about your family," the mother said. "I was adopted, and I've been told my birth parents came from Ireland. I was hoping I could look up their history, but I haven't had time this trip. I picked up this pamphlet, though." She was

215

searching through her purse. "It's an application for a heritage tracing. You're lucky, you have all your history around you."

Lucky? I felt suddenly guilty, pretending to have an accent, pos-
ing as a child from a nuclear, grounded family. These three people
were more of a family than I'd ever been a part of.

"Do they work?" the mother asked me.

"What?" I said. I was starting to feel carsick, and her voice was
fading, like she was backing slowly away.

"These heritage tracing places. Do they work, or is it a tourist
scam?"

"I wouldn't know," I said. I rolled down my window, exposing
my fevered face to the damp, cool air. "My mother's dead," I added,
in my own voice. No one heard me but the daughter; she clung to
her boxed girl and looked at me wide-eyed, waiting to see what evil
thing I might do.

I met a boy on the train. He sat down across from me in my
booth, sprawling his skinny arms across the breadth of the table between us.

"Do you fancy a bit of company?" he said, once he'd settled
himself. He had greasy hair pulled into a painful-looking ponytail;
his teeth and the delicate inner skin of his lips were brownish-yellow.
His eyes, though, like saucers of black ink, could have been mine.

"Why not," I said, doing my best to stare level at him.

He took out a blue pouch and rolled two cigarettes out of twiggy
tobacco, offering me one. I inhaled, and the woodsy smoke seemed
to seep over my brain at the same time as it filled my lungs.

He talked, for what seemed like a long while. The smoke was
muddling my head, so that I could hear only rhythmic snatches of
sound like the break of a wave, and then I went under again. The
few words I heard him pronounce seemed to have no reference to
each other. I must have talked back. Must have invited him over to
my side of the booth, must have allowed the bonfire taste of his
tongue to invade my mouth. It could have been me that eased open

his fly, though I was only conscious of sliding my fingers into the gap.

"Jesus!" he yelped, and pulled back. He was pressing my blue-tinged fingers in his palms. "I thought you'd slapped a fish in there," he said. "You've the coldest hands on earth."

"That's because I'm dead," I heard a voice say. His smile faltered.

"What?" he said, dropping my hands. He slid out of the booth, zipping up his fly. There was an older couple at the other end of the car, looking at me. *Slut*, their silent voices said.

"You're one fucked-up girl," the boy said to me. I wondered, but didn't ask, what his problem was. He strutted away down the aisle and forced open the door that led to the dining car, letting it slam shut behind him.

He'd left his pouch of tobacco and papers. For the rest of the journey I rolled loose, misshapen cigarettes, inhaled red embers, and pressed my cold fingers against my fiery forehead.

In Dublin, I walked down streets crowded with people who moved like Bostonians, swiftly and expertly weaving their way. At the *Irish Times* office, a woman called four different extensions to find out who the hell Seamus O'Flaherty was.

"Sorry, dear, it's me first day," she whispered, her hand over the mouthpiece.

I sat down on a padded stool, a ringing in my ears.

"Nope, he's not in today," the woman finally said. "He's on assignment, in Belfast."

"Still?" I said. Belfast was where those starving prisoners were, in the article he wrote when I was a baby.

"They keep the journalists busy in the North," the woman said. She squinted at me. "Are you all right, pet?"

"When's he coming back?" I said, standing up. I had to grab the corner of her desk, I was so dizzy.

"He's due back tomorrow," she said. "Do you want to ring someone?"

I walked out of the lobby without answering her. There wasn't anyone for me to call.

Out on the street it had begun to rain. I stood for a moment, then leaned against the side of the building, sliding down until I was sitting, clutching my knees. I couldn't go anywhere else, or ask any more questions. I will sit here, I thought, and wait. I tried to remember the poems I had once taped on my wall, but all that came to me were the words from the funeral. I could hear phones ringing hysterically inside the lobby. I put my forehead in the crook of my arm and closed my eyes on the sparks that were taking over my vision.

I must have fallen asleep, because when I felt the hand on my shoulder, I looked up and it was nighttime. Liam was leaning over me, raindrops smearing his worried face.

"Gráinne," he said, helping me stand up, "are you all right? Why are you sitting here in the rain?"

"I'm waiting for my father," I said. My voice sounded odd, though I had stopped using Clíona's accent.

"When's he due back?" Liam said.

"Tomorrow." I tried to clear my vision by pressing my thumbs against my eyelids. "How did you get here?" I said.

"I hitched." Liam smiled. He looked tired; I recognized the recent death inked below his eyes—I'd seen it on Stephen's face when I'd moved in to kiss him. I shrugged Liam's arm off my own.

"I don't need the whole stinking island following me," I said. I believe I was slurring. Liam pushed my hair off my forehead, letting loose rivulets of water at my temples.

"Always have to be the tough one, don't you, Queen Gráinne?" he whispered. He was looking at my mouth and for a second I thought he was going to kiss me. I wasn't prepared for how my knees turned watery. But before I could adjust, he pulled me along, so we were walking in the direction of the rain.

"We'll have to find accommodation," he said. "You'll be dosed if you don't get out of those wet things."

He brought me to a damp-smelling bed-and-breakfast above a fish-and-chips shop. The lady who showed us the dingy room looked at me with disapproval. Once she'd left us alone, Liam made me change out of my clothes, turning his face away and handing me his flannel shirt. I could barely manage the buttons; my fingertips had no feeling left in them.

He tucked me under the blankets of one of the twin beds and turned out the light. My pillow smelled faintly of vinegar. I watched his shadowy form as he removed his shoes and jeans and slipped under the covers of the bed beside me. He lit a cigarette, briefly illuminating his ivory cheeks. I watched the burning coil move from his mouth to the ashtray and back again.

"Liam?" I whispered.

"Yeah?" he said. The darkness of the room was so heavy, I imagined he could hear my thoughts.

"Thanks for coming after me," I said. It wasn't what I'd meant to say, but Liam, as though he didn't know this, answered me anyway.

"I needed to get off the island for a while," he said. "I couldn't breathe there. It's been like the plague or something, the last few days."

I knew what he meant. Since Owen drowned, the islanders hadn't only been sad, they'd been sick. Despite their laughter, they didn't just pay their respects and go home, but carried death around like a virus.

"I was just thinking how strange it is," Liam said. "I grew up being told my father might drown every time he went off to sea. Islanders drown every year, sometimes a whole family of men at once. Da always said a prayer at dinner before he left, asking God to bring him home safely. So I should have expected it, you know? But I never really believed it could happen to him." Liam wiped his nose with the edge of the sheet.

"You were lucky in a way," he added. "Your mum was sick first, so you had time to say good-bye."

When he said that, my ears filled again, and the sounds of the room slowed and rose in volume, so it was like I was listening to the world from under the sea. The pillow beneath my cheek was cold and soaked with salty water.

"Liam?" I said, my own thick voice echoing in my ears. "Do you ever feel like you're drowning? You can't reach the surface and you're filling up so quickly with water that you know soon there won't be room for anything else? But you're not in the water." I gasped, swallowing the smoky air. Was it possible to forget how to breathe? I wanted to ask him. Was that how my mother and his father finally died? "You're drowning," I whispered, "but you're not in the water at all."

I stopped talking when Liam pulled back my covers and crawled into bed beside me. He pressed his body full-length against mine, and I could feel him hard against my hipbone. I took his hand, moved it up to my breast, automatically surrendering myself to what might happen. But he pulled his hand away. He crawled over me and lay so my back was to him, holding my hands still against my stomach.

"Don't, Gráinne," he whispered, but he did not move away. I stopped thrashing and let the warmth of his body pour into mine. "You're all right," he said, over and over in the darkness, and I wanted more than anything to believe him. I did not sleep, but only lay there, wrapped and motionless within him, tracing the rhythm of his breath as it parted, then smoothed again, the delicate hairs above my ear.

In the morning, as we walked back to *The Irish Times* building, I watched the rush hour mob of professional people. As in Boston, the crowds were a complicated choreography of briefcases, clicking shoe heels, and blank, unwelcoming faces. I searched for my father in the lineup of suited men. Was that what he would look like—

like every father of every friend I'd ever had—polished, secretive, and distracted?

Then I caught Liam staring at me.

"When was the last time you ate something?" he said.

"Why?" I said. I was concentrating on walking in a straight line.

"You look funny," he said. I wiped the sweat from my upper lip.

"I feel fine," I said. Liam shook his head and, taking my hand, pulled me across the street and into a café.

"Sit down here," he said. "You can watch out that window for Seamus. I'm getting you a sandwich." The maroon-painted room was thick with smoke, and everything was swaying a bit besides, but I managed to focus my eyes on the doorway where my father would appear. I imagined him descending from a double-deck bus like it was a ship, his face sea-burned, his clothing smelling of wood-smoke and fish. Like Liam's father must have been—before he was carried in a coffin—coming home from a trip at sea.

Liam came back with two ham-and-cheese toasties and tea. "Eat that," he said, and he wouldn't look away, so I took a bite and watched the door.

It seemed like I was chewing forever, and the hunk of sandwich wasn't breaking down at all. I swallowed, and the food pushed like clay down to my stomach. My face was burning, and my scalp was fiercely itchy.

"Excuse me," I said, and I stumbled to the ladies' room. I threw up, the remains of the sandwich plopping into the toilet bowl, and then I heaved for a few minutes, terrified that the reflex wouldn't stop, that I would never be able to breathe again. When my stomach stopped lurching, I splashed my face at the dirty sink and dried my cheeks with rough paper towel. I walked out to Liam, weaving with difficulty through the maze of tables with their expectant place settings.

"I don't see him yet," Liam said. "Jesus," he added, standing up and peering at me. "You're really pale. Are you sick?" I told him I was going out for air, trying to move my lips as little as possible. I opened the café door and immersed myself in cold wind. A calm came over me, in which I told myself I was perfectly fine. I turned to go back inside, and the sidewalk rushed at me like a wave, and then I was drowning in blackness.

"Wake up, Gráinne," Liam was saying. I wanted to tell him to be quiet, because his shrill tone was hurting my head. "Wake up!" I opened my eyes, and saw not Liam, but another man leaning over me. It was my father, looking like a pirate, his black and silver curls tied at the nape of his neck, and a leather strap spread from one shoulder to under his other arm. I thought for an instant it held a sword, but saw it was attached to a zoom-lens camera. There were lines at the edges of his eyes when he smiled; I hadn't expected that.

He was lifting me up. He did it effortlessly, and for a moment I thought it was a dream, or a memory, of myself at three years old.

"Hello, little one," my father said, his voice like a low, moany song, and the last thing I thought, before I fell back into darkness, was that his body was unnaturally warm.

CHAPTER 26

Grace

Gráinne was three and a half by the time Grace found a man to take her off the island. Max was a rich American tourist, traveling around Europe on his yacht, who descended on Inis Murúch like a loud obnoxious king, waving fifty-pound notes and buying rounds for the whole pub. The islanders groaned with contempt for him when he wasn't listening, but accepted his pints with blank, friendly grins.

He locked his eyes on Grace the first time he saw her. She was careful not to flirt with him too openly in the pub, but pretended to meet him by chance on his walks in the uninhabited portions of the island. He reminded her of Mr. Willoughby with an American accent: a man used to getting what he wanted if he paid enough. She suspected he'd inherited his money, because he never spoke of work. She had no feelings for him besides the self-satisfaction his attention aroused in her. She wanted him for his boat and his money, which she figured would be easy enough to get. It felt wonderful to have a goal again, so simple and unobstructed.

For the last year, with a gradual laying of bricks—the silent, stubborn bricks of Seamus and the sharp weapon-bricks of Grace—a wall had grown between the two of them, a wall that sometimes shocked them, as each was convinced that the other had built it alone. Grace fought Seamus, screaming vicious insults and throwing pottery, but he refused to fight back. He watched her calmly until she exhausted herself and left the house when she started to cry. He spent many long nights in the pub, but when he came home he was never drunk. She would have preferred him drunk; she could have been condescending then, could have beaten him down. But he slipped into their bed with bright and focused eyes, and she gave in once his heat reached her. They bruised each other making love, woke without speaking of their sore hips and swollen, bitter mouths. They glided by one another like blind ghosts during the day, focusing their attention on Gráinne, taking turns with her as though they were already separate, single parents. When Seamus was out of her sight, Grace wondered why she'd ever agreed to marry him. She hated herself for the way she lost her grip in that bed and laid her love open for him to see like a gaping wound. She knew she needed to get away, far enough so the gravity of his body wouldn't pull her back.

One afternoon while Seamus was fishing with Owen, Grace swam through the harbor to Max's boat, where he was waiting. She fucked him on a hard bed in his private cabin. It was like lying underneath a dead man compared to Seamus; Max's body was sticky-cold and his stomach had the texture of a jellyfish. They smoked, naked above the bedclothes, and Grace painted him a portrait of an abusive, ignorant Seamus, to get Max to shake his head and grumble that she deserved more. He actually thought it was his own idea when they decided that Grace would go on to Spain with him. They could bring the baby as well, Max said, there was room enough. Grace left the boat after dark, and floated through the water to the hotel. She was excited as she pulled on her clothes and walked in to pick up Gráinne, like a prisoner who had finally sawed through the first bar of her cell.

In the hotel pub, there was a party going for her stepbrothers Conor and Marc Jr., who were turning seventeen and were headed for England in a week. Clíona was laughing loudly between the twins, who were now a head taller than she. She reached up to straighten their fair hair, gazing with pride—as though, Grace thought with disgust, they were her own sons. "Sure, she can send them out of Ireland with her blessing," Grace mumbled under her breath, "because they're men, and island men are spoon-fed everything they want."

Gráinne was playing under the bar stools with Liam. Someone had given them chocolate cookies, and Gráinne was smeared with brown frosting.

"Will you have a pint, Grace?" Marcus said cheerfully, pulling the Guinness tap with its squeal and hiss of air. He looked delighted, his blue eyes drinking in the family he believed was sound.

"I won't, Marcus," Grace said. "Come on, sweetie," she said to Gráinne. She tried to wipe the chocolate from the girl's face, but the napkin shredded into lint that stuck to her little chin like feathers to tar.

"Ah, come on now," Marcus said. "One drink won't kill you." He put the half-poured stout on the grate to settle, the tan cloud showering like fog in the glass.

"I said I don't want it," Grace snapped, and Marcus's face fell. He shrugged, shaking his head, and moved down the bar to Clíona and the twins. He's never liked me, Grace thought. I just came in the package with his mail-order bride. She was meanly satisfied that after tomorrow his face, and all the faces that looked like his, would never peer at her again.

That night, Grace crawled under her daughter's covers and whispered that they were going on an adventure.

"What's adventure?" Gráinne said. Her little voice was like an islander's, rising and falling in a watery tune.

"An adventure means you and I leaving this island and traveling to exciting places."

"Like my uncles?" Gráinne said.

"They're only going to England," Grace said. "Wouldn't you like to see the world?"

"Ah, sure," Gráinne said. Lately, she'd been imitating Clíona's expressions with frightening accuracy. "Will Dada come, as well?"

"Not right away," Grace said. "But who's your best friend in the universe?"

"Mummy," Gráinne said, yawning.

"And you're Mommy's. Why do we need anyone else?" Gráinne fell asleep before she could answer, her warm wet breath staining Grace's neck.

In her half sleep at dawn, Grace felt Seamus get out of their bed, heard him showering and knocking around the kitchen. She lay like a child on Christmas morning, longing to spring out of bed but frightened it wasn't time yet. She pulled the covers up over her nose; once Seamus left, the duvet and pillows always turned chilly. She waited for him to come kiss her good-bye, but heard the crinkling of his jacket and the slip of a metal key off the hook.

"Seamus?" she called out in a weak, worried voice. He came into the curtained bedroom with his hat on, his camera bag pinching his shoulder. It was too dark to see the expression on his face.

"Weren't you going to say good-bye?" she said. He was going to Belfast again; when he came back, he would find her gone.

Seamus didn't say anything, and her excitement went cold; she suddenly felt trapped again, like a paralyzed invalid in the bed. He stepped up to her quickly, his shadow rushing down, and kissed her so deeply she felt her insides crack like silvery slivers of coal cleaved by heat. Then he was gone, and though he hadn't spoken, the room fell into silence. Why, when she was the one who was leaving, did she feel abandoned? She kicked off the blankets and slapped her feet on the damp carpet, trying to concentrate her tricky mind on what she needed to take with her.

Grace's plan was to leave late that night, when no one would be around to stop her. At dinnertime, when she had everything packed and repacked, Mary Louise stopped by with Liam. Grace was annoyed.

"Can't you come back tomorrow?" Grace said. "Gráinne's not feeling well and I want to put her to bed early."

"She looks well enough," Mary Louise said, watching Gráinne grab Liam's hand and run off to her bedroom. Grace swallowed her fury.

"I just wanted to bring the boy over to say good-bye," Mary Louise said. Grace slammed the door, but Mary Louise had already slithered in.

"How did you know?" Grace said. "Is your life so pathetically boring that you need to spy on me?"

"Ah, Grace, don't be angry," Mary Louise said. "I saw the signs. I'm not so dim as you think."

"Did you tell anyone?" Grace said.

"No, and why would I? No one can stop you when you fix your mind on a thing."

"I guess you think I'm a bitch for abandoning my husband," Grace said, mimicking what she thought of as Mary Louise's whiny tone.

"Not so," Mary Louise said. She was looking at the pictures on the sitting room wall: Seamus's parents' wedding next to his own. "That's just your way," she said. "You're not one to settle; you fancy yourself in prison if you're obliged to anyone else." Mary Louise turned to look at her. "It's your mother you take after."

Grace laughed meanly. "I'm nothing like my mother," she said. "She's even more settled than you are."

"You didn't know her years ago," Mary Louise said.

227

"Yeah? Neither did you."

"Aye, but I heard stories." Mary Louise smiled. "And I can see it in her still. There's the same restlessness there; she's made different decisions is all."

Grace shook her head and told Mary Louise to leave. Who did she think she was, saying she understood Grace or her mother? Mary Louise called to Liam that it was time to go, and Liam and Gráinne came to the door, holding hands and whining that they wanted to play for a few more minutes.

"Sure, I'll miss you Grace," Mary Louise whispered. "Though I know you won't say the same about me." Grace wanted to ask her: Why have you always been so stupidly nice to me, when it's obvious I hate you? But she knew what the woman's naive answer would be: You're my sister. Grace watched them walk down the path and closed the door with a satisfied bang.

When Grace arrived at the quay at midnight, Clíona was waiting grimly by the yacht.

"Jesus Christ," Grace said. "What do *you* want?" All her plans for a secretive escape were being twisted into good-byes. Clíona picked Gráinne up out of the stroller, and they went through their silly little routine: a hug, a kiss, and a squeeze, and at the squeeze part they both squealed and crushed each other. Grace looked on with disgust. If she traced back over her whole life, she could not remember her mother ever touching her, except to smack her in anger.

"What did you do now?" Grace said. "Bribe Max? Murder the captain? Are you going to lock me up in the church until I promise to be a good girl?"

"No, Grace," Clíona sighed, putting Gráinne down, "I'm through fighting you." Max came up the steps, looking furtive and guilty, and loaded Grace's bags and the stroller onto the deck.

"So why are you here, Mother?" Grace said. Clíona looked at her with the same hard, expressionless gaze.

"Don't be thinking Seamus will come after you," she said. "He's too much pride."

"I'm not doing this so Seamus, or any of you, will come after me," Grace said, though the same jolt of fear she'd felt with Seamus that morning hit her with Clíona's words. He *will* come after me, she thought. And everything will be different.

"Spare me the lecture," Grace said. "I already got one from Mary Louise. What, does the whole island know I'm going? I'm surprised they're not all here, picketing."

"Sure, they all knew you'd leave someday," Clíona said. "It's plain to anyone you hate it here. Haven't you been wandering around with that same sulky face these five years?"

"I don't sulk," Grace said.

"You do, sure, always have. No one could ever make you happy, except that wee one." Gráinne was looking at them with a worried expression that made her babyish face look old. "I hope you can make yourself happy," Clíona said. "That's all I came to say."

"No, it isn't," Grace said. "As usual, Mother, you came here to try to ruin things for me."

Her mother backed away, leaving the entrance clear to the boat.

"I don't suppose you'll write and tell us where you are," Clíona said.

"No."

"Ah, no," Clíona echoed softly. For a moment she looked thin-shouldered and old, but she straightened her posture and did up the top snap of her rain jacket.

"Good-bye so," she said lightly. "I wouldn't stay with your man there too long," she said, gesturing toward Max, who was waiting with a melodramatic expression. "He looks a bit feckless, that one." She turned around before Grace could answer, and walked gracefully up the pier, her jacket flaps fluttering in the wind.

"Are we going or what?" Max said, and Grace, closing her eyes against her mother's iron figure, handed Gráinne over the wooden rails.

As the yacht rounded the harbor entrance by Granuaile's castle, the turrets glinting silver under the full moon, Max poured Grace a glass of wine and toasted her escape.

"I thought I'd have to wrestle with that bitch on the dock," Max joked. Grace didn't answer. She was looking at the castle walls, imagining a stone-finned woman, and Seamus's light hand. She saw herself as a little girl, laying a hopeful place at the kitchen table.

"You sure you want to do this?" Max said.

Grace snapped to attention, smiling sexily. "Of course," she said, kissing him.

He gave a satisfied grunt and put his hand on her ass. "Jesus!" he yelled, and Grace almost giggled until she saw he was looking behind her.

She turned and saw Gráinne, balanced on the back rails, leaning precariously over the rushing water.

"Move back, baby," Grace yelled, running toward her, but Gráinne let out a musical laugh and toppled overboard.

"Oh shit!" Max yelled. "Stop the fucking boat, the kid's fallen off." He climbed the slippery ladder to the navigation deck.

Before they could even turn on the searchlights, Grace was in the water, gliding below the surface, her arms strained and blindly groping in the cold sea. She grabbed hold of a little body and pulled it up, keeping Gráinne's head up as she paddled back to the boat. The captain lifted Gráinne, and Max dragged Grace on deck with a wet plop.

"Is she breathing?" Grace cried, pushing Max away. Gráinne started coughing, and Grace wrapped her with shaking hands in the deck blanket.

"Should we go back?" the captain said.

Max looked unsure. "No," he said. "She's all right, isn't she Grace?"

Grace turned her back and told him to leave her alone. She peeled Gráinne's wet clothes off and rubbed her viciously with a monogrammed blue towel, as Gráinne looked at the water with a calm, detached expression.

"Don't ever do that again," Grace yelled. "You don't jump off a boat. You could have drowned, do you understand me? You'd have drowned if I hadn't found you."

"The lady *told* me to do it," Gráinne whined. For a minute, Grace thought she meant Clíona.

"What lady?"

"The mer-lady," Gráinne said. "I wanna swim with her. She pulled me."

"There's no such thing as mermaids, Gráinne," Grace said. "That was me that pulled you out of the water."

"No, there!" Gráinne insisted, pointing at the dark water.

Grace looked and thought she saw the bluish curve of something diving, probably a dolphin. Or, God, a shark. She shivered, holding Gráinne tighter.

"I don't care what you think you saw," Grace said. "Never go in the water without me."

"She's following us," Gráinne said, wriggling away and peering over the rails.

"Stop it, Gráinne," Grace said.

"She's lonely," Gráinne said. "I sing to her." She started singing in her little island voice, the lullaby her father had taught her in Irish. Grace had no idea if the words were even right—they sounded like gibberish. But Gráinne sang with confidence, wooing and moaning at the water.

Grace started to cry. "I'm sorry, Gráinne," she whispered, hugging the girl from behind. "We'll be all right, kiddo. Just me and you, for a while. You won't miss him for long, I promise."

She rocked the girl until long after the island faded out of sight, and Gráinne sang faintly, the same tune over and over like an echo, until Grace could no longer distinguish whether the music came from her daughter, or rose from the sea below.

CHAPTER 27

Gráinne

I was in my mother's bed, huddled at the corner, my hot cheek against the cool wall. I was aware of a man's presence; I couldn't see him, but there was that sweaty, musty smell that made me think it was one of my mother's men. I could hear my mother's voice coming from the dark corner of the room; she was reading poetry from one of my notebooks.

> *Shy one, shy one*
> *Shy one of my heart,*
> *She moves in the firelight*
> *Pensively apart.*

"Mom!" I called, and she came over, her face barely visible in the blue night-light I hadn't used since I was five. She sat down on the bed; there was no man there, it was only the two of us.

"Are you feeling better?" she said. Her hair was down, like curls of blood around her neck. I tried to get up but I couldn't move.

"I'm not sick," I said, though I wasn't entirely sure my voice was working.

My mother kept reading the poetry, from typed columns on sheets of white paper, forming the words through a secret grin.

> *She carries in the dishes,*
> *And lays them in a row.*
> *To an isle in the water*
> *With her I would go.*

"Mom," I said. I was crying, but my mother continued to smile. "Don't you know you're going to die?" I said. She stood up then and walked away, as though I'd stumbled on a rare untouchable topic.

I got out of bed and noticed I was wearing Stephen's flannel shirt, which smelled of low tide, and my mother's sand-caked sneakers. I left the room and found myself in the cottage at Singing Beach. On the braided rug was a path of shorn hair, seaweed, and blood–red jellyfish, leading to my mother and Stephen's bedroom. I followed it, the debris slipping under my feet.

I opened the door slowly, afraid of what I might find. It wasn't the cottage room but a hospital: a tall silver-railed bed, IV poles and red flashing buttons on the walls. I got into bed to wait for my mother, and someone who looked like my grandmother but didn't seem to recognize me started to hook me up to tubes and strap my legs with seat belts to the railing.

"There's nothing wrong with me," I said, but she shoved the prongs of an oxygen line up my nose. There was an IV needle stuck to my inner arm, and I could see it pumping—sliding in and out like it was having sex with my vein.

"Where is my mother?" I said, and I heard myself wheezing, saw my breath like sea fog in the air.

"You're all right, Gráinne," the woman sang. She leaned over me with a needle, pulled a ropy black thread through a gash in my breast.

"Stop that," I said, and when I pushed her away, both she and my wound disappeared.

There was a telephone next to the bed. I lifted it and dialed my home number. It rang continuously, but behind the ringing I could hear my mother's laughter, and the rhythmic moan and breath of a man.

"I should answer that," I heard Stephen say, his throat thick with sex, the way it had been long ago, when I'd listened to them making love in the next room.

"Don't stop," my mother moaned, and the thumping quickened.

"Gráinne!" Stephen erupted with his orgasm, and I almost dropped the phone. I could feel the damp heat of his lips seeping through the receiver. "Don't," he whispered. "God."

The ringing continued, like the sound of a whistle gnawing at my ear.

When I hung up the phone, they came in, my mother and Stephen, looking worried and guilty. My mother lowered the bed railing with a click and sat down beside me. She had a towel with her and began rubbing it over my wet hair in soothing strokes.

"Don't ever go in the water without me," she scolded.

"Mom," I said. I was crying so hard that the whole bed was soaked, as if it had been walloped by a sea wave.

"Shhh," she said. "We'll have time to talk when you're better." I pushed the towel away so I could look at her.

"But you're dying," I said. "Stephen took you to the hospital." She laughed, looking at Stephen, and he was laughing along with her.

"Don't be silly," she said. "I'm not the one dying." She began to cough. She hacked with a liquid sound until her face turned purple, and what looked like a jellyfish erupted from her throat and fell with a squishy plop on the bed.

"You're all right, Grace," Stephen said, moving in to hold her. He kissed her earlobe. Her hair was thinning fast; corkscrewed strands of copper fell from her shoulders like rain.

She took the towel and scooped up the bloody mess. I saw a nipple protruding from the towel folds and I could tell by the way her gown sank on one side that only puckered skin and stitches remained. She had vomited up her breast.

"This is my body," she said, holding the bloody towel high in front of her. "It will be given up for you."

"Please don't go, Mom," I said, reaching for her. I couldn't move far because of the straps on my legs. "Please stay with me," I said.

My mother grinned as if nothing was wrong and she thought I was just being a pain in the ass, so she needed to humor me.

"If you close your eyes," she said, "I'll read to you."

Once I'd closed them, I couldn't seem to open them again, and it was not her voice which continued, but a man's voice, sounding far away.

Again and again when I am broken
my thought comes on you when you were young,
and the incomprehensible ocean fills
with floodtide and a thousand sails.

I struggled at the belts, and when I got free, I was on the beach, the waves crashing stormily in the dark night. My mother's voice was there, rising from the water, and I ran down toward it, the sand squealing and singing beneath my rubber soles.

"Mom!" I screamed. I couldn't see her, only the bluish curve of something dangerous in the water.

She sang out lines to me.

Dance there upon the shore;
What need have you to care
For wind or water's roar?
And tumble out your hair
That the salt drops have wet;
Being young you have not known
The fool's triumph, nor yet
Love lost as soon as won . . .
What need have you to dread
The monstrous crying of wind?

I dove into an oncoming wave, which broke across my shoulders like a hard wooden plank. I tried to swim toward her voice, but the sound of the sea in my ears deceived me. Another big swell pushed me under, and the current, like hands on my ankles, pulled me deeper out to sea. I reached my arms out for my mother, and she found me and pulled me to shore. I was lying on pinching sand, coughing up black water and bits of seaweed. Words still pounded in my ears. It was no longer my mother's voice, but the man's, moany and vaguely familiar, who sounded like he was pushing the poetry through tears.

The shore of troubles is hidden
with its reefs and the wrack of grief,
and the unbreaking wave strikes
about my feet with a silken rubbing.

When I opened my eyes it was Liam, and not my mother, leaning above me in the moonlight.

"You've a cut over your eye," he said, pressing his shirtsleeve gently to my forehead. "I thought you said you couldn't drown if you knew how to swim," he joked, touching my cheek with his free hand.

My mother's still out there, I wanted to say, but he plummeted down and kissed me, and the salt and warmth of his lips swallowed my words without answering them.

While we lay there, sucking deeply on each other's mouths, Liam's hands all over me, swelling my skin to the point where I wanted to burst, my mother's voice called me for the last time.

> *Will you defy the barbarous sea,*
> *challenging the misfortune of ocean,*
> *will you sail again peacefully with the tide,*
> *will you swim like a love-making tune?*
>
> . . .
>
> *Perhaps there will appear to us a gentle dream*
> *in which will be seen on the floor of oceans*
> *a black shapely one and a fair one*
> *encompassed with a sea of brightness.*

When I opened my eyes I saw my father, holding a thin book near a lamp that lit the hospital room with a foggy yellow glow. His hair was down, black and silver curling like night around his earlobes. He was reading to me.

> *How did the springtide not last,*
> *the springtide more golden to me than to the birds,*
> *and how did I lose its succour,*
> *ebbing drop by drop of grief?*

He glanced up then and smiled at me—and I saw myself, shifting and drowning in the black mirror of his eyes.

"Am I dying?" I said, my throat squeezed thin and dry.

"God, no," he said. "You're malnourished and anemic, but if you smarten up and eat a little you'll recover in no time."

I started to cry, wanting to be back in the dream with the chance of meeting my mother if I swam out far enough. "Mom's gone," I said to him.

"Yes," my father said. "I know, Gráinne."

"I didn't say good-bye," I whispered. His face blurred under my watery lashes until it seemed I was looking through the screen of the sea, making a soundless confession.

"Ah, now, your mother was never the one for good-byes," my father said. "She prefers to slip away unnoticed, like the tide, and come back when you least expect her."

"But she's not coming back to you," I said, imagining him looking out over deceiving waters. "Not ever."

"Aye," my father said and he put a warm palm on my forehead, as if he meant to ease my life with the pressure of skin. "I know that."

"Why didn't you come for me?" I said.

"I'm sorry, Gráinne," he said. "I wanted to. I was afraid it would be like last time."

And I saw him then, with younger, more hopeful eyes, taking a sand-filled teacup from my hand, snapping my picture from behind the mask of his camera. One of my mother's boyfriends—there and then gone, without memory, without significance, without, I had thought, any connection to the family that was the two of us.

My father, Seamus O'Flaherty, sat with his hands fiddling and tapping against his knees. He had long, brown hands, with calluses lined up like a mountain range on his palms, ink staining the rough bump on his pen finger. His knuckles, like mine, were thicker than the flesh of his fingers—the type of hands that suggest the raw bones of a skeleton.

It was my father's hands that I watched as he told his story, and my mother's hands that I thought of as I translated his words into myth in my mind—her hands gentle on my hair, before they were waxed reproductions tied up in a rosary. Her hands as they might have been, when she was a girl my age.

There was a girl who grew up with no father, whose only family was a mother who loved her harshly. A girl who was only ever touched by the sea, or by the hands of boys enchanted by her. A girl who laid an empty plate for an imaginary pirate queen, an invitation to a fierce spirit she hoped was like her own.

There was a young man, an ocean away, who had only a father; his mother was the harsh land and grieving water which surrounded him. A young man in love with the myth of his island, who watched for magical sea-women in the rhythm of the tide.

When they met, the girl was thin as a rail, her eyes bruised in sorrow. She had been taken from her home and transplanted to a place where her language sounded strange and her body refused to stay warm. She knew only how to swim and how to use her fingers and mouth in passion. She had lost a child, and was afraid of losing herself.

When he first saw the girl, the young man knew how to pull a living from the sea, and how to weave a story so it sounded like a song. He could read the soil and stormy weather, speak the language that had been beaten from his ancestors. He could travel to any country, translate other lives onto paper, but could not live in any land but his own.

They fell in love—she with his body, he with her spirit. It was his heat that breathed her own life back into her, his voice that raised her eyes over the water. He fed her the land and the language he loved, thinking her fierceness was a sign of the sea-woman he had dreamed of as a boy. They took from each other what they could not create in themselves: a partner to fit in the empty slot of his world, a lover to accompany her back to the sea.

When they married, their love was immersed in fear. She was afraid of being his prisoner, he was terrified of the day she would leave him. Each of them waited for the other to change.

They had a child: a girl with the dark sea coloring of her father and the fierce look of her mother. The child had her father's reticence and dreamy fascination with language, as well as the blunt, de-manding temper and adventurous streak of her mother. She was them and she was not them; she illuminated each to the other and she stretched forth ahead of them, beyond their reach or understanding. The man and woman loved their child as they could not love each other: with the grief and the joy that they could not keep her for long.

The woman never learned to love the man's island. Year by year it grew smaller, colder, more her prison than his paradise. She left him as he'd always predicted she would—slipping away by night, disappearing like a mermaid sliding under the sea. Perhaps she hoped he would follow her, even as she knew he would not be able to. She left him regardless, left him because her love for him was not as strong as the pull of her own spirit. She took their daughter, not knowing—or did she?—that one day she would send the girl back.

The man, paralyzed by grief, sustained by false hopes, waited. He waited for the woman to return, waited for their natures to shift just enough to allow them to be happy together. He waited, as it turned out, for too long.

By the time he traveled across the ocean after his family, like the journalist he was, in search of the story, his baby girl was five years old. This is the part that only he knows, the part of which no one was aware.

He approached her in a park in Boston, where she played quietly in a sandbox while her baby-sitter read on a bench nearby. The girl was laying pretend tea out in plastic flowered cups. He told the sitter he was a friend of her mother, and asked the girl for permission to join her.

"Are you one of my mother's boyfriends?" his daughter said, the suspicion of a city child in a face that was, in vivid flashes, her mother's.

"I was once," the man said. She filled a cup with sand, balanced it on a saucer and passed it to him with polite grace. She laid a place reverently to her left, and then one for herself.

"Will there be someone joining us?" the man said, thinking of

*the table they once shared, the three of them, in what he had wished
was happiness.*

*"That one's for my father," the girl said. She formed her words
with care, as if each one was as important as the other.*

*"And where is your father?" the man said, but what he was
thinking was: Look at me, Gráinne, please truly look at me. I'm
right here.*

*"He's at sea," the girl said, pretending to sip her sand. "He's
a pirate, so he's very busy; I keep his tea ready for him." She looked
up, concerned. "Don't tell Mommy," she added. "She gets upset."*

"And how will you know him when he comes?"

*"Oh, he's very handsome," she said, with the exaggerated
patience children bestow on grownups. "And he'll be wearing pirate
clothes, of course."*

Her voice no longer had the lilt of the island in it.

*As he watched her tending the empty place—filling a tiny plate
generously with grass and stones and arranging it next to the teacup—he remembered a story his father had told him as a child. A
story about Jesus and his last instructions before his death.*

*"Lay a place at your table for me," Jesus said, "for when I
come again to the world. And if a stranger appears, give him my
share—for every time you refuse a stranger, you refuse me." The
man's father, in the tradition of the islanders, had always set a third
place for their supper. What the man, as a boy, had imagined but
never told his father was this: that the plate awaited a woman rising
out of the sea to join them.*

*I am a stranger, he thought as he watched her little hands refill
the imaginary father's cup. She is not my daughter if I am not with
her.*

*Her coloring was still his own, but in this city light looked noth-
ing like the sea. He remembered how it used to be when they looked
into each other's eyes: they had seen themselves looking back through
those tiny round mirrors. Now, she did not see herself in him. He
snapped a photo with his journalist's camera, to capture her.*

241

That night he stood in a shadow outside their living room window, watching his wife and his daughter laugh and recount their day to one another. He looked at the doorbell, labeled with her maiden name. He could ring it, walk back into their lives, leave behind his land and its language and everything that defined him. He could try to live in a city which would suffocate him, try to get used to sandboxes instead of beaches, paved parks instead of bogland.

Or he could steal his daughter away, teach her again to love her homeland, to speak in the music of the water surrounding her. Watch her grow up motherless.

In the end he did nothing. Because he knew he could never have what he wanted: his home as well as his family. Because he looked at the two women of his life and saw they were not his to keep. In the end he returned to the only woman he had ever understood: Inis Murúch, the Island of the Mermaids. Where he set his table, each evening, for a family of three.

He returned knowing that one day he would see his child again, and that he would have to explain his absence in her life. Knowing also that he would not be able to answer in the blunt way of her mother, but in the myth and mystery of his language, and that no explanation would ever be enough.

I am not sure if these were my father's exact words. But with my eyes closed and the image of my mother skimming across my mind like a mermaid cloaked in mist, these are the words that I heard.

"That is where my door to the story closes," my father said. "The rest of it—your mother's life and your own—that is your story, Gráinne."

I looked down at my untouched hospital food; the soup had fogged-over the cutlery and tray with a beaded moisture. I thought of the place setting I used to find in the cottage, everything laid out in some secret, ancient preparation by my mother. Of her gray-paneled door, left ajar and expectant, and how I'd sneaked past it, afraid my motion might swing it open. As if opening that door would release my mother's soul, like the souls in cages under the sea, and then she would be lost to me forever.

"Why won't you eat?" my father said. "Can you not see what you are doing to yourself?"

How could I tell him? That if I ate, time would begin again, and I would know I was alive. And if I was alive, then it was my mother, not me, who had died. My mother who had died without me.

"Close your eyes, Gráinne," my father said, when he realized I was crying too hard to answer him. "You can begin again in the morn."

And he sang to me then, in a language I had forgotten, until the tears dried to salt on my cheeks, and I fell into a dreamless sleep.

When I woke again, it was daytime, and Liam was sitting in a padded blue armchair by my bed. I had the strange feeling that I'd fallen asleep with the wind and rain storming at my windows, and woken to a calm blue morning.

"Hey," I said, testing out my voice. He looked up and smiled. Excitement ran like a drug through my veins, and I felt like jumping over the bed rails. No one, not even Stephen, had ever smiled at me like that before.

"I was worried about you," Liam said, standing up and resting his arms on the silver bars. "You're looking more like yourself now."

"Is that good?" I said, rubbing crusty sleep from my eyes. I couldn't possibly look attractive, unwashed and swaddled in a yellow johnny. There was a tube attached to my arm and a faint bruising ache where the needle was embedded in my skin. Liam put a hand to my face, stroking a crumb of sleep away with his finger.

"Aye, that's good," he said, but his voice caught and he moved away. There was a low rumbling in my stomach.

"I think I'm hungry," I said.

Liam brightened. "It's about time," he said. "What do you fancy? I'll get you anything."

"Something salty," I said.

He came back bearing white paper bags crammed with fried fish and chips. We sat cross-legged on the bed, eating with our fingers. I couldn't eat it fast enough, and the smell of salty fish in the room made me dizzy and aroused. Liam fed me a piece of cod from his bag, letting his thumb linger on my lip.

"Where is he?" I whispered, looking toward the door.

"Seamus?" Liam asked. He looked feverish, his eyes glazed—like light reflecting off water. "He'll be back this afternoon." He was staring at me, without shyness, so intensely I stopped chewing and could hardly breathe.

"Gráinne," he said, and I knew he was going to kiss me, no fantasy or mistake this time. His lips were warm and tasted of oil and salt and fish, with another richer flavor beneath that I knew, with a thrill of recognition, was the taste of him. The chips bags spilled in our laps, then Liam was lying down with me, and his hands on my breasts, stomach, and back were not groping or alien, but so natural my body seemed to reach out of its skin toward him; it could hardly get close enough.

When the nurse came in and caught us there was screeching and scolding, and I laughed until my stomach ached, watching Liam trying to look apologetic while holding his hands over his groin and licking his swollen, delicious lips.

CHAPTER 28

Clíona

It's the ringing of the telephone that wakes me. I've fallen asleep on the sofa—something I've been doing lately while Mary Louise watches the hotel on slow afternoons. Never before have I been the napping sort, but I suppose it comes with age.

It's Seamus ringing to say that he and Gráinne will be in on the four o'clock ferry. The girl's well enough to travel again. I'm happy, if a little nervous, that they will both be here for Christmas dinner tomorrow.

After I hang up the phone, my head still feels strange, ringing with the echoes of my dreams. I dreamed about my mother, scolding me when I was a wee girl. More of a memory really. I must have been just this side of seven years when I convinced my brother Colm to take me out in the curragh to gather seaweed for the fields. I plopped over the side after overextending myself to reach what I thought was a lovely-looking piece. Colm fished me out and when he brought me home soaking to Mum, she was livid.

"Ah told ye ne'er to go out in that boot!" she said, in the Northern accent she had which was so different from my own, and every other islander's. "Are ye wantin the mermaids to git ye?" At the mention of mermaids, I started crying. I'd heard enough stories of how heartless the creatures were, how they clamped onto you with their webbed hands and held you under, laughing bubbles as you choked for air. I tried to hold back my sobs; my mother hated it when her children cried. She spanked me that day, hard and un-relenting with my father's belt. My father never hit us, but she liked to use his belt for the appearance of authority, as on our island it was usual for the men to punish the children. Whenever she asked my father to unbuckle it, he did so slowly, as though he were the one about to be spanked.

I hated my mother that day—hated her most of the thirteen years I spent with her, that's true enough. Now I can look back and see that I'd frightened her, that the terror of me drowning had been hidden behind her rage. But at the time I only saw a mean, ugly woman who never smiled and hardly ever left the yard, for she hated to meet her island neighbors. My mother was never at home on Inis Murúch. Mind you, it's a lovely place, and I'll live here until the day I die and am buried in the graveyard up the road. But I'll admit that island people can be hard on strangers. My mother lived here for near-on twenty years and I don't think she had a friend besides my father. Islanders can spot it a mile away if a newcomer has any contempt for the place, and my mother had plenty. They won't forgive that.

I can still see every detail of my mother's funeral, as if it is hap-pening right before me. She was laid out on the bed for the viewing. I myself had helped the island woman wash her yellow limbs and prepare the hair above a face gone stiff in that familiar displeased expression. All the islanders who had never welcomed her moaned pretend sympathy to my father.

"Ah, she was a good wife to you, Jared," they said. "It's hard-pressed you'd be to find a better woman." The urge to contradict and expose them boiled in my throat.

I had nursed my mother as she wasted away those last three months, the cancer spreading so quickly I don't think it left a bit of healthy flesh in her body. She had been mean until the end, and sometimes confused myself and my sister for the island women she despised.

"Say it to my face, you bitch!" my mother had growled at me one morning, before she'd lost her ability to speak. "I know well enough how you hate me. You'll be thrilled when I'm gone, so you can get your trampy hands on my husband."

"Mum," I said, backing away, the brush I'd been using on her hair held at a useless angle in front of me. "It's me, Mum. Clíona."

"I know who you are, girl," my mother said. Spittle ran down her chin like the foamy suds of washing-up liquid. "You're the daughter who wants me to die."

I cried then, begging her not to say such things, clinging to her with more affection than I ever had in my life. Because she was right, you see. I did want her to die.

At the funeral, Mrs. Keane came over to me to offer her sympathies.

"You'll miss her something awful, won't you girl?" she said.

"No," I said coldly. "I can't say I will."

Mrs. Keane was appalled. Of course, she was probably thinking even harsher things about Mum, but had the manners not to say so. "God help you, you're a vicious child," she said, turning away.

The whole island knew what I'd said before the day was through. I suppose that's how I got my reputation of being a hard woman, which still sticks in the old one's minds today.

"Clíona O'Halloran will tell you straight," they say of me, though I can be as circumspect and hypocritical as the next person.

I was true as my word, sure. I didn't miss my mother, not for years. Not until my father died. I long for her now, with the pain of a child and the understanding of an old woman.

Brónach—the Irish word for sorrowful—was my mother's Christian name. It is only after my own life as a mother that I can see how the name suited her. If I could have just one moment back, one time when she was screaming at me in rage, then I could say: I'm sorry you're lonely, Mum. Maybe it would have made a difference; we might have wound up the best of friends, like Grace and Gráinne.

I wonder, sometimes, if Grace missed me when she was dying, if for the first time she saw me as I truly am.

I sometimes think God planned our lives all wrong. What's the use in learning the truth so long after the opportunity to use it has gone by? I suppose that's what the afterlife is for, though it's not so easy, even for a Catholic woman, to keep in mind the promise of resurrection when you're drowning in the deep sea of your own mistakes.

I stand on the quay and watch the ferry slide past Granuaile's castle, the tiny figures of Seamus and my granddaughter standing on deck, pointing and leaning toward one another so they can be heard over the roar of the engine. Seamus, though he's been halfway around the world, will always be an islander. I suppose it's the only thing Grace could never love about him.

When they climb off the boat, Seamus steps forward and gives me a hug, right there in front of Eamon and the other men on the dock. He lifts me a little off my feet, until I screech in protest.

"You're an awful man," I say, prying myself away, but he's laughing and I can't help but smile at him. He's happier than I've seen him in years.

Gráinne, poor girl, looks about half her age, pale and skeletal, her short curls standing up in the wind.

"I guess you're mad at me," she says, a gleam in her dark eyes.

"Ah, you're all right, girl," I say. "It would be nice if you told a person, before you went traipsing off to the city." I leave it at that.

I don't blame her for going to look for Seamus, it seems the best thing really. I can see the affection they once had for each other is there still, just clouded a little by intervening years.

When we get to the hotel, Seamus leaves us alone, walking toward his own house. Gráinne and I sit in the conservatory, the last of the sun glinting off the glass behind her head.

Her hair has grown enough that it resembles the short, violet-black curls she had as a baby.

I hear one of the two hotel girls call out "Clíona," and Mary Louise's murmur silencing her.

"What does your name mean?" Gráinne asks, as I pour her a cup of tea.

"It comes from an old legend," I say. "Clíodhna eloped against her parents' wishes and sailed off in a curragh with her man. He left her by the shore of an island—some say this one—to go hunting, and a freak wave crashed in and dragged her under. He thought she'd drowned, but later the islanders said they'd seen her, and that she had become a fairy of the sea."

Gráinne is quiet for a moment, and I can hear Grace's contempt in my mind. "Figures," Grace once said, "you'd be named after a loser."

"She was probably better off," Gráinne says.

"Come again?" I say. I'm confused, not sure if she's referring to my daughter or my namesake.

"Well I'd rather be off with the mermaids then stuck with some guy who treated me like that," Gráinne says, sipping her tea, that look of fierceness in her eyes. Her features are Seamus's, but the expression is the image of her mother.

"It's just an old story," I say. "I think it's told to discourage girls from running away." I didn't mean to imply anything, but Gráinne's brow furrows viciously.

"I wasn't running away," she says. "I just wanted to talk to my father."

"I know," I say.

"But if I did want to leave," she adds, stiffening her bony shoulders, "I could. You can't keep me here. I know you tried to keep my mother here, but you just can't do that."

"I'd like you to stay, Gráinne," I say slowly, carefully. "Most island children leave when they're eighteen. Some come back, but the majority find something to keep them away. I made a mistake with your mother, Gráinne. I did not want to let her go. And I lost her—lost the both of you—because of it."

She cringes, the poor thing, when I say the word "lost."

"I hope one day you will feel at home here," I say. "But I won't force you, sure. I never meant to force you." She looks confused, like she expected a big row and my agreement has left her speechless. I'm a bit surprised myself. At how easy this feels.

"I guess I'll stay for a while," she says quietly, and I nod, passing her a scone—which she actually eats.

You're the strangest of the lot of us, I want to say to her. A bit of everyone and every place of our lives in you. I was an Irish woman lost in America; your mother was an American girl trapped on Inis Murúch. You, Gráinne, are a little of both, and have been dragged between the two like a hooked fish. You may never feel at home here, I want to say, or anywhere. But sure, you're the kind who can make a place for herself, wherever you are.

Gráinne is looking out the glass walls at the sun, which is setting like a pool of blood on the water. The gaze is not quite her mother's. Gráinne doesn't seem to be looking at what's beyond that sea, so much as she's looking at the water for its own sake. Sure, this could be just an old woman's wishful thinking.

All the words I long to say to her crowd and clot in my throat. I cough them aside and hope my eyes will speak for me.

"More tea?" I say, and she lifts her saucer with a shaky hand. I steady it with the spout and pour the red-brown liquid, steaming, over the lip of her cup.

CHAPTER 29

Gráinne

On Christmas Eve, my sixteenth birthday, my father and I went for a walk along Mermaid Beach, which was a mirror reflection of the singing sand my mother had died by. For days I had asked him questions, and he'd answered in a voice I now remembered having loved as a girl. I could fill things in now, and the image of my life and my mother's stretched across boundaries I didn't know were there.

"Was your mother happy?" my father asked, as we marked the wet sand with the patterns of our soles.

"Yes," I said, immediately. We were almost always happy, my mother and I. Though she had brief periods of sadness, her "damp days" she called them, that I now associated with a memory I hadn't shared.

My father didn't look surprised or even resentful that she'd been content without him. I know my mother well enough to see that she loved this man, probably more than she loved Stephen. I also know that love had nothing to do with her being able to stay with him. "Always love the man second," my mother had told me. "You come first."

I looked down at the brown blanket of shore, decorated by miniature Play-Doh-like curls left by the sandworms.

"Do you still like living here?" I asked my father.

He smiled, understanding what I meant. He must see my mother behind every rock, glimpse her curving form in every wave.

"I do, sure," he said. "Do you?"

"Um," I said, taken aback, "I don't know. I haven't really been *living* here."

"What is it you've been doing these last four months?" my father said, his eyebrows lowering toward his grin.

"Waiting," I said.

"Waiting for what?" he asked, as though it were a simple question.

Waiting for a boat that carried my father, for Stephen to write, Liam to kiss me. Waiting for my mother to stop dying and come to my door.

"Just waiting," I said.

My father's eyes seemed to look inside me, as if my skin had the transparency of water. "Take a wee bit of advice from an old man who knows about waiting," he said. "Now that you're back here, you can start living. Then you'll decide if you like it."

I thought about what my grandmother had said, how she hoped I'd feel at home here. If I stayed with this family, would my voice always sound so conspicuous in my ears? Would I always be an outsider?

My father turned his face into the sea wind as we walked.

"On this island, Gráinne," he said, "you can watch the moon and the sun rise and fall, with nothing to separate you from them but the water. Silver and gold and green. Some find this island too small. I feel as though I live on the grandest place on earth."

We stopped by a large barnacle rock. On its flattened top, where the tide never reached, was a miniature lawn of deep green grass, pimpled with lichen-stubbly stones.

"At the high tide," my father said, "your mother would stand up there, looking toward the mainland, and dive into the water. Sometimes I'd follow her down and watch her, half expecting that she would never again emerge from the sea."

We both looked out over the silver-rippled waves. I could see her, my mother with her hair like a sunset on her shoulders, her legs melding into fins as she dove.

"I still watch for her," my father said.

I imagined my mother's response, sharp and teasing; she would diffuse the emotion, turn her eyes to his and flirt him into distraction.

I wanted to take his hand, to put my head against his warm, beating chest and cry. Me too, I wanted to say.

My father touched my head, briefly because there was still an awkward grief between us that would be there for a while. The waves sizzled whispers at our feet.

At Christmas dinner, there were more of my relatives in Clíona's house than I could possibly keep track of. Marcus's twin sons were home with their wives and a pack of blue-eyed, rambunctious children. My grandmother's sisters, slightly less good-looking versions of her, squeezed me and bluntly grieved that they'd missed me for years. I glided through the crowded room, smiling and answering questions, trying to pretend I was used to such a big family. Clíona moved at my side, introducing the faces by their connection to me. This is your antie, your cousin, your uncle twice-removed. This was what she wanted for my mother, I thought, and what she now wants for me. To be able to look into faces and see my own features, to be told that my love of poetry comes from my great-grandfather, my swimming from my father, my tendency to brood from the

O'Malley side. Only my mother hadn't wanted it; she preferred to define herself. The only person she'd ever admitted a connection to was me.

Liam, whom I hadn't seen since he left Dublin in November, arrived with his mother and the line of brothers. My father put a firm arm around Mary Louise's waist.

"I'm so sorry about Owen," he said, looking into her eyes. "He was a good man."

"You've always been a friend to us, Seamus," Mary Louise said. I could tell by her face, which was tired but composed, that she was not in danger of becoming weepy.

"Who'd have thought it," she said, trying to smile. "Both of us widowed at our young age." I saw Liam watching them, calculating possibilities. He closed his eyes, and I knew he was picturing his father.

Later, while my father and Mary Louise chatted, Liam and I snuck out the back door and went behind the storage shed, where he kissed me for a long time.

"You'll never guess what Seamus gave me for Christmas," he said, when our mouths were red and tender. He took a thin cardboard package from his inside pocket. *Fetherlites*, it said, with a fogged portrait of a man and woman, looking at each other in ecstasy.

"Condoms?" I said, laughing.

"Can you believe it?" Liam said.

"Why not?" I shrugged. My mother had given me condoms; they had lain unused in the drawer of my bedside table.

"I thought maybe it was some sick test," Liam said. "Fathers don't give their daughter's boyfriend rubbers. Not here, anyways."

"Maybe they should," I said.

Liam smiled. "Fair enough," he said. "We've got them so. If we need them." He looked at me mischievously. "Do you think we'll need them, Granvaile?" he said, putting his arms around my waist.

I pulled him in closer, inhaling the smell of his mouth and skin. "I'd say we will," I whispered, and I knew I sounded sexy.

I could hear the water lapping the shore by the hotel, and I knew the tide was low because there was the smell of exposed seaweed—a thick, sensual smell, as though thousands of mermaids had left the evidence of their lovemaking in the sand.

Before she got sick, I used to crawl into bed with my mother in the morning, after whatever man she'd been with had left for his life. I would nuzzle her neck, inhaling the sea-smell of her, the salty excitement that perspired from her skin. I used to think that when I finally felt passion it would smell like that—like my mother. Now I knew that the sex on my mother was only a layer, like perfume. What was underneath was what I missed the most. Underneath the myth of her was an odor so particular nothing could re-create it: the smell of her flesh and her soul, still new beneath her scales.

"Hey," Liam whispered. "Where are you?"

The mist was so thick I couldn't see the ocean or the mainland behind it. There was nothing to orient me in the bubble of fog, but Liam, whose face looked clear and sharp, kissed me again with his swollen, salty mouth, his hands fluttering lightly up and down my sides, and for the first time in a long while, what lay beyond this island of singing rock and grieving, hungry sea didn't matter.

CHAPTER 30

Gráinne

I set the table for Christmas dinner: eleven adults and fourteen children, Clíona tells me. At the end of the table nearest to the door, I add an extra plate, glass, side plate, napkin, gleaming silver cutlery.

After we have eaten, the sounds of laughter and bickering gone, the music of Liam's flute only an echo, I will clear the table, leaving the unused place. Later, when all the others have gone to sleep, crammed five to a room on extra cots from the hotel, I will sneak down here, and wait in the darkness.

She will enter quietly, her bare feet squishing liquid prints upon the carpet. When she sits beside me, I will smell the dank, sexual odor of seaweed, of low tides, of the bed I was always welcome to crawl into as a child. In the shadows of blue moonlight, her hands will appear webbed, her long fingers connected by paper-thin fins. As she eats, her copper curls dripping beads of water onto the tablecloth, I will tell her about Liam, about the particular scent of his skin, about the kisses, and the condoms waiting in his pocket. She will laugh music, tease me, offer advice. I will tell her of my grand-mother, my father, my cheery mob of a family—where the women adore the men, but only pretend to depend on them. About how their voices rise and fall like water, about how a part of me wants never to go back to a place where people don't speak in tunes.

I will tell her I am no longer afraid of her dying. I know now that there are far worse ways of losing people, even when they're right in front of you.

She will nod, smooth my short curls back from my forehead, kiss my raw red scar.

Gráinne, she will sing, naming me again.

She will recite poetry, without any pages to guide her.

> *A face haunts me,*
> *following me day and night,*
> *the triumphant face of a girl*
> *is pleading all the time.*

I will know exactly who she means.

Perhaps one of my little cousins will come downstairs for a glass of water or a secret snack, and see the retreating shadow of a woman, hear the gulp of water and the far-off moan of wind.

"Who was that lady?" the little girl will say, and I will settle her in my lap.

She is the pirate queen, Granuaile, who barges in, hungry and battle-worn, leaving her sword to glint by the fire.

She is the sea-woman, Muirgen, who transforms from the ocean at night, to steal one last look at her sleeping human children.

"She," I will say, "was my mother."